"What do you want, Logan?"

"I'm just being friendly. Here."

Logan offered her the bag. Jessie took it. Their fingers bumped. So did her pulse rate.

"Why?"

He laughed—a low rumble of sound. "Are you always suspicious when people are nice to you?"

"You've made it clear you don't like or trust me. So why are you really here?"

"Because Miri's important to me, and she likes you."

He tied off the kayak, then climbed onto the dock. His legs were long and tanned and lightly swirled with dark hair. Even his bare feet were sexy.

So he was attractive. Big deal.

That didn't mean she was attracted to him... Definitely not.

Dear Reader,

Have you ever dreamed of winning the lottery? I think most, if not all, of us have. We believe that a few million dollars will solve all of our problems. When I started reading the real stories of big lottery winners, I learned that isn't usually the case. Winning the jackpot is, in fact, a curse for most winners. That's how this story began.

When elementary-school teacher Jessamine wins, her life is turned upside down. She's forced into hiding and must reevaluate the things that are most important in her life—and those are not the material things she can buy. Then she finds a man she can love, but how can she ever be sure he loves her and not the fortune she's won?

I hope you enjoy Jessamine's journey.

Emilie Rose

USA TODAY Bestselling Author

EMILIE
ROSE

The Lottery Winner

HHARLEQUIN® SUPERROMANCE®

Recycling programs
for this product may
not exist in your area.

ISBN-13: 978-0-373-61003-7

The Lottery Winner

Copyright © 2016 by Emilie Rose Riddle

HARLEQUIN®
www.Harlequin.com

USA TODAY bestselling author and two-time RITA® Award finalist **Emilie Rose** lives in North Carolina with her own romance hero. Writing is her third career. She's managed a medical office and a home day care—neither offered half as much satisfaction as plotting happy endings. Her hobbies include gardening, fishing, cooking and traveling to find her next book setting. Visit her website, emilierose.com, or email her at EmilieRoseAuthor@aol.com.

Books by Emilie Rose

HARLEQUIN SUPERROMANCE

Second Chance Mom
Starting with June
The Secrets of Her Past
A Better Man

HARLEQUIN DESIRE

The Ties that Bind
The Price of Honor
Her Tycoon to Tame

SILHOUETTE DESIRE

Wedding His Takeover Target
Executive's Pregnancy Ultimatum
His High-Stakes Holiday Seduction
Bedding the Secret Heiress
More Than a Millionaire
Bargained Into Her Boss's Bed
Pregnant on the Upper East Side

Visit the Author Profile page at Harlequin.com for more titles.

I thank the Lord for blessing me with this amazing career and for filling my head with characters and stories that need to be told.

CHAPTER ONE

JESSAMINE MARTIN TRIED to appreciate the fingers of peach and salmon creeping over the rooftops as she walked along the Key West boardwalk, but she was too busy waiting for the new pay-as-you-go phone in her pocket to vibrate to concentrate on which tints she could blend to attain those specific hues.

She missed her family and work. As noisy and chaotic as teaching art to elementary school kids might be, the routine was normal, comforting. This unrelenting solitude wasn't. She couldn't even keep track of what day it was unless she checked her watch. Monday. She used to love Mondays. They represented the beginning of a week doing what she loved. That had changed the day the school board demanded she leave.

She wanted her old life back.

Gulls squawked and waddled away as she passed, and fish churned the waters of Key West Bight, waiting for the tourists who weren't up yet to buy food pellets from the gumball machines and toss them into the water. After six weeks of walking this stretch, she could identify some of her nonhuman companions as regulars by their size, colors and scars. So sick of her own company and lack of purpose, she was almost desperate enough to talk to them.

The waterfront was quiet at the cusp of dawn. Only fishermen moved about, preparing their charter boats for a day of excitement and adventure, traveling out to the Gulf for fishing or to the Tortugas for diving. Her day would be filled with more of the same monotonous schedule she'd adopted since arriving. She'd read another of the paperbacks she'd picked up at the Key West library or do a little painting or sketching if she could rouse the muse. But even her muse yearned for the stark lines of South Carolina's rolling hills, bare deciduous trees and thick pines.

The phone buzzed against her hip. She snatched it up so quickly she nearly dropped it as she fumbled to find the right button to answer the unfamiliar device.

"Is everyone okay?" she blurted.

"All good here. How are you, Li'l Bit? Enjoying your vacation?"

She bit her tongue on the automatic impulse to tell her brother for the zillionth time not to call her Li'l Bit and that this was in no way a vacation. But at this point, she didn't care what Brandon said as long as he called. "Have there been any more…incidents?"

"The extra workers Dad hired and the Cherokee County deputies are keeping an eye on the orchard. And the Gaffney police have units watching your house and Leah's and the kids' day care."

She'd been horrified when her brother told her even her sister's family was in danger. Jessamine couldn't live with herself if something happened to her precious niece and nephew.

"Can I come home?"

Silence filled her ear, and she pictured his grimace. Could she blame him? Same question. Different day. "Not yet," he responded finally. "That dumb redhead with the local news showed up at Mom and Dad's last night with a camera crew. She noticed that your car's been in the same spot in the driveway for weeks and suggested the disappearance of the state's largest lottery winner is due to foul play. She wants permission to search the orchard. She expects to find your body buried under the peach trees."

Not the answer Jessamine had wanted. "I wish I'd never bought that stupid ticket. I only wanted change for a five."

"Don't be a drama queen. Millions of people would kill to be in your shoes. Literally, Jessamine. Remember that. Watch your back. And remember, you wouldn't be in this predicament if you'd learn to say no instead of giving that mooch money every time she asks."

Mortification burned her face. *Guilty as charged.* "I've learned my lesson."

"I hope so, because being a people pleaser will take you down. Seventy percent of lottery winners end up bankrupt or dead within a few years."

She groaned inwardly. He'd clicked into special agent mode, reciting the overprotective, stern lecture she now knew by heart.

"Brandon, please stop telling me that every time we talk," she interjected when he paused for breath. "I heard you the first fifty-something times. You're only contradicting yourself when you tell me to relax and have fun then try to make me scared of my own shadow."

"I don't want you to become a statistic."

"I won't."

Okay, so maybe she hadn't initially believed his warnings that lottery winners and their family members were exponentially more likely to be victims of violent crimes, kidnappings, blackmailing and lawsuits. At first she'd gone about her life as if nothing had changed, blaming his excessive paranoia on his job as a computer crimes investigator with the South Carolina Law Enforcement Division.

Then, after the public announcement of her win, the media storm had hit and her life had exploded. Her back door had been kicked in while she was at work and her house ransacked. Many of her belongings had been stolen. And then her car window had been shattered—*twice*. One of those times had been the day after she'd gotten it back from the repair shop. Next there was a burglary at her school, specifically of her classroom, which had prompted the school board to demand she take a leave of absence until her presence no longer posed a danger to the students. But the final straw had been when her parents' house had been broken into while her mother was home alone. At that point her brother and father had "strongly encouraged" Jessamine to take a long vacation for everyone's safety.

So here she was. Stuck in paradise. And miserable.

"You still lying low?" he asked.

"Even you wouldn't recognize me."

"Good. Alternating your routine?"

She winced and studied the hungry seagull easing closer. As much as she liked to experiment artistically, she was a creature of habit. Routines were soothing and comforting, and comfortable was something she hadn't been since arriving here. So…she might have wavered on that edict a little—which Mr. Rules and Regulations wouldn't appreciate.

"I'm being very cautious. So, what else is new?" she asked in an effort to divert him.

"Mom enrolled in the concealed-carry class yesterday."

Yet another piece of normal chipped away. Jessamine sank onto a dew-dampened bench with her back to the hungry fish. Her mother detested guns. And now she was going to carry one. Because of Jessamine. "The burglar really shook her up."

"Getting out of the shower and finding a strange man going through your bedroom drawers tends to have that effect on people. You, Mom and Leah need to be careful. You and Leah should take the CC class, too."

That would mean having a gun in her house. She had no problem with firearms. She'd grown up around them. Her father and brother were avid hunters. They'd taught her to shoot a weapon competently and hit a target. But she didn't need to own a gun. "I don't want to do that."

"Leah has agreed to take it with you."

She rocked her head side to side to ease the tension knotting her neck muscles. "How can *me* winning the lottery ruin so many lives?"

"Nobody's life is ruined, kiddo. Your notoriety is a temporary inconvenience. Once it blows over, you'll be fine. We all will be, with some minor adjustments and a few extra precautions."

She shooed the inquisitive bird. "How can you be sure?"

"Because Big Brother will be watching. Not just the guys in uniform doing drive-bys, but also with the security systems we've installed at the folks' and your place."

"Afraid to step outside is no way to live."

"I hear ya." He paused. "Jessamine, Dad and I have come to a decision."

His ultraserious tone and the use of her given name rather than the hated nickname trapped the breath in her lungs. "One I'm not going to like, I gather."

"Depends on how you look at it. Remember we used a chunk of your first check to rent that house for you for three months? Well, we want you to stay there for the duration. It doesn't make sense to throw that money away when we're still working the kinks out of security here."

Her spine snapped straight. "But you said the only reason to pay for three months was because it was cheaper in the long run than renting week to week."

"And it was—*is*. It's also the only way to guarantee you'd be in the same secure place while you're away."

"You said a month. Six weeks at the most. It's been that. I've already missed Thanksgiving."

"Turkey is turkey. It tastes the same every year. Look, we can't make you stay, but everyone in the family will sleep easier if you do."

"But what about Christmas? And Mom's birthday?"

"Dad's taking her away somewhere secret for her birthday. He won't even tell me where. She won't be home. We'll have Christmas when you get back, and then we'll really have something to celebrate." His radio squawked in the background. "I gotta go. Love you. I'll check in again tomorrow before my shift."

And then the phone—her only connection with home—went dead. She lowered her hand and stared at the silent device. Loneliness welled within her.

Christmas was only twenty days away. And her mother's birthday was three days afterward. She'd never spent either day away from her family. Pressure built in her chest, rising up to clog her throat. She wanted to scream but settled for stomping her feet. The gull got spooked and flew away. She glanced around to make sure no one had witnessed her tantrum.

Everyone dreamed of winning the lottery. It was supposed to be a good thing. For her, it had been a curse. If she could've afforded to give away the money, she would have. But she couldn't. Her parents' health insurance premiums had risen so drastically in the past year that they'd had to drop coverage, something they couldn't afford with her dad's Parkinson's disease. He needed to stay on his medicines to slow the disease's progression. Jessamine's unexpected windfall had allowed her to reinstate their policy and get her father back on his prescriptions. Her new income had also paid for the security systems each house had suddenly required because of her blasted win.

And then there was her job—or lack of one. Would the school board let her return to work when this media thundercloud blew away? She loved teaching and missed her students. But this last round of budget cuts had been hard on the noncore classes, and she'd felt vulnerable even before her temporary dismissal.

She bounded to her feet then, and with leaden steps resumed her route toward Trumbo Road. If she didn't get moving, she'd start bawling. She'd been exiled from her home and job, cut off from her friends—although she wasn't sure who the real ones were anymore—and even her church family. She'd attempted to find a church to attend down here, but folks in this surprisingly tight-knit community were too inquisitive of newcomers. After visiting three she'd quit looking and settled into her own Sunday morning routine of sorts. The weeks ahead loomed like an eternity. But she'd get through them. Somehow.

Maybe when she got back to the house she'd paint the Key deer. Again. Or the hibiscus. Again. The coconut palms? A dark swoop crossed her peripheral vision, then a bird splashed down. No. Her miserable mood would be better illustrated by painting the cormorants. A quartet of the prehistoric-looking black birds frequently parked on the end of her dock and spread their drying wings like gargoyles waiting to swoop in and carry her off. And their screeching calls to each other... She shivered despite the sun's warmth on her skin. The avian squatters creeped her out. She avoided the dock whenever they were present.

She reached the tall white fence marking the end of her route. The restaurant on the other side was quiet now. When she made her rounds again at dusk, the Fisherman's Widow's inside and outside tables would be packed. People would be laughing, silverware clinking, and the kitchen would be emitting heavenly scents. She hadn't risked eating in a restaurant thus far, but she was tired of her own cooking. Maybe she'd order takeout tonight.

And then she connected the dots between her brother's words and her financial status. She was supposed to be operating on a cash-only basis. Adding another six weeks to her stay put her in a dicey situation. She hadn't budgeted for three months. She'd replenished her art supplies a couple of times, and in the Keys they had cost double what they did at home. That meant she'd have to be very, very frugal if she wanted to have enough money to cover the rest of her stay. Even then, she'd probably run short. And without access to her accounts, she definitely wouldn't have money to buy Christmas and birthday gifts.

The irony of being a lottery winner and having her future secured with quarterly checks for practically the rest of her life but being short on actual cash right now didn't escape her. Her brother had cautioned her not to use a cash machine or credit cards or she might alert someone to her location. She could ask him to send more prepaid debit cards, but he couldn't access her accounts, either. In his rush to get her out of town, he'd failed to arrange that. He or her parents would have to use their own money to buy the prepaid debit cards until she could pay them back. Not an option she'd take until she was desperate.

So…she admitted with a sigh, no takeout. No matter how tempting. And no more art supplies.

She turned to head back for her car. A muffled cry stopped her. Was it a hurt animal? She listened until she heard it again. The whimper sounded human. She immediately recalled stories of babies discarded in Dumpsters—the restaurant's was on the other side of that fence. But it hadn't sounded like a baby. Had it? Undecided, she rocked from her heels to her toes.

She'd worry all day if she didn't check.

Tamping down her brother's dire warnings of kidnapping schemes, she clutched the can of pepper spray in her pocket, rounded the wall and approached the garbage container, then cautiously leaned forward to peer inside the open doors. She saw nothing but the dirty metal bottom. Relieved, she exhaled then recalled the trash trucks had been pulling out of the street when she'd arrived. She heard the noise again. It hadn't come from the smelly green box beside the building after all but from behind the restaurant. Had one of the delivery people fallen? She bit her lip.

Should she check it out or mind her own business? She knew what Brandon would say. *Not your problem. Go home.* But she couldn't walk away from someone in need.

As quietly as she could, she inched down the sidewalk past the closed kitchen door to the rear of the building. A woman sat at one of the patio tables with her hands to her face and her chin to her chest. Her short curly hair was a pale shade between blond and silver. Another sob escaped followed by hiccuped breaths.

Compassion compelled Jessamine forward even though caution urged her to retreat. "Ma'am, are you okay?"

The woman gasped and startled, twisting to face Jessamine. She swiped her eyes, revealing a face with enough wrinkles to make it interesting. She was petite and looked to be in her fifties or sixties. "I'm alive. So I guess I'm still in the game. Who are you?"

"Jess—" Had her story reached the Florida Keys? Would she be recognized and hounded here? "Jessie," she amended, giving the nickname her college roommate had used.

"Hello, Jess—Jessie. I'm Miri. Short for Miriam. You're new around here, aren't you?"

Keep it simple. Then leave. "Yes. I heard you

crying and wanted to make sure you were okay. Are you hurt?"

"Not physically. But I've seen better days. Would you like to join me or are you in a hurry to get to work?"

She should lie and leave. But the thought of going back to the empty house, as nice as it might be, didn't appeal. "Um...not really."

"Then pull up a chair. I'll get you some coffee. My private stash. Good stuff. I don't share it with just anyone."

Jessamine searched for the words to politely refuse.

"Please, Jessie. Today's the anniversary of my husband's death. I'm feeling sorry for myself. I need better company than my own right now."

That made two of them sick of their own company. Empathy twined through Jessamine like the flowering vine she'd been named after. She studied Miri's blotchy cheeks and red-rimmed eyes. How could she say no to a grieving widow? A couple of minutes wouldn't hurt, would it? "Maybe a quick cup."

Miri sprang to her feet and rushed into the building, leaving Jessamine open to an ambush of second thoughts. Brandon would needle her for being a people pleaser again.

The woman quickly returned, shouldering her way through the door carrying a coffeepot and an extra mug. "Sit. Please."

Hoping she wouldn't regret her decision, Jessamine perched on the edge of the chair.

Miri took her seat then poured the dark brew. "I'm sorry you caught me with my pants down, so to speak. You'd think I'd be used to waking up alone by now."

Jessamine clutched the mug rather than offer the hug she suspected the woman needed. The rich aroma teased her senses. She took a sip and let the dark brew roll down her throat. She hadn't bothered making coffee since coming to Florida. It seemed a waste to make a whole pot for one cup. But she immediately decided that would change—starting tomorrow.

"I'm sorry, Miri. How long has he been gone?"

"Three years. I miss that old fart."

The acidic comment startled a smile from Jessamine.

"You ever been in love, Jess—Jessie?"

Jessamine's smile fell. She averted her gaze. Her thumb found her bare ring finger. Yet another thing the lottery win had cost her. She would never know if a man loved her or her annuity. "I thought I was once."

"Then maybe you know how it is. You love 'em. You curse 'em. But Jack was mine. And now he's not. We fought. And we loved. But we fit. Know what I mean?"

She and Aaron had never disagreed on anything until he'd asked her to choose between him and her family. Not something she wanted to contemplate right now. She gulped coffee and scalded her tongue. "How long were you together?"

"Thirty-five years. Sounds like forever, and yet it passed in the blink of an eye. We met when I came down for spring break during college. The weather was horrible, and the boats were stuck in port. He bought me a drink and asked me to dance. Lord, that man could not dance, but he'd been watching me and knew I loved to. So he tried. It wasn't pretty," she added with a sad smile. "By the end of that week I was in love. I didn't want to go back to finish my senior year, but he insisted. Said if I didn't come to my senses and still wanted to marry a fisherman after I graduated, he'd be waiting. I came back and he was."

Why couldn't she find a love like that? One who put her best interests first? Dark hair blew across her face. Her heart leaped and her breath caught. She spun around to see who'd sneaked up on her, but no one was there. Then she remembered the dye job. Cursing her brother's horror stories, she exhaled, tucked the strand behind her ear and caught Miri watching her. Jessamine wanted to squirm but reached for her coffee instead.

"The weather brought Jack to me. And it took him away. He was struck by lightning during a freak sudden storm over the Gulf Stream. He fished, captained a charter boat service. I cooked his catch to help pay the bills when business was slow. That's how I ended up with this place. I started with a food cart on the wharf, then moved up to this board-and-brick location twenty years ago."

Miri's resourcefulness reminded Jessamine of her mother, who baked and sold pies and canned peaches and preserves to supplement the orchard's income. "Do you have children?"

"We were never blessed with our own, but when my sister passed I took over raising her boy. Logan grew up and moved away. But now he's back."

Something ominous in the last phrase piqued Jessamine's curiosity, but she let it go. It was none of her business. As much as she wanted to linger, she could hear her brother scolding, *Making friends isn't a good idea.* She set down the mug and rose. "Thank you for the coffee, Miri. I'm sorry for your loss. It sounds like you had a great marriage."

"Oh, we did. But it's not just missin' Jack that has me upset. It's the torrent of other pressures… Oh, never mind. I've enjoyed your company, Jessie. I'm sure you have better things to do than listen to an old lady's problems."

She didn't. Glancing at the sun and acknowledging she wouldn't be back in her compound before it fully rose, she sank back onto the chair.

"You're not old. You're what my mama calls 'experienced.' So what else is wrong?"

"Truthfully, my nephew is driving me nuts. Logan moved back here after Jack died, and Lord, that boy hovers. He watches every move I make and tries to tell me how to run my business. I didn't mind at first because…well, he needed to feel useful, but now…" She put a hand to her forehead and rolled her eyes. "I've had enough. Then yesterday, my best waitress called in to tell me her obstetrician has put her on complete bed rest for the remainder of her pregnancy. I was already one server short with our busy season just around the corner. If Logan gets wind that Carla's gone—he never liked her because she's…well… different—I'll never hear the end of it."

Don't say anything. But Jessamine's mouth opened anyway. "I waited tables all through college. I'm sure it wouldn't be that difficult to train someone. You could probably have two new servers in no time."

Miri's hazel eyes sharpened. "Carla did all the training. Has for years. Do you have a job, Jessie?"

Jessamine's toes curled in her sneakers. "Um… not at the moment."

"Want one?"

Say no. "I won't be here much longer."

"Are you on vacation?"

"I'm kind of on a...sabbatical." The word her father had used popped out.

"You could help me train the new hires."

No. No. No. "Miri, I appreciate the offer, but you don't even know me. I could be a criminal."

"Are you?"

"No." Jessamine sighed. Why couldn't she lie?

"Then I know what I need to. You're kind, compassionate and an experienced waitress. Please, Jessie. I'm desperate."

She shouldn't risk the exposure. "I really don't need a job."

"Just a week. Two at the most. Keep my customers happy and my nephew off my back while you train your replacements."

Jessamine searched for an excuse and came up empty. *You don't owe this near stranger an explanation. Just. Say. No.*

"We serve lunch and dinner Friday through Sunday but only dinner the rest of the week. I pay well. C'mon, Jessie. I need you. It would be a load off my mind if I didn't have to close my doors because I don't have enough staff to open tonight."

Jessamine could practically hear the vacuum sound as she got sucked in. Filling out forms with her name and address wouldn't be smart.

"Please?" Hazel eyes pleaded. "You'd be working with two other waitresses. One's very experienced. The other's not bad."

Jessie was sick of her own company. Her vacation felt like solitary confinement. And tips were often cash. If she helped Miri, she could solve her own problem this time instead of relying on her family to send her money—money they couldn't spare. She caved like soggy papier-mâché.

"I can help. But only if you'll let me work for tips alone. No paycheck. No paper trail."

Miri's pale eyebrows shot up. Her gaze turned speculative. "Okay. You're hired. I'll get you a copy of Carla's schedule. Be right back."

Miri disappeared into the building. Again, Jessamine heard Brandon's voice. *Not smart, Li'l Bit. You should have said no. Run while you can.*

But her body hadn't obeyed the order by the time Miri returned and slid a paper and pen across the table. "I'll need your phone number and clothing sizes."

"I, um…"

Her cellular and home phone numbers had been hacked within hours of the lottery win announcement, and the begging calls had come around the clock from strangers, "friends" and relatives so distant no one could remember them. Their sob stories of children with cancer or single moms living in cars had been so convincing and heart wrenching that Jessamine had wanted to help them all. Her father's intervention was the only thing that had stopped her from blowing that first check on strangers. He'd warned her she'd soon be broke if she didn't toughen up.

Then her brother had confiscated her old phone and disconnected her house phone. He'd taken her to buy a box of disposable units from different stores, then he'd given her strict instructions to use a phone for two weeks then discard it and open a new one. She no longer kept a phone long enough to learn the number.

Miri waited. "I, um...don't know my number."

"None of us do anymore. It's a push-button world these days. I'll need it if I need to call you to change your schedule. No one will have it except me. I'll wait while you look it up."

Suspecting she might be making a mistake she'd live to regret, Jessamine reluctantly pulled out her phone, turned it on and wrote down the number that appeared on the screen. She added her clothing sizes and handed the paper back to Miri. The woman folded it and tucked it into her bra.

"I'll keep it right here. No one will get it." Miri reached across the table and covered Jessamine's hand. "Do you need a safe place to stay, Jessie?"

The question threw her. "I have one. Thanks."

"Are you sure? Because I have a guest room over my garage. You can stay as long as you want. And Jack left me a .30-30. Kicks like hell but gets the job done."

Miri was offering protection and even willing

to use a rifle to provide it. She must think Jessamine was running from someone—an abusive ex or something. The thoughtfulness of a stranger made her eyes sting. She squeezed Miri's hand. "I'm good. But thank you."

"Then I'll see you today at three. I'll have a uniform for you and we'll go over my system. Jessie, I can't thank you enough for helping me through this rough patch."

Jessamine rose and beat a hasty retreat, kicking herself the whole way back to her vehicle. She debated not returning tonight. Miri only had her phone number. No last name. No address. Jessamine would simply have to toss this phone to avoid any calls.

But she'd promised. Miri needed her help training waitresses and running interference with the bossy nephew. Jessam—*Jessie* could do that. And then she'd go home with a clear conscience.

But she had to learn to say no. Starting now.

THE PRETTY BRUNETTE caught Logan's eye even before he took his customary seat at the oyster bar. She was lean but in shape, and she had great legs. Sleek muscles flexed beneath the smooth, tanned skin revealed by the Fisherman's Widow's uniform of a tank top and denim skort. A thick, loose braid hung to the middle of her back with escaped strands of hair draping her cheeks.

She'd waited tables before, though not here. It

showed in the easy way she carried five loaded plates on one arm, refilled glasses with a flick of her wrist and kept the hush puppy baskets full. She had an engaging smile for the customers, but tension lingered behind it.

That stiffness, combined with the way her hypervigilant gaze snapped toward the entrance each time the front door of his aunt's restaurant opened, kept him ensnared. It was as if she feared who might walk in. He'd entered through the kitchen, so she'd missed his arrival.

His aunt came through the swinging doors and set a plate on the bar in front of him. "See what you think of this. I'm experimenting with the mahi."

He eyed the dish. He'd spent a large part of his life being her number-one guinea pig. Most times, that was a good thing. "What is it?"

"Coconut-crusted mahi sliders with pineapple chutney."

Sounded edible. He took a bite. The tender, flaky meat practically melted in his mouth, and the seasonings were the perfect balance between sweet and hot. He chewed, then swallowed. "This recipe's a keeper. Who's the new waitress?"

Miri's gaze swung across the crowded dining room, stopping where his hovered. "Jessie. She's a sweet girl. Experienced, too."

"Where's Carla? Late again?"

Miri hesitated, and he braced himself for the

excuse du jour. "Carla's doctor ordered her to stay off her feet for the rest of her pregnancy."

"She's barely pregnant."

"She's six months along, and her blood pressure spiked."

He should have known the woman would find the one excuse for which she legally couldn't be fired. He didn't like her *or* her overly tattooed and pierced stoner boyfriend. They had a habit of borrowing money from Miri and never paying it back. Advances on her salary, his ass. The amounts were never deducted from the next check. His aunt was a pushover and a sucker for a sob story.

But on the positive side, Carla would be out for months. If he was lucky, she'd stay at home with her kid and never return.

"What do you know about the new girl?" With only one road on or off the islands, you tended to recognize residents quickly. "She's not from here."

"She's honest and a good waitress."

"How do you know if she's honest? Did you do a criminal background check using the link I gave you?"

That earned him a scowl. "She says she isn't a criminal, and I believe her."

He didn't like where this was going. "Did she pass the drug test?"

"I just hired her this morning, Logan. We haven't had time for that yet."

"You're supposed to screen them before they start. Did you at least check her references?"

Miri grabbed a towel and wiped the bar, avoiding his gaze. "No time for that yet, either."

"Give me her application. I'll do it now. She can stop by the lab in the morning." He rose and dug in his pocket for his cell phone.

"Sit down and put that thing away. Finish your dinner, Logan. I'll get to the paperwork when I get to it. I needed Jessie tonight. You can see we're still a couple of servers short. Everyone's having to work seven days a week. Jessie's covering double the tables she should be, and she's doing it well. She even knew the computer system."

"She's another one of your strays, isn't she?"

"Why must you always think the worst of everyone I hire?"

"Because you usually hire everyone else's rejects. Is she staying in the apartment?" He'd spent time there too before he'd finished renovating his cottage.

"No, smarty-pants. Jessie has her own place. Stop trying to do my job. I've been running this business without your guidance for decades. I know how to hire employees. And quit being so suspicious of everyone. You'll make yourself miserable if you don't."

"I'm looking out for your best interest. Do you see how she's watching the door?"

"Let it go, Logan."

"I'm worried about you."

"Don't be. I'm fine. The Fisherman's Widow is fine. We don't need a watchdog." Miri sighed. "You act like I have no sense at all."

"You don't when it comes to people. You're too softhearted. You surround yourself with leeches and losers. You let them take advantage of your generosity."

Red flagged Miri's cheeks. "You have no room to accuse *me* of choosing my associates unwisely."

He winced. Miri didn't have a mean bone in her body. That was as close to a low blow as she'd get. Because it was true—*he* hadn't always been wise. His failure to see the situation right in front of him was the reason she had no cash reserves or retirement funds.

"Speaking of leeches and losers…that one's a prime example," Miri added in a waspy tone. He twisted to follow her scowling gaze and spotted the private detective he employed crossing the dining room. She shot I a scathing look when he took a seat. "I wish you'd hold your business fleecings elsewhere."

The PI ignored Miri's insult and smiled. "Well, if it ain't my little ray of Florida sunshine. Always a pleasure to see you, too, Miri." He delivered the words in an exaggerated version of his New

Jersey accent, which seemed to irritate Logan's aunt even more.

"What kind of name is I, anyway?" she snapped.

"Nobody can spell Ignatius. I save 'em the trouble by keeping it short and sweet. Kind of like you do, Miriam Louise."

Logan's aunt stiffened at the use of her given name, then stomped back into the kitchen. Logan shook his head. "Why do you needle her?"

"She started it. She treats me like a dog shit on her shoe. That whole lip-curling thing bugs the crap out of me. And what in the hell is wrong with using my initial?"

Miri got along with everyone. Why not I? The two had been at each other's throats since their first meeting over a year ago.

"Anything?" Logan asked the PI.

"Nope. Trail went cold in Porto Alegre, Brazil."

"Two people can't just vanish." Frustration killed Logan's appetite. He pushed the unfinished meal aside.

"Your wife and business partner have. For now. They'll turn up eventually. Finding them depends on how much money you want to spend. Me, I'd say good riddance and cut my losses."

"Ex-wife and ex–business partner," he corrected. "I can't let this go. They destroyed my reputation when they embezzled our clients' funds. No reputable firm will hire me."

"What's wrong with the setup you got here? You get a free meal every night. You got a decent place to stay. You set your own hours and make enough to get by doing people's taxes. What else do you need?"

"I want them to admit what they did and clear my name."

"Hate to tell ya, Nash, but even if we find 'em and they're extradited to the States and they sing like canaries, it won't get the stench off ya. Stuff like that tends to stick."

Logan refused to accept that. He'd done nothing criminal, and he had to prove it. "That's a risk I'm willing to take."

I shrugged. "Your dime. But don't say I didn't warn ya. You gonna finish that?"

"No."

I snagged the dish, pulled it closer and shoved an untouched slider into his mouth. "Damn, that woman can cook," he said.

"What do you make of her?" Logan nodded toward the brunette waitress.

"Hot. Yours?"

"Nah. Miri's new hire. See the way she watches the door?"

I nodded. "She got outstanding warrants? Or an abusive ex?"

"I don't know."

"I'd find out. Something's got her jumpy."

"I will. Don't doubt it. I'll be damned if someone else steals from Miri on my watch."

CHAPTER TWO

JESSIE REFILLED THE last saltshaker and wiped down the table, then straightened and stretched the kinks from her spine. Her body ached from the unaccustomed exercise—but in a good way. She blinked her tired, gritty eyes. It was time to go home and remove these irritating contacts.

She stopped beside the final open window and let the peace of the empty dining room settle over her. Water lapped outside the building, and a gentle breeze drifted in. She loved the concept of a restaurant constructed on a pier so low to the water that the fish swam close enough for the customers to drop food to them and watch them gobble it up.

The music went silent, and the lights illuminating the water went dark, jarring Jessie into action. She closed and latched the window. If her brother found out she was outside the compound after dark, he'd never stop lecturing. But she should be safe. No one except her family knew she was in Key West, and it was only a half mile's walk to where she'd parked her rental car at the opposite end of the well-lit boardwalk. She'd thought it better to keep the vehicle as far away from the restaurant as possible just in case Brandon's paranoia wasn't all in his head.

Miri came out of the kitchen, followed by the good-looking guy who'd been seated at the oyster bar most of the evening. Something about the way he'd scrutinized Jessie's every move tonight had made her nervous. That uneasiness intensified now with him only two yards away. He wasn't part of the kitchen staff, so who was he?

"You did a great job tonight, Jessie."

"Thanks, Miri."

Miri indicated her companion with a flip of her fingers. "Jessie, my nephew, Logan Nash."

The one who drove the restaurateur nuts with his interference? He looked only a few years older than Jessie. His hair was as black as the cormorant's wings and his eyes, as blue as the noon sky, stared at her with suspicion.

Jessie wrung the wet rag in her hands and nodded but said nothing and didn't offer her hand. He nodded in return.

"Will you be back tomorrow?" Miri asked.

A wad of bills weighted Jessie's pocket. Tonight's tips would be enough to get by for a while. But for how long? Not six more weeks, for sure.

"I ask because someone is coming in for an interview in the morning," Miri added when Jessie hesitated. "If she works out, I'll have her shadow you tomorrow night."

Jessie dug her nails deeper into the cotton. She'd promised to train her replacements. And Miri needed a buffer between her and the human cormorant. Should she risk it? Going back to solitary confinement after an evening of interacting with people sounded like torture. But no one should recognize her here. Not with her disguise.

She took a deep breath and answered, "I'll be here," before she could change her mind.

"Great, hon. You don't know how much I appreciate it."

Logan tugged the bank bag from Miri's hands. "I'll give Jessie a ride home on my way to drop off tonight's deposit."

Objections blossomed in Jessie's head. Miri's startled expression, which quickly transformed to one of worry, confirmed Jessie's reservations. "Thanks, but I, um…have my car."

"Miri's is the only one in the lot."

"I parked nearby."

"I'll walk you to it."

His forceful tone made her hackles rise. It was one thing for her father or brother to boss her around—or, as they said, "strongly encourage"—but she wasn't taking orders from a stranger. "I appreciate your offer, but I'll be fine."

"It's almost midnight."

"I have pepper spray."

His nostrils flared in obvious irritation and his mouth opened, but Miri laid a hand on his arm.

"Leave her be, Logan. After her busy night, Jessie probably needs to clear her head. I always do. Thanks for taking the deposit. I'll see you tomorrow." She crossed to the front door and held it open in a blatant invitation for Logan to leave.

Blue eyes drilled Jessie's again. "You need to hit the clinic for a drug test before you come in tomorrow. All of our employees are tested."

Jessie glanced at Miri, who shook her head. "I'll manage *my* employees, Logan. Now go."

His lips thinned. He looked ready to argue, but then said, "Good night."

He left and the wind leaked from Jessie's lungs. Only then did she notice her racing heart and damp palms. "So that's him."

Miri nodded. "I commend you on not getting into a car with a strange man, especially one who's being a bossy britches, but you can trust Logan. He's a good one. Just a little overprotective."

"About that drug test...I'm trying to avoid a paper trail right now."

"I suspected as much. Forget it. After the way you hustled tonight, I know you're not using anything."

"If you have any doubts about me working here—"

"I don't."

"Thanks."

"Want me to give you a ride to your car?"

Jessie shook her head. "It's okay. I'm just down the boardwalk."

"I'd feel better if I watched you till you're out of sight." After locking the front door she led Jessie out the rear to the patio. She pulled out her phone and punched buttons. Seconds later Jessie's phone vibrated against her hip. "Now you have my number. Save it and call if you need me. For anything, hon, and at any time. Day or night. Be careful. I'll see you tomorrow."

Then Miri sank into a chair. She reminded Jessie so much of her mother sitting on the patio and watching as Jessie walked to the end of their long driveway to wait for the school bus that it made her eyes sting.

"Good night, Miri. And thanks for…understanding."

"There's nothing wrong with needing a second chance."

Jessie didn't correct her. She backed away and waved then turned and strode off before she gave in to the overwhelming urge to hug the restaurant owner, confess all and ask her advice. But it was better if Miri didn't know. Knowing could add her to the list of people adversely affected by being connected to Jessamine.

For the first time since being forced from her job, she felt a sense of purpose. She couldn't protect her mother from the chaos at home, but she could protect Miri from her mess here and from her overbearing nephew.

It wasn't until Jessie slowed to turn off Highway 1 that she realized she'd said no to Logan Nash. Funny how easy it had been to say the word to him. But he'd definitely gotten on her bad side, and like a student who seemed destined to cause trouble, he needed watching.

FOR THE FIRST time since arriving in Florida, Jessie awoke refreshed and eager to start her day. Attributing her good night's sleep to the hustle at work, she started a pot of the exotic coffee provided with her rental, showered and dressed while it brewed, then grabbed her mug, her caddy of art supplies and her easel and headed out onto the deck.

Her brother had called twice while she was in the shower, and she debated calling him back. But for once she didn't want to talk to him. Calling meant she might have to lie about where she'd been last night or what she'd done. Instead, she texted him to let him know she was okay and slipped her phone back into her pocket.

A flash of movement caught her eye. A trio of Key deer, none any bigger than her at-home neighbor's rescued greyhounds, strolled through the backyard a dozen feet below. The four-legged family had become part of her morning routine.

Except for the waterfront space, the rental

property was completely fenced in, but the deer somehow found their way in and back out again on a regular basis. Back home in South Carolina, the deer invading her daddy's orchard were considered a nuisance and were dealt with accordingly, but here Key deer were a protected species. And they were welcome company. She would miss them once she returned home.

On her first day on the island she'd learned that the animals liked people food when she'd left her lunch on the table beneath the palms and gone inside for two minutes. She'd returned to find them eating her sandwich. Captivated, she'd fed them her apple, then later when she'd slipped into the library to research them, she'd discovered she'd broken the law. Feeding the deer was illegal, for their own safety. She hadn't fed them since, but they always showed up looking hopeful. It made her wish she'd replaced her camera. It, along with her laptop, had been stolen in the first break-in, and searching for new electronics hadn't seemed important with everything else going on. But she'd sketched her visitors multiple times.

"Sorry, guys. No food again today."

Their big brown begging eyes filled her with a load of guilt that she tried to ignore, then the buck led his little group off into the dense green foliage bordering the fence. Juggling her load, Jessie carefully descended the stairs and dug her toes into the still cool crushed shells, then glanced toward the private pier and stopped in her tracks. The cormorants were back doing their creepy statue imitations. She couldn't bring herself to join them. Instead she set up her chair and easel in the shade beneath the coconut tree and picked up her binoculars.

One of the birds turned his head and stared at her very much like Miri's nephew had last night. A shiver skittered down her spine. "I'm naming you Nash," she told the vile creature.

She filled her palette then quickly painted in the background. From this distance, the island was a blur of greens and the water blues and grays. Then she picked up a finer brush to begin the focal point. Her fingers flew across the canvas, adding detail to the birds and the long and narrow dock. As the sun climbed overhead and forced her to squint, she wished she'd brought her sunglasses outside, but she rarely bothered early in the morning. The lenses muted too many of the colors.

The rumble of a boat motor penetrated her concentration. She watched it until she was able to identify it as a regular fishing boat rather than one of long, low speedboats or diving boats that often cruised by. There was nothing remarkable enough about it to make her interrupt her work. She'd love to hire someone to teach her to dive, but her brother's warnings and her cash situation kept her from putting thought into action.

The craft passed less than fifty yards from the end of the dock, startling the cormorants into flying away. The driver and passengers waved—most boaters did, she'd discovered—and she waved back. Eager to claim her turf before the birds returned, she grabbed her gear and hustled down the sun-bleached planks to the wider rectangle at the end.

Waves from the boat's wake gently rocked the floating platform. She set her gear on the fish-cleaning table. The water lapping at the pylons was clear. She could see the bottom and the crab trap someone had left behind. One lone crab beat against the metal cage. Grabbing the rope, she hauled it up, opened the door and tipped over the trap. The crustacean scuttled over the edge of the boards to freedom. She pitched the wire cube back into the water with a splash. No way was she boiling a live crab and listening to it beat against the pot until it died. She shuddered.

Two cormorants swooped overhead. She waved her arms, and thankfully they landed on the dock next door—a safe two hundred yards away. She settled her canvas against the easel. The picture was coming together so quickly that it reminded her of the old weekly public television show she used to watch as a child. The instructor had whipped out a painting in an hour. She wasn't that fast, but there was definitely something freeing about painting here with no interruptions and no audience.

The sun's glare was intense, and once again she wished for her sunglasses. Tomorrow she'd remember to bring them, but she didn't dare leave today or the birds might return. She checked her watch. Another hour before she had to shower and report for work.

If she was lucky, Logan Nash wouldn't show up tonight.

SUE SLID A disposable takeout container onto the bar in front of Logan. "Miri said to tell you to take your dessert and go home. What did you do to tick her off?"

He shifted on his bar stool and drummed his fingers on the envelope containing the rejected forms. "I tried to get the new waitress to fill out her employment forms."

He'd left his office early, bringing with him the necessary paperwork, and he'd waited out front, planning to corner Jessie before the restaurant opened and insist she complete the sheets. But Miri had spotted him and run interference, insisting that if he couldn't stop hounding Jessie then he needed to go home.

He couldn't figure out why his aunt was so determined to protect the waitress. So here he was again—stuck on a bar stool for an entire night watching the brunette's suspicious behavior and learning nothing.

"What do you think of your new coworker?" he asked the sixty-something waitress who'd been with Miri since the day she'd opened Fisherman's Widow.

"Jessie? What's not to like? She hustles. I don't have to cover her tables. She runs my stuff when I get behind before I even have a chance to ask. And she has the patience of a saint training the gal, who is not the brightest bulb in the box, if you catch my drift."

He'd come to the same conclusion about the new trainee. But he wasn't interested in her. "Where did Jessie say she's from?"

Eyes narrowed beneath Sue's penciled brows. "She didn't say. In case you missed it, that flood of cruise ship passengers ran us off our feet tonight. No time for chitchat. I'd tell you to ask Jessie yourself, but you need to respect Miri's wishes and quit trying to chat up the new employee, Logan."

"I'm not interested in her that way." He debated telling Sue that Jessie hadn't gone for the required drug test or filled out the employee paperwork. The newest hire had done both. But dissing one employee to another was undoubtedly a violation of some kind. "Just keep an eye on her."

"In case you haven't noticed, we've been too busy for me to mind anybody's business except my own. You should do the same," Sue delivered then sailed out the front door.

He lifted the lid of the box. Key lime pie. One of his favorites. But eating it would have to wait. Jessie's trainee and the other waitress had left before Sue. That meant Jessie and Logan were the only ones left in the public area of the building. He had to act fast if he wanted to get what he needed from Jessie before his aunt interfered again.

He grabbed the envelope and headed for the outside dining area, where Jessie was boxing the last of the condiments to bring inside for the night.

She glanced up when he pushed the door open and stilled. Brown eyes tracked his progress across the planks with something akin to dread.

He held out the manila envelope and a pen. "You haven't filled out your paperwork. You can't be employed here without filling out an I-9 and a W-4."

She ignored the offered items. Her breasts rose and fell on three breaths. Something he shouldn't be noticing. "That's between Miri and me."

"I'm her accountant. I'm required by law to have this information on all employees. I need it for payroll."

She blinked thick lashes. Slowly. As if buying time. "I'm not on her payroll."

That knocked him back a step. "What does that mean?"

"I work for tips."

"You're busting your tail for eight hours a night with no expectation of a paycheck? What are you after? Cash under the table?"

His sarcasm turned down the corners of her mouth. It wasn't until she pressed her lips together that he realized how full they were. "No. Just tips."

"That's ridiculous. It's not even close to minimum wage."

"I'm a friend helping a friend. Is that so hard to believe?"

His suspicion multiplied tenfold. "Why?"

"Why help Miri?"

He nodded. And waited. And waited.

"She's a very nice person. And she's hard to say no to."

Good answer, but she'd taken too long to come up with it for it to be genuine—a clue he'd been too dense to notice when his wife had started hiding things from him. "What are you getting out of it?"

"I told you."

"Tips are taxable income. I still need your information."

"My accountant will deal with it in April."

She had to be another one of Miri's projects. He dropped the pen and papers on a nearby table and caught her wrists. Ignoring her gasp, he rolled her hands thumbs out to examine her inner forearms. No ugly track marks marred the ivory skin that clearly showed undamaged blue veins beneath the surface.

And then her warmth leached into his palms and up his arms. It spread across his shoulders then sank through his chest and gathered into a ball of heat in his gut. Desire? No way. Then he noticed her calluses. Not heavy ones, but Jessie definitely used her hands on a daily basis.

She yanked free and wiped her palms on her hips as if he'd dirtied her. "What are you doing?"

With effort, he hacked through the haze that had befuddled his brain. "Looking for signs that you use."

"Use?" Her brow pleated. A beat of silence passed. "Drugs?"

Her wide eyes and shocked tone didn't fool him. "It wouldn't be the first time Miri helped someone get clean. They usually stay at her house, and it usually backfires. I end up having to help her evict them."

"I'm not staying with her. And I don't and never have used drugs."

"Then why are you avoiding the drug test and paperwork? What are you hiding?"

Her cheeks flushed. She averted her face, but he didn't believe for one moment she was that fascinated by the dark waterfront. "I told you. I'm just a friend with time on my hands."

"I don't believe you."

Worried eyes focused on him. "If Miri hires known drug users, then why are you so insistent on me taking the test? Wouldn't it be a moot point?"

He bit back a curse. She was a wily one. Then the piped-in music went silent, a signal that the kitchen had been cleaned to his aunt's exacting expectations and it was time to lock up. He gritted his teeth. He'd learned nothing about Jessie's motives or agenda. Sure enough, the kitchen door swung open and Miri walked out. She scanned the empty dining room, spotted them outside and headed in their direction with the kind of scowl he knew boded ill—for him. She plowed open the back door with a flat palm.

"Sue was supposed to send you home," she told him.

"I'm waiting for you to lock up."

"Since when do you hang around until I close?" Her gaze fell on the envelope, and her expression grew even fiercer. Miri had been a great substitute mom. He'd rarely seen her lose her temper, but when she did, it was a sight to behold. From a distance.

"Logan, butt out of my business."

"I'm covering you—legally."

"We're not breaking any laws. But you're

tempting me to take my iron skillet to your head. Now go home before I ban you from my restaurant." Her scowl could curdle milk. "You ready, Jessie?"

"Yes. I'll, um…I'll set these in the cooler on my way out." Jessie ducked her head, grabbed the box of condiments and swept past him, her long dark braid swinging like a pendulum above her hips. Nice hips. Curved, but not round.

He shouldn't be noticing.

Miri shot him one last warning glare then followed her. When Jessie returned from the kitchen, Miri rested a hand on her shoulder and leaned closer. "Let me get rid of him and I'll walk you out," Logan heard Miri whisper conspiratorially.

Yeah, they definitely had something going on that needed monitoring.

"Thanks, Miri, but there's no need. I parked closer tonight," Jessie replied with a quick glance in his direction. He averted his gaze and pretended he hadn't been eavesdropping. Then she hustled out the front door. He held it for Miri then waited while she locked it.

"I'm not kidding, Logan. You're overstepping your bounds."

"I hear you, but—"

"There is no but. Go home."

He wasn't going to talk sense into her tonight. He kissed Miri's cheek. "See you tomorrow."

He pivoted toward his car.

Follow Jessie home.

The idea stopped him midstep. He palmed his keys and rolled the thought around in his head. He was already paying I as much as he could afford to track Elizabeth and Trent. If he wanted info on Jessie, he'd have to get it himself.

He stared into the gloom of the streetlights and spotted Jessie heading toward Margaret Street. Traffic was light but not so light that he couldn't blend in. Miri got into Jack's old truck and drove away in the opposite direction.

He hustled to his car and waited until Jessie was a block down before starting the engine. A vehicle passed him, then a second. He pulled out behind them, going slowly as if searching for a parking space but keeping Jessie in sight. She slid into a small sedan. Hanging back, he let another car pull out and get between them, then he followed Jessie's vehicle onto Highway 1.

"This is nuts," he muttered after she passed several mile markers. "I'm acting like a stalker."

But Miri's safety depended on him protecting her from further harm—financial or otherwise—and there was something about the new waitress that didn't add up. A furtiveness that worried him since he'd seen, ignored and been burned by a similar situation.

The car between them peeled off. Finally, Jessie signaled and turned left. That posed a problem. There would be less traffic off the highway, making it harder to remain undetected. But at least he was familiar with the area since he often explored the Keys. She kept her speed slow. The street was long and straight. She'd be onto him if he stayed behind her. The first road to his left was horseshoe shaped. If he took it, he'd come out farther down the main road. He might lose her, but it was a risk he had to take. He turned and hit the gas. She passed in front of him just before he reached the stop sign. He braked and watched her taillights. Her indicator flashed by a driveway near the end of the road. He waited until she disappeared through the fence before rolling forward.

An electronic gate slid closed, blocking her driveway. Making note of the house number, he drove past and circled back, pulled off the road and killed his headlights. Each of the houses on that stretch was surrounded by tall fences of either stone or block. That worked in his favor by concealing him. He checked both directions to see if anyone was watching. It was all clear, but he felt like a criminal. With his heart racing, he exited the car and ambled up to the iron gates to look through the white bars. Nice house. But not movie-star expensive. Still, an acre of waterfront property wasn't cheap. Jessie's car was the only one parked beneath the house. She climbed the stairs to the front door and tapped in a code, then disappeared inside. Lights came on.

To the left of the house, he spotted a hot tub beneath a thatched roof with a pool beyond it. A lamp-lit pier stretched out into the water.

He scanned his surroundings again and spotted the discreet real estate agent's sign. A rental, but still an expensive place, and not something a waitress could afford unless she had a rich husband or a sugar daddy. He'd noticed she wasn't wearing a ring.

How could Jessie afford a house that rented for thousands each week? Her calluses and demeanor led him to believe she wasn't a socialite, and her shoes were the same brand he saw in big-box stores—not designer or high-end. He ought to know—his ex had worn both. Besides, if Jessie were rich, why would she be so damned good at waiting tables?

Tonight's investigation was only leading to more questions. Something about Jessie didn't add up. He had to find out how she was paying for her expensive accommodations—for Miri's sake. If Jessie's money came from swindling others or selling drugs, then he'd have to stop her before she snookered his aunt.

CHAPTER THREE

THE HEAT OF the overhead sun penetrated Jessie's floppy straw hat. Rivulets of sweat trickled down her bare back. It might be December, but the Keys were experiencing a heat wave.

A boat motor droned in the distance, but she was too caught up in putting the last strokes on her cormorant to look up. She'd lost count of how many boats had passed since she'd raced out here early this morning trying to get ahead of her unwanted squatters. Nightmares starring the birds had kept her awake, and she hoped getting this painting out of her head would give her peace.

She added one last daub of raw sienna to the beak, then sat back to study her work with as much objectivity as she could muster. Not bad. The bird itself was finished and lifelike enough to be creepy. She checked her watch. Noon. If she stopped now, she could take a swim before showering for work.

She washed out her brush then removed her hat and crossed to the edge of the dock. Arching left then right, she stretched the kinks from her spine. She curled her toes over the edge, anticipating a dip in the cool, clear water, but then she spotted the nurse shark lurking by the crab pot and backtracked. Locals claimed nurse sharks didn't bite, but she wasn't testing that theory. She'd settle for cooling off in the pool.

She gathered her painting supplies. Only then did she notice a boat engine's noise—it was closer than any previous boat had come. Curious, she turned to see a center-console boat with one man on board heading straight for her dock. Her brother's daily warnings echoed in her mind, and alarm skittered through her. Was some guy going to try to kidnap her and demand her lottery winnings for ransom?

Nervously, she mentally measured the distance to the house. The pier was more than a hundred feet long and it was fifty more across the beach to the bottom of the steps. Could she reach the house and lock her doors before the stranger caught her? No. Worse, she'd left her pepper spray inside, and her nails were clipped too short to do much damage. But she refused to become a statistic. She'd have to stand and fight and hope he didn't have a gun. She had nothing except her easel to use as a weapon. Her best bet would be to introduce him to the nurse shark then run.

Praying she was just being paranoid but determined to be the best witness she could be if she wasn't, she studied the vessel's shirtless occupant. He was tallish with short, dark hair, and muscled enough that he'd be hard to fight off. Mirrored lenses covered his eyes, but his attention appeared to be fixed on her.

"Jessie?" he called out.

Logan Nash. Shock made her stomach drop. She should have recognized that square chin.

A different kind of panic set in. She wasn't wearing her colored contacts or much of anything else. Ducking her head, she scrambled for her hat and sunglasses, shoved them on and cursed the fact that she hadn't brought out her cover-up or even a towel. She'd bought the skimpy bikini top and low-slung boy short bottoms soon after arriving. She'd been pretending to be someone else, and she'd decided she wanted to dress like someone else, too—someone who didn't always wear a modest one-piece. Of course, this swimsuit didn't cover enough skin for anyone else to see her in it.

The craft thumped against the dock's rubber edge, jarring her deep inside. He killed the engine then shoved his glasses into his thick hair, revealing blue eyes that skimmed over her then the house. "Your place?"

How had he found her? And why? "For now. What are you doing here, Logan?"

He dropped his glasses back over his eyes. "I was riding by and thought I recognized you."

He tossed a rope toward her. It landed a yard away. She left it there. Without invitation he stepped onto the platform, rocking the surface beneath her feet, then he looped the rope through one of the metal cleats stationed around the deck and straightened.

She couldn't see his eyes and felt exposed on so many levels as she stared at her reflection in his mirrored lenses. Dropping her gaze, she found herself entranced by the smooth curves of his pectoral muscles, the light dusting of dark curls. She'd only seen him in polo shirts and khaki pants before now, and she wished she could have kept it that way. He had the body of an athlete, from his broad shoulders to his tapered waist and long legs. Lordy, he'd be a joy to paint.

No, Jessie! She gulped, trying to dislodge the knot in her throat, and wrapped her arms around her middle.

He abruptly stepped around her to the easel holding her picture. "Did you paint this?"

"Um. Yes," she forced out, feigning calm she didn't feel.

She didn't like him knowing where she lived. How would she get rid of him? "It's a beautiful day to be on the water, but it's supposed to storm later. Better get your trip in before it hits."

He glanced her way, a crooked smile on his face. Her stomach swooped. "I can spare a few minutes."

He was close—too close. And too naked. She could feel the heat emanating from him and smell his suntan lotion. The air turned thick and humid, making it hard to breathe. She shuffled backward, putting space between them, then wished she hadn't when the distance widened her view, making it impossible to miss that he had those little dents disappearing beneath the front waistband of his trunks. Seeing those hollows up close and in person on someone you knew was a lot different than sketching them from a distance in a nude art class. The inclination to trace them came out of nowhere and was totally foreign. Her stubby nails bit into her palms.

Aaron had been a dedicated gym rat, but despite the hours he'd put in, her ex-fiancé hadn't had a body like Logan's.

Logan shoved up his glasses once more. "You're an artist?"

"Oh. No. I'm an art—" *Teacher.* She bit her tongue on the word. "Dabbler."

"This is really good, Jessie. You must make a lot of money selling your dabbles."

She blinked in surprise. "Oh, I don't sell them. Painting's…just a hobby."

A line creased his forehead, and his narrowed gaze focused on her. He jerked a thumb, indicating the canvas. "Do you have more of these?"

"Yes. Why?"

"May I see them?"

She pressed her bare toes against the warm dock. She didn't share her art with anyone except her family, and these days she rarely showed them her efforts.

"Maybe some other time. I need to get dressed for work."

"The restaurant doesn't open until four today. You can spare five minutes. I'll even help you carry your stuff inside so you can do it in one trip and save time."

She didn't want him in her house. "That's nice of you, but I don't think—"

"If the rest of your work is as good as this I might have a profitable proposition."

Intrigued despite her aversion to him, she wrestled with her conscience. In the end, she caved because she didn't know how to politely refuse. "A quick look."

Carefully grabbing the still-wet cormorant and her paint palette, she turned and made her way to the house. He grabbed the easel and followed. Inside, she propped the canvas against the sunroom wall beside the other pieces, set the palette on the newspaper she'd left on the table and automatically reached to remove her sunglasses. Then she remembered her lack of contacts and left her shades in place. She paused to let her eyes adjust, but even then the lenses were too dark to wear inside. As much as she hated leaving Logan unsupervised in her house, she had to get her contact lenses or risk tripping over something. She ran a mental checklist. There shouldn't be anything left in plain sight that he couldn't see.

"Set that over there and have a seat. I'll be right back."

She hustled into her bedroom, shut and locked the door, then entered the bathroom and did the same. That had been too close a call. She whipped off the sunglasses and hat and checked the mirror. Familiar blue eyes stared back at her—not the cobalt blue of Logan's. She'd inherited her daddy's pale, silvery-blue irises. She quickly inserted the nonprescription colored contacts, then she shoved the box of dark chocolate-macchiato semipermanent hair coloring beneath the sink. Covering her blond roots would have to wait until Logan was gone. She took a moment to don a cover-up then plopped her hat back on her head and checked her image again. Her brown-eyed disguise was back in place. Even her mother wouldn't recognize her.

She went to find then get rid of Logan. He wasn't in the sunroom. Panic welled within her. Where was he? And what was he doing? She raced into the kitchen. Empty. Through the dining room. No Logan. She found him in the living room. He stood, fist to chin, studying the paintings and drawings she had scattered about.

He didn't acknowledge her arrival, and his lack of response kinked nerves in her belly. Sharing her work—her serious work, not the stuff she doodled with her students—was hard. Really hard. The sensation of nakedness returned full force. She scanned her collection.

"I, um…like to experiment with different mediums. Acrylics, charcoals, watercolors, pastels…"

"You did all these?" he asked without lifting his gaze from her favorite representation of the deer family.

She took a deep breath. "Yes."

His gaze drilled hers. "Why don't you sell them?"

"Who would want them?"

"Jessie, your execution is excellent, and these have the local flavor that tourists love to take home to remind them of their trip. Would you be willing to sell them?"

She'd never sold a painting and couldn't believe anyone would want to pay good money for one. "I guess…I might."

"The same paintings have hung in Miri's restaurant for as long as I can remember. They're dated and faded. We could swap some of her old art with yours and market these to tourists. I'm sure you've seen similar setups in other restaurants with discreet price tags nearby."

She struggled for words and found none. As a child she'd dreamed of becoming an artist, but once she'd reached college her father had said, "Choose a steady, reliable career that pays the bills and comes with benefits. Artists starve." She'd compromised and decided to teach art. Teaching gave her an opportunity to instill her passion for creativity in others. Between the hours she taught and those spent preparing for each class, she'd had little time to pursue many personal projects until she'd been banished to the Keys. Now all she had was time.

The interest in her work was shocking, but doubly so from Logan Nash. "Why are you being nice when you've been nothing but confrontational up until now?"

"Because fresh art might bring more business to the Widow."

"Miri already has more traffic than three waitresses can handle."

"The staff shortage is a temporary situation."

Fear battled eagerness. "I wouldn't know how to price them."

"I do."

His offer sounded too good to be true. "What's your take?"

"My take? You mean like a commission? Nothing. And I doubt Miri will want one, either. But none of these are signed. Sign this one." He pointed to her favorite Key deer picture. "Bring it to work tonight."

Her heart beat double time. She bit her lip, dug her toes into the plush rug and searched his face. He looked sincere, and she *really* wanted to believe his compliments. She was tempted—so very tempted—to test her fledgling artist's wings.

What would her father and Brandon say? She

ached to call and ask their advice. But she couldn't. Telling them about this opportunity meant telling them about her job—something they definitely wouldn't approve of.

"Jessie, at least show this one to Miri. If she doesn't agree that your work could be an asset to the Widow, then you've lost nothing."

Except her pride. Logan had gotten her hopes up. How would she feel if no one wanted it? She had to take the chance or forever regret it. "Okay."

He nodded. "See you in a few hours."

She walked him out then caught herself checking out his broad shoulders and strong back as he descended the stairs. She shut the door a little harder than necessary and locked it, then pressed a hand over her pounding heart. She didn't release her pent-up breath until he'd boarded his boat and driven away.

Logan liked her work. Someone outside her family actually liked her work. What's more, he thought that others might, too. Joy and pride bubbled inside her. She danced in place, then sobered.

Putting herself out there meant possible criticism. Could she handle it? Then again, if this venture was a total flop, her family and friends—if she had any left after the lottery debacle—would never have to know. She'd go back to real life and leave her childish dream of becoming an artist behind forever.

WHEN THE KITCHEN door swung open, Miri checked the clock. The restaurant didn't open for two hours. But instead of one of the kitchen staff, Logan's investigator walked in. Ignatius was the last person she wanted to see.

"He's not here," she told him and experienced a twinge of shame at her nasty tone. Being a business owner meant being polite to everyone—even parasites. That was especially true in Key West. As cosmopolitan as the city seemed, it was truly a small community.

"I'm not here to see Logan. I'm here to see you."

Suspicion trickled through her like water through a cracked levee. "Why?"

He removed his ball cap, revealing a thick head of salt-and-pepper hair, and shifted on his feet. The big goofball looked so uncomfortable, her protest that the public wasn't allowed in her kitchen stayed locked behind her clenched teeth.

"Today's my daughter's birthday. She and her girls are meeting me here for dinner tonight. I need it to be...special."

Not even close to what she'd expected him to say. "I appreciate your business. I'll do my best to resist the urge to poison you."

"No. You don't..." He hadn't laughed. Had she expected him to? "I'm not explaining this well. Bethany and I... We don't... We're not close."

That wasn't a surprise. "What did you do to piss her off, Ignatius?"

"Don't call me that. It reminds me of Catholic school."

"It's your name. *I* is only a letter. What did you do to turn your daughter against you?" she pressed.

His cheeks turned ruddy. "I wasn't there for her and her mother when she was young. I worked all the time, trying to make detective. Then when Bethany was sixteen, Eileen split and moved down here. I couldn't afford to come down more than once a year, so I didn't get to see my daughter or granddaughters much. Other than birthday and Christmas cards and social media, we don't communicate."

"Why try to change that now?"

"Because Sydney and Chloe are the spittin' image of their mama, and when I see their pictures online I realize how much I missed of Bethany's childhood. I want a chance to do right by those girls."

Sympathy surged like a storm tide inside Miri. She wished Logan's father would have a similar revelation before it was too late. "How old are they?"

"Ten and twelve."

She gave him bonus points for knowing their ages. "Have you bought your daughter a present?"

"Yeah." He dug into his pocket, pulled out a

small, unwrapped jewelry box and shoved it toward her. "Just picked it up."

She took it and lifted the lid. A gold heart necklace with three different-colored gemstones sparkled on the satin liner. The little tab said fourteen karat. It wasn't junk.

"Those are Bethany and the girls' birthstones," he added. "I special ordered it."

Kudos to him. He'd spent time and effort and had even planned ahead. She'd have expected him to just grab the closest thing—from the clearance rack, if his clothes were anything to go by. She snapped the box shut and handed it back. "She should like it."

"Ya think?" He sounded so hopeful. Someone ought to tell him he was too old to have that puppy-dog look in his eyes.

"I think she will. What about a cake? Not that our desserts aren't delicious, but a cake would be a personal touch."

His dumbfounded expression gave her the answer. He hadn't thought of that. Two of the kitchen staff came in. She greeted them then motioned Ignatius toward the dining room. She wanted him out of the sanctuary of her workspace.

"I have a friend who's a baker. I'll get something special from her. What's Bethany's favorite dessert?"

He shrugged, and his cheeks darkened again.

"Does she hate anything?" Another shrug. "Allergies?" Same response. Miri sighed. She didn't know whether to feel sorry for the guy or be angry with him for knowing nothing about his child. "Which birthday is it?"

"Thirty-nine."

"Not a milestone, then. I'll put you in Jessie's section. She has a way with our younger customers that'll put the girls at ease. And I'll seat you right over there." She pointed at the table she usually reserved for honeymooners. "It's quieter so you can talk, and you can see the fish on two sides. Your granddaughters won't have to fight for the best seat."

"I...thanks, Miri. I appreciate it."

"Now I need a favor from you."

"Name it."

"Drop Logan's case."

His expression turned from gratitude to pugnacity in a blink. Probably his cop I'm-writing-you-a-ticket face. "If I do he'll just hire somebody else."

That wasn't what she wanted to hear even if she suspected it was true. "He's so focused on finding his ex-wife he won't even date anyone else."

Green eyes searched her face. "Have you dated anyone since your husband passed?"

Taken aback by the unexpected attack, she struggled for an answer. "We're not talking about me."

"You're accusing the man of not moving on

with his life. I'm just saying, you might want to look in the mirror."

She straightened to her full height at the offensive remark and opened her mouth to tell him where to go. But then she spotted the bartender close enough to overhear. With tremendous effort, she reined in her temper. Having a business to run required her to mind her manners no matter the provocation. Word got around. She couldn't afford to tell the fathead what she thought of his rotten psychoanalysis skills. Not here. Not now. But one day...

"Leave dinner to me. We've got you covered."

"Thanks, Miri. I owe ya."

"Yes. You do."

Logan plowed through the kitchen door into the dining area like a man on a mission. His eyebrows jacked up when he saw Ignatius, but he didn't slow until he was beside them.

"You look all nice and tanned. Did you take the morning off?" Miri asked him.

"I've been out on I's boat. Did you know Jessie's an artist?"

She struggled with the news that Logan and Ignatius knew each other well enough to share expensive toys, then the rest of his comment sank in. "And you know that how?"

"I saw her work. She's very talented."

Compliments after he'd been pressuring her to fire Jessie? Miri picked up a weird vibe. Logan might not be a teenager anymore, but she could still read him pretty well. "Where did you see her art?"

He glanced at the PI, confirming her suspicions that these two were in cahoots, then Logan met her gaze. "At her house."

She didn't like the sound of that. Jessie had been very careful about not disclosing her address, and she and Logan didn't get along. Jessie wouldn't have shared that information with him.

"How do you know where she lives?" she pressed, suspecting she already knew the answer.

He paused. "I followed her home last night."

"Logan Na—"

He flung up a hand. "She's staying in a very expensive gated waterfront rental home. A place a waitress can't afford on tips alone. If she's into something illegal, I don't want you caught in the web. Today I checked out her house from the water side and saw her painting on the dock."

Shocked to hear her suspicions confirmed, she snapped, "Logan Chancellor Nash, you ought to be ashamed of yourself." Then she remembered the bartender. Luckily, he'd gone to the back for stock.

"I'm protecting you."

"By stalking my waitress?" she whispered then glared at Ignatius. "You used to be a cop. Tell him that's illegal."

"You peek in her windows?" Ignatius asked.

"Of course not."

"You planning to harm her?"

"No."

"She know you followed her?"

"No."

Ignatius shrugged. "Not a problem then, as long as it doesn't become a habit."

Miri wanted to kick the infuriating idiot in the shin for encouraging her nephew. "It's a problem for me!"

Logan ignored her outburst and turned to his friend. "I didn't see anything suspicious. There were no signs of drug paraphernalia in her house, and no sign of other cars in the driveway. But how's she paying for the place? Rich husband? Boyfriend? Lover? Selling drugs?"

"Valid questions," Ignatius replied.

Miri poked a finger at Logan's chest. "That's none of your business. I've told you before, leave Jessie alone."

Heaven help the poor girl if she discovered Logan's actions. She was already spooked about someone or something.

"She didn't know what I was really looking for when I asked to see more of her work. She invited me inside. I checked out most of the house," he added for Ignatius.

"Being sneaky and devious doesn't make it right, Logan."

"I told her to bring one of her paintings here today to display and sell."

Yet another sign of his presumption. "This is my restaurant. Don't you think you should have consulted me first?" Not that she wouldn't have helped Jessie if she'd known.

"When you see her work, you'll want to replace every picture in this place."

No, she wouldn't. There were memories attached to each one. But she couldn't say that, because it would only make Ignatius think he was right and that she hadn't moved beyond her grief over losing Jack. "What hangs in *my* restaurant is still *my* decision."

"Right. I told her you wouldn't want a commission, but if her painting sells, then you could invite other local artists to display here and take a percentage of the sales price."

No doubt her pigheaded nephew meant well. He was probably trying to replace her nest egg. He'd never accept that she didn't blame him for his exes' dirty work. But as long as she had enough money to keep a roof over her head and Sue in a job until they were both ready to retire, then she had enough.

"I swear, Logan, sometimes your heart's in the right place, but your methodology is all wrong. Don't help me anymore. Do you understand?"

"I hear you."

But she knew he'd ignore her as he'd always

done. He was one stubborn son of a gun. She only hoped he didn't run Jessie off before she could help the girl—whatever her problems.

JESSIE TURNED THE corner onto Margaret Street, spotted Logan outside the Fisherman's Widow and missed a step. She couldn't get inside the restaurant without going past him.

Wind ruffled his dark hair and his white, rolled-sleeve button-down shirt accentuated his tan. He resembled one of the rich guys who frequented the yachts parked along the wharf. But she now knew what he looked like in nothing but swim trunks, and that was…a distraction that made her sketching hand twitchy.

She saw the exact second he spotted her, because his posture changed. Looking as alert as a hunter with its next meal in the crosshairs, he watched her cross the street. She covered the automatic urge to tug at the short hem of her uniform skort by blotting her damp palms on her hips. The encounter ahead wouldn't be fun.

"Where's the painting?" he demanded.

"I didn't bring it." The fire of excitement had fizzled soon after he roared off in his boat. Doubts about putting herself out there had dogged her as she showered and dressed for work. Then she'd realized his demand that she bring the painting wasn't even about her.

His eyebrows lowered. "Why?"

"While your offer is generous and flattering, it's Miri's restaurant. I want to check with her first."

His eyes narrowed. "Did she call you?"

"No. Why?"

"Never mind. She has to accept that the stuff on the walls needs replacing."

"That's your opinion. She might disagree."

He strode to the door and yanked it open, motioning for Jessie to go first. He loomed behind her like a hovering hawk as she went to the kitchen in search of Miri. On the way, she checked out the current wall art—something she'd only done superficially before because she'd been too busy watching the patrons. Each piece was of good quality. But all needed some TLC.

Miri glanced up from the pie crust in front of her when they entered. Her rolling pin stilled.

"Tell her to bring her painting," Logan demanded, and Miri's expression turned uneasy.

Jessie gave Miri a sympathetic smile. "I thought Logan should ask why you've never replaced the ones you have."

A tiny smile curved Miri's lips. "Jack gave them to me. Each one commemorates a moment of our lives together."

Jessie shot Logan an I-told-you-so look. "Her art has sentimental value. You can't just discard it."

Logan rocked his jaw back and forth. "I'm trying to update this place and make both of you some money."

"I don't want it at Miri's expense."

Miri laid a hand on Jessie's forearm and gave her a squeeze. "You're a dear and I love you for thinking of me, Jessie. But I want to help you. Truly, I do. And if you're as good an artist as Logan says, this exposure could be good for you—even if I have to buy easels to display them. Please, bring your paintings."

Miri's encouragement fanned the ember Logan had lit. How could she make this a win-win situation? "I have an idea. Follow me."

Jessie grabbed a clean rag, dampened a corner of it, then led them to the oil of one of Key West's historic Victorian homes that hung behind the cash register. "Tell me about this one."

Miri's face softened. "That's the bed-and-breakfast where Jack and I honeymooned. It's the first piece of real art he bought me."

"Then it definitely should stay. It's a quality piece. But I'm guessing these have been here since the days when smoking was allowed inside restaurants?"

Miri nodded.

Jessie gently rubbed one side of the frame where it wouldn't be visible to guests, then displayed the sooty residue for Miri to see. "All it needs to revive the original colors is a professional cleaning. I could hang one of mine while yours is out for restoration. I'll help you find someone reputable to do the job, at minimal cost. It'll come back as good as new."

She knew how to do it because she'd interned at an estate auction house her senior year of high school, but she couldn't volunteer to do the job without giving too much away.

Looking sad, Miri shook her head. "I never even noticed the grime. All I see is the memory. Thank you, Jessie. That's a grand suggestion."

"Miri, the alcohol delivery's here," one of the kitchen workers called.

Miri held up a finger. "Be right there. I'll take this one down tonight after we close if you'll bring one of yours in tomorrow morning for our weekend crowd to enjoy."

Jessie's heart quickened. "I'll do it."

Then Miri left Jessie alone with Logan's blue gaze lasered on her. "How did you know about the soot?"

"My dad used to be a smoker." True, but not the whole truth. "Excuse me. I need to set up for opening."

"Why can't we clean them?"

"Because restoration takes skill, patience and the right chemicals. Doing it wrong will irrevocably damage the work. The process varies with the condition of each piece and type of paint."

When his eyes narrowed, she wanted to slap a hand over her mouth for revealing too much, but teaching was as natural to her as breathing. She made her escape before he could ask more and hoped Logan didn't pick up her slip.

CHAPTER FOUR

JESSIE GRABBED THE tray of salads, turned and almost slammed into Sue. The older waitress blocked her path. "You do know who your birthday party guy is, right?"

"A friend of Logan's?" She'd seen the man at the oyster bar with Miri's nephew that first night. Miri clearly didn't like him, so Jessie had kept her distance and she didn't ask questions.

"He's a private investigator who sometimes works for Logan."

Invisible spiders climbed Jessie's spine. Had Logan hired a PI to check up on her? "Why does Logan need a PI? I thought Miri said he was an accountant."

"He is now, but he used to be a big-time financial adviser before his ex-wife and his ex–business partner ran off together. He was devastated by the betrayals of the two people he trusted most. Came here to lick his wounds, I suspect."

No wonder Logan was so distrustful. "Thanks for the heads-up, Sue."

"Just watching your back, sweetie. Us gals need to stick together."

"Hush puppies," called the cook, and Sue hustled off to get the sweet cornmeal appetizers while they were still hot.

As Jessie made her way across the dining room, she realized Miri and Sue must have discussed her. Approaching the table warily, Jessie noticed the unhappy faces. Logan's PI nervously pleated his napkin. His daughter appeared resigned to a miserable meal, and the girls looked bored out of their minds. In her experience, bored kids created trouble. If Jessie didn't intervene, they wouldn't be here long enough to cut the beautiful cake Miri's friend had delivered. She detoured by the hostess stand and grabbed a few items.

At their table she served the adults their salads, then set crayons and extra place mats beside each girl. She received identical you've-got-to-be-kidding-me looks. "I know you're too old to color a kids' menu, but some of the fish swimming by the windows are too cool not to sketch."

"I can't draw," the older girl grumbled mulishly.

"Sure you can." Ignoring the folded arms and pouty bottom lip, Jessie tucked the empty tray under her arm and flipped a place mat to show its blank back.

"First, pick your fish. Then get his basic overall shape in your head. See if you can guess which one I'm drawing." She used her order pen to draw an elliptical shape. "Then just add to it."

She filled in fins, eyes and a mouth. It was a fast, rough sketch, but good enough to identify which type of fish she'd chosen.

"That one!" the younger girl cried out, pointing.

"Right. You'll be surprised how easy drawing something is once you break it down into its separate parts."

"You're pretty good," the older girl said, showing interest.

"I've had a few years of practice. And you know the secret?" Jessie leaned down but whispered loud enough that both girls could hear. "Nobody starts out good."

The younger girl grabbed a crayon and pointed it at a barracuda. "I'm drawing the long one. I like his teeth."

"I'll bring over more place mats if you run out." Filled with satisfaction for the first time since her exile, Jessie looked up and caught the woman's grateful smile, then the PI's speculative gaze.

Nerves twisted her stomach. That was twice today that she'd unintentionally revealed something that could blow her cover, but her love of art—specifically, sharing it with children—was hard to suppress. She had to be more careful.

JESSIE GLANCED IN the rearview mirror and caught sight of the picture of the Key deer in the backseat of her rental car Friday morning. Another wave of guilt swamped her.

She'd started her morning with lying to her brother, and there was no way she could feel good about that. When he'd asked her plans for the day, she'd evaded the truth by telling him she was looking forward to painting No Name Key rather than confessing her excitement over displaying her first picture in public. It wasn't a complete lie. She was eager to paint the island across the waterway and maybe even visit it to explore. But not today. Or tomorrow. Or even Sunday.

She worried during the entire drive south about displaying her work in such a public setting. It would be the first momentous occasion of her life that her family hadn't been a part of, and if it blew up in her face, she'd have no one but herself to blame.

Her anxiety crested when the restaurant came into view. With any luck Logan would be at an office somewhere and not lurking at the Widow. The man had to work sometime, didn't he? Heart in her throat, she turned into the small parking lot and parked beside Miri's truck. After scanning the area, she extricated the canvas and headed for the building. So far, so good. No Logan.

As promised, Miri had left the side door unlocked for her. The dining room was empty, but Jessie heard the hum of conversation and the clank of pots in the kitchen. The wall behind the register was empty save a brass hanger protruding from the whitewashed bead board. She hefted the frame and positioned it over the hook. Then she stepped back to study the largest painting she'd done to date. The splash of colors looked good. Pride and excitement bubbled inside her. She ached to snap a picture, send it to her family and share the moment.

The canvas tilted slightly to the left. She reached to adjust it. A long arm stretched past her, and a big hand covered hers. Her heart lurched with panic. She ducked away and spun around, slamming her left elbow against the hostess stand. Pain shot to her fingertips. But it was only Logan, not some nameless assailant sneaking up on her. Darn her brother and his daily dire tales.

"You nearly scared me to death. Don't you have a job you should be at?" How had he gotten so close without her hearing him? She cursed the sudden dryness of her mouth and wiggled her tingling digits. Hitting your funny bone was not at all funny.

One dark eyebrow dipped. "I set my own hours. Why are you so jumpy, Jessie?"

"I don't like people sneaking up on me." He was too close. The space behind the stand wasn't built for two—one of whom was a broad-shouldered man whose subtle citrus and spice cologne filled her nostrils, making it difficult to breathe. She needed to escape, but he blocked her path.

"I didn't sneak. I walked from over there." He pointed to a two-top tucked in a shadowy corner by the bar—not his usual spot at the bar. An open folder, an empty plate and a glass confirmed his statement. "Are you always this nervous?"

Only since winning that stupid lottery. "I'm anxious about displaying my work." She stifled a wince at yet another half truth. "If you'll excuse me, I need to move my car from the parking lot."

She wanted to leave before she had to tell more lies.

"It's fine beside Miri's."

A tremor slithered through her. She was supposed to be aware of her surroundings. Had he watched her arrive and she hadn't even noticed?

He extracted a pen and a small manila card from his shirt pocket. "What did you name this one?"

She hadn't. "How about *Morning Visitors*?"

He wrote on the card, then asked, "Jessie what?"

"Just Jessie." She'd signed the paintings with her Key West moniker. No last name. No initials. Not that she believed anyone would recognize her style or trace her through it, since she hadn't exhibited anything since her senior year of college. But she couldn't take that chance.

He wrote something else then stepped toward the painting, startling her into jumping back. He taped the card to the wall, and when she saw the figure he'd written below her name, her mouth fell open. "Y-you can't ask that much for an unknown's work."

"You'll get this easily. You could get more if the buyers could get a picture with you in front of it."

"No! I, um… I don't paint for the money."

"That's a naive outlook. Or that of a woman with other means of support. Do you have a deep-pocketed sugar daddy?"

"That's rude of you to suggest, and it's really none of your business."

"It is if you're doing something illegal to support yourself that could jeopardize my aunt."

She stiffened at the implication, but she couldn't explain. "I wouldn't do that."

"You expect me to take your word for it when you won't provide even basic employee information? I'm not as gullible as Miri. You're hiding something. Do you have a record?"

"I've told you I don't. Why can't you believe I just want to be left alone to paint?"

"Because that's bullshi—"

The kitchen door whooshed open. Miri joined them, pressing her hands to her cheeks. "Oh, Jessie. That's wonderful."

Jessie's face warmed despite the cold chill in her core caused by Logan's distrust. "Thank you."

"I can't wait to brag to everyone about what a talented artist you are."

Alarm rocketed through her. "No! You can't."

Jessie caught Logan's narrowed gaze on her and fumbled to recover. "I'd...um...die of embarrassment. My art is...personal. Please don't say anything."

Miri nodded with understanding in her eyes, hitting Jessie with another twinge of guilt. The hole she was digging with her dishonesty kept getting deeper. What would the people at church say about her behavior? But she wasn't hurting anybody. Right?

"It'll be our secret, hon."

"You should go to her house and see the rest of her work," Logan insisted. "If cleaning your old ones is going to take a while, you'll want to send them in multiples. That'll allow Jessie to display more pieces."

Another frisson of anxiety swept Jessie. Logan obviously didn't like her. Why was he trying to help her? Or was he only trying to get back into her house to find something incriminating?

"I don't go to anyone's house without an invitation," Miri snapped.

Jessie liked Miri and trusted her as much as she could trust anyone she'd met only four days ago, but inviting people into her hideaway wouldn't be a good idea. Plus, Logan, Miri's overprotective guardian, would probably accompany her.

"There's no need for you to trek out to my place. I'll bring in as many paintings as you want to see.

And I brought the name of a restoration specialist," she added, trying to change the subject.

She'd had to look up the company online at the library and go by their credentials and reviews from past patrons, because she didn't dare speak to anyone in the art community here. She handed Miri a paper containing the name and address without looking at Logan, even though she could feel his stare.

Miri tucked it in her pocket then hooked her arm through Logan's and pulled him toward his table. "Get your stuff and go to work, Logan, so we can do the same here. Jessie and I will discuss what we'll hang and what we'll remove after I consult with her specialist."

Jessie exhaled, willing her nervous tension to float away on her breath the way she'd done in her student teaching days. No luck. She never should have let Logan into her house.

Miri came back after seeing out her nephew. "Jessie, no matter how high-handed Logan gets, promise me you'll remember he's a good boy. He means well."

Why did that sound like a warning?

BY THE TIME the dinner rush ended Saturday evening, Jessie was a nervous wreck. She wanted to retreat to her walled compound and not emerge for a week. She was so exhausted her old solitude was starting to appeal.

Not only had they been run-off-their-feet busy yesterday and today, but every time a customer had paused in front of her Key deer painting, adrenaline had surged into her veins, making her heart beat double time. The piece hadn't sold. She hadn't expected it to. Not really. Especially at the ridiculous price Logan had slapped on it. And yet a lingering disappointment and sense of rejection weighted her.

A ding from the bartender's bell signaled that Jessie's drink order for table twelve was ready. She hustled over to pick it up and spotted Logan at a back corner table. He hadn't been there earlier. She knew, because she'd been watching for him. His unrelenting scrutiny made her nervous. He caught her eye before she could escape and signaled her over.

Seriously? Could he not see she was too busy to wait on him?

"Where's the new girl?" he asked when she stopped by his table.

"She dropped a tray during the lunch rush and ran out. She hasn't returned."

His lips turned down. "I hope Miri had the good sense to fire her. I haven't seen Pam, either."

Pam was a quiet, stay-to-herself woman who raced away the minute she clocked out. Jessie'd had little interaction with her. Today she'd learned why. A single mother, Pam tried to spend as little time away from her three kids as possible. Otherwise, her husband would claim her unfit and sue for full custody. She was what Logan had referred to as one of Miri's projects.

"Pam's at home with a sick kid."

"Are you handling this crowd alone?"

"Sue's working."

"You're delivering a lot of her orders."

He'd been watching her. Goose bumps lifted her skin. "It's easy for me to bring them when I'm on my way into the dining room anyway."

The long hours were getting to the older woman. Jessie had caught her leaning heavily against the kitchen wall while waiting for orders a few times.

The front door opened, and a party of ten entered. She needed to get back to work. "Did you want something? I'm really busy."

Logan gathered his belongings and rose. "An order book."

She blinked in confusion. "Excuse me?"

"Get me an order pad. I'll help. Sue doesn't need to push so hard."

She agreed wholeheartedly, but… "Do you know how to wait tables or operate the computer system?"

"Yes and yes."

Dumbfounded by his unexpected assistance, it took her a moment to kick into gear. The bartender gave her the pad. She passed it to Logan.

"Which section should I take?"

She told him.

"Got it." And then he walked off, leaving her with a tray of drinks to deliver and a load of questions.

Who was this man? The suspicious control freak who watched her and tried to micromanage Miri, or a devoted nephew who would do anything to help his aunt? She had to find out.

THE MUSIC WENT silent then all but the main dining room's lights went dark. Jessie dropped the last refilled saltshaker into the holder and stretched her tired back.

Miri came out of the kitchen carrying a bottle of wine. "Girls, we deserve a glass."

"Amen," Sue said and ducked behind the bar to snag three glasses and a corkscrew, leaving Jessie with the impression the women had shared nightcaps before.

"Jessie, dump that and join us," Miri insisted. "I sent Logan off with the night deposit ten minutes ago. We should have a few minutes' peace. C'mon," she added when Jessie hesitated.

This was the perfect opportunity to find out whether he was Jekyll or Hyde. After seeing how well he'd interacted with tonight's guests, Jessie was more confused than ever. She carried the box to the kitchen and returned.

Miri eased into a chair as if her body ached.

"I haven't had to bus tables in ages. I forgot how hard it was."

Sue sank across from her even more slowly. "Tonight required more hustle than I had in me. Busy season's starting. Better find some new blood soon. I'm not sure how many weeks like this I can handle. And we still have tomorrow to get through. I couldn't have made it without your help, Jessie. Don't think I didn't notice you grabbing my orders." She pulled a wad of bills from her pocket. "You deserve half of this."

Touched by the gesture, Jessie shook her head. "No, Sue. Thank you, but I don't want your tips. My mama always taught me to pitch in when needed. That's all I was doing."

Blushing, the woman hesitated, then nodded and repocketed her money. "Your mama raised a fine girl."

Miri filled and distributed the glasses then lifted hers and sampled the golden liquid. "Mmm. This is good. I'll have to stock more of it."

"I'll second that," Sue added after tasting.

Jessie searched for a way to settle her curiosity. "It was nice of Logan to help. He really seemed to know what he was doing."

Miri nodded. "Logan came to live with me and Jack six months after his mother died. He did everything from fishing and filleting with Jack's crew to bussing tables then waiting them here. He's a hard worker. I'll give him that."

"Wasn't his dad around?" Jessie asked.

"Carter buried himself in his grief and his work after Virginia passed and forgot all about parenting his son. By the time I figured out Carter wasn't going to snap out of it, Logan had become a pro at fetching his own groceries, fixing his meals and getting himself to school. He covered for his father so well not even the school counselor suspected anything was wrong."

Sue nodded. "And Carter didn't even notice. That hasn't changed."

Jessie'd had students in similar, or even worse, situations to Logan's, and she sympathized. She'd been blessed with involved parents, and hers had always been there to offer encouragement, guidance or a reprimand when needed. She depended on them as sounding boards—which was why living solo was so hard now.

Sue's reply raised more questions about Logan, but Jessie didn't want to seem too curious. "How old was Logan when he came here?"

Miri chuckled and shook her head. "Thirteen going on thirty. He tried to be the man of the house whenever Jack was away. Made for some interesting territorial squabbles between him and me."

"Those squabbles returned when he did. Makes both of you hard to live with," Sue added with the kind of candor only true friends could share. "Where'd you grow up, Jessie?"

Jessie ducked her head and bought time by sipping her wine. The cool liquid slid down her throat like ambrosia. She hadn't had any one-on-one time with Sue and should have anticipated questions. How much could she safely reveal? "I grew up on a farm. You?" she asked hoping to derail the questioning.

"I'm a local. Been widowed more years than I was married. I didn't pick a good husband the first time or the second. Decided to forgo a third attempt. No kids. Got a boyfriend?"

So much for changing the topic. "Not anymore."

"You end it? Or did he?" Sue persisted, making Jessie squirm.

"I did."

"Miss him?"

Jessie closed her eyes and tried to recall Aaron's features. But instead of her ex-fiancé's, the image burned on her retinas was one of tanned flesh tightly wrapped over muscles. Logan. In swim trunks. She gulped her wine and shook her head to banish the image. "Not even a little bit."

She realized that at some point since leaving home she'd quit second-guessing whether she'd wronged Aaron by choosing her family over him, as he'd accused. Her father was right. If her fiancé had truly loved her, he would have signed the prenuptial agreement her family insisted she ask for instead of throwing a tantrum and demanding she choose between him and them.

When had that forgetting him part happened?

"What about your parents, Jessie? Are they missing you?"

"Oh, Sue, leave her be," Miri objected.

Jessie wanted to hug Miri for intervening. "They know where I am and are probably jealous of my beach vacation."

"Some vacation. You're working your patootie off," Sue grumbled.

"I don't mind. I'm actually happy to help." Thrilled to see the bottom of her glass and the end of this conversation, Jessie rose. The room swayed, forcing her to grab the back of her chair.

Miri sprang to her feet and caught Jessie's elbow. Her eyes widened with alarm. "Are you okay?"

Jessie blinked to clear her head. "I'm fine. I guess I shouldn't have had wine on an empty stomach."

"When did you eat last?" Miri asked.

Jessie scrolled though her memory then grimaced. "Breakfast?"

Tsking, Sue rose. "You never took a lunch or dinner break?" She didn't wait for Jessie's answer. "Sit down, child. I'll get you a bowl of clam chowder."

"You don't have to do that, Sue."

"You took care of me. Now I'm returning the favor. Sit. I ain't letting you leave till you eat some'n." Then she hustled off to the kitchen.

Jessie glanced at Miri for backup, but Miri only shrugged. "You might as well listen to her. She's a mother hen. Don't know how I would have gotten through losing Jack without her. Down here in the Keys, we look out for our own."

But she wasn't one of theirs and never would be. Jessie eased back into her seat.

"And, Jessie, don't let me hear about you skipping breaks again. I know we were busy and your intentions were good, but I can't have you neglecting yourself. The employment folks would have my head—if Logan didn't get it first."

"I'm sorry. I won't."

"I'll go back through the applications tomorrow and see if I can find any that come close to my minimal standards to give 'em a chance. I hate that we lost BeBe, but waitressing wasn't really her thing, was it?"

"No."

Sue returned with a bowl of soup and a basket of crackers. "I heated it up a bit."

"Thank you, Sue." Jessie's stomach rumbled in anticipation. She put a spoonful of the thick, creamy, clam-laden chowder in her mouth and moaned. "I know now why your recipe's so popular, Miri."

"It's Sue's mom's recipe. But thanks. Eat up."

The women chatted while she ate, making Jessie miss Sunday afternoons at home with her extended family. Her aunts always gathered around the table to sip coffee and chat while the men retreated to the den to watch whatever sport was on TV. She was halfway through the bowl when the front door lock clicked open.

Logan strolled in, took one look at the bottle on the table and grinned. That grin sent her stomach and appetite AWOL. "Up to your old tricks, I see."

Miri rose. "Just taking the edge off our aches. Too bad there's none left for you. I'm going to run Sue home. Will you make sure Jessie finishes every last drop of her dinner, then see her back to her place?"

Jessie dropped her spoon in dismay. "That's not necessary. I only had one glass of wine. I can drive."

"You almost passed out on me. Either Logan follows you or I drive you. And, honey, I'm dead on my feet. What's it going to be? Me making the trip tonight and then again tomorrow to pick you up, or Logan following you home?"

Stuck between a bad choice and a worse one, Jessie realized she'd have to lie. Again. Not a habit she enjoyed acquiring. But she'd figure out how to ditch Logan after the older women left. There was no way she'd let him follow her home. "He can see me home."

Nodding, Miri left with Sue on her heels.

The moment the door closed behind them, Jessie stood and faced Logan.

"What happened?" Logan demanded.

"Nothing except I forgot to eat today. That and the wine made me a little light-headed. But I'm fine now that I've eaten and I'm steady on my feet. There's no need for you to follow me home."

"I said I would, and I'm not lying to Miri."

"I'm trying to save you a drive far out of your way."

"You heard her. If something happened to you, blame would be on my doorstep. I already know where you live, Jessie. What are you afraid of? That I'll interrupt something at your place that you don't want me to see?"

"Why do you insist on thinking the worst of me?"

"Because you're not telling the whole truth. Are you?"

What could she say? "Let me wash my bowl before we go."

So much for her plan to ditch him.

CHAPTER FIVE

JESSIE DROVE TOWARD Big Pine Key with her eyes repeatedly flicking to the rearview mirror. Her wipers intermittently swept the misty rain from her windshield.

She didn't like Logan following her home—she had to find a way to get rid of him. She flipped on her blinker when she reached her turnoff. He did the same. An eerie sense of déjà vu hit her. Suddenly his headlights looked familiar.

She'd been too irritated to notice earlier. But she could thank her paranoid brother for making her hypervigilant of such things as a bulb being out of line on the driver's side of a car tailing her.

Logan Nash was a sneaky, devious, lying bastard.

She whipped into her driveway, stopping inches short of the closed gate, then launched from her car when he pulled in behind her. She was too peeved to care about her hair and clothing getting wet.

Logan opened his door and stepped out onto the crushed oyster shells. "I'm supposed to see you inside. Miri's orders."

As the youngest of three and a teacher of sometimes challenging kids, she had no problem going toe-to-toe with anyone. She did that now and quickly realized her mistake. Logan was too close. Too big. Too intimidating. But she couldn't back down—not even when his narrowed blue gaze made her pulse skip and her mouth go dry.

The closest streetlamp was a hundred yards away. Confronting a near stranger who had followed her home before and been inside her house to see that she lived alone was probably not her brightest move. And her pepper spray was in her purse in the car. She should be afraid. But fear wasn't the reaction Logan elicited. Anger? Definitely. Agitation? Without a doubt. Awareness? In double doses. No doubt about it—if Logan Nash wasn't such an ass, he'd be attractive. Acknowledging that only upped her anger thermometer.

"You followed me home Tuesday night," she accused.

He shoved his hands in his pockets and rocked back on his heels, not looking the least bit daunted by her charge, but at least the action gave her a few precious inches of space and breathing room. "Why would I do that?"

"You tell me. Your driver's side headlight is angled too far in. A car with the same problem tailed me from Key West Tuesday. Spotting me on the dock was no coincidence. Was it?"

His hesitation was slight but noticeable. "It's my job to protect Miri."

"From what? I'm no threat!"

"I've yet to meet a criminal who admits guilt before being caught red-handed."

"I am *not* a criminal."

"You've conned Miri into not running a background check on you, verifying your references or requiring a drug test, and you refuse to provide your tax information—a federal violation. Why would you do that unless you're hiding something?"

He had a point. "We've been over this before. I don't know what else I can say to reassure you I won't hurt Miri."

"You could tell me how a waitress can afford to stay there." He pointed to the shadow of her rental.

She'd have to give him something to get him off her case before he sicced his bloodhound on discovering the truth—if he hadn't already.

"I came into a little money and paid for an extended vacation so I could paint." Truth. She was getting the payout little bits at a time for the next fifty years or so.

"A vacation from what?"

"My job."

"Doing what?" When she remained silent he said, "See? Still keeping secrets. And you expect me to trust you?"

"I'm not your ex-wife," she snapped then immediately wished she hadn't when he jerked to attention.

"You've been gossiping."

Her face burned, making her thankful for the murky light. He'd think she was interested in him. "I overheard. I'm not the least bit interested in getting into your business. I wish you'd stay out of mine."

"Wouldn't you do whatever was necessary to protect your family?"

She had and still was. But she couldn't say that. "You've seen me home, Logan. Good night."

When he made no move to leave, she climbed back into her car and waited for him to do the same. Then she pushed the remote to open the gate and drove her car through. When he rolled forward as if to follow her, she stomped her brakes just inside the fence. Behind her, Logan did the same. She pressed the button again, and the tall gate closed in the foot-wide gap between their vehicles. Her last view before she hit the gas pedal was his scowl in her red taillights. She'd probably pay for her escape tomorrow.

But he wasn't getting back into her house.

MIRI INTERCEPTED ANOTHER dark look between Logan and Jessie as they prepped the tables prior to opening for Sunday lunch. Jessie's pointedly cool manner toward her nephew was impossible to miss.

Sue hiked her penciled eyebrows. "What gives?"

Miri shrugged. "Having Logan follow Jessie home last night might have been a mistake."

But she'd had no choice. Although Jessie hadn't had enough to drink to be dangerous, she had been woozy, and Sue didn't see well enough to drive in the dark when it was raining—even if she refused to admit it. Both women had needed tending.

"Ya think?"

"It's a shame, because he needs someone like her."

"A woman with a mysterious past?" Sue asked with a touch of sarcasm.

"Oh, hush. You know what I mean. She's a hard worker, and even if she won't tell us what's going on, she's proven she has a heart of gold time and time again. And just yesterday, when that elderly man accidentally tipped her with a hundred-dollar bill instead of a ten, she chased him down the sidewalk to return it."

"We'd be in a world of hurt without her—especially with Pam out again." Sue shifted, looking uncomfortable. "I understood your need to start opening seven days a week after Jack died. You had to keep busy and you were afraid of losing the Widow. And I managed okay when we had a full staff and I had days off, but these last couple of weeks have been hell, Miri. I can't do it anymore."

Alarm shot through her. Sue couldn't quit. She was more like family than an employee. "I'll find someone—several someones—*soon*."

"It's time to find something to do besides work until you collapse from exhaustion every night. You need to start living for something or someone other than this place." The criticism stung. "Look who's talking."

"Hey, I tried to find love again. Twice. But the last one almost got me arrested. If you and Jack hadn't vouched for me I'd have been locked up with that miserable, lying piece of trash."

"We knew you didn't know he was making meth in his welding shop."

"You and Jack stood by me through some ugly and difficult times. That's why I've stuck out the extra hours this long without griping. But I need my days off to recuperate. My knees and back are hurting so bad at night I can't sleep."

Desperate, Miri grabbed Sue's hand. "It won't be much longer. I promise."

"You're missing the point, and I love you enough to beat you over the head with it until you get it. But I guess I have to be blunt. For years you've condemned Carter for burying himself in his work after Virginia died, but you've done the same thing. Your brother-in-law isn't the only workaholic in the family."

She couldn't have been more offended if Sue had spat on her. "I am not a workaholic!"

"Yes. You are. Snap out of it before you alienate everyone who loves you."

Flustered but unable to come up with an argument to prove Sue wrong, Miri dismissed the idea. "We have a line forming outside. I have to open up."

"My point exactly," Sue muttered. "You dodge your problems by working."

Miri ignored her and called out to the woman working stiffly alongside Logan, "Jessie, don't forget to take your breaks and eat something today."

Jessie's face flushed. "I won't forget."

"I'll see that she doesn't," Logan stated.

Making note of Logan's protectiveness, Miri crossed the room and unlocked the door. Ignatius stood at the front of the line. She couldn't stifle her involuntary recoil. A confrontation with him was the last thing she needed after Sue's bombshell.

His smile fell. "Good morning to you, too, Miriam Louise."

He plowed forward, taking the door from her and forcing her out of his way in his bulldozer manner. He held it open with one hand. The other he kept behind his back.

"Please come in," the pushy bastard invited the

dozen or so people behind him as if he owned the place.

It took everything Miri had in her to bite her tongue on the urge to tell him to take his bossy attitude and his name-calling and go away as she greeted the guests streaming past. Assuming he'd take his usual perch at the bar, she ignored him and seated the others. When she returned to the hostess stand he was waiting.

"These are for you," he said, producing an enormous and beautiful bouquet of mixed blooms. That he'd been able to conceal something that size made her realize how broad his shoulders were. Not that she cared.

"For what?"

Instead of being insulted by her suspicious reaction, he laughed. "Relax. I'm not asking you out. These are a thank-you for making dinner with my daughter so special. She said she wants to do it again. So do the girls. That means a lot to me, Miri."

His earnestness deflated her anger. "You're welcome and thank you, Ignatius."

She enjoyed his wince at his full name—but she owed him. Burying her face in the blossoms, she inhaled their heady fragrance.

He cleared his throat. "I thought you might want to go out on my boat on your next day off."

Good grief. Give the man an inch… "That sounds like you're asking me out."

"Nah. Logan mentioned how much you enjoyed fishing with your husband but that you'd had to sell his boat to hold on to this place. I thought you might like a day on the water. We can fish or not. Up to you. I'll even pack a picnic so you won't have to deal with the food."

Distrusting his offer, she squinted at him. "That still sounds like a date. And I don't date, Ignatius. Not because I'm hung up on the past. But because I don't have the time, need or desire for another man in my life."

"Sheesh, woman. Then pack your own lunch and pay half for the gas. I'm just trying to give you the chance to enjoy something you used to like."

His exasperation made her feel ungrateful and embarrassed. "Thank you. But I don't have days off. We're open seven days a week. Do you want a table today or are you sitting at the bar?"

"Neither. I did what I came for. Have a good one, Miri." He tapped two fingers to his forehead, then left, doubling her shame. He'd made a special trip, and she'd treated him like a bill collector.

But no matter what he said, his invitation smelled fishy. She watched him leave, noting his confident stride. He wasn't bad looking if you liked your men big all over. And he was still fit despite his retirement. But she couldn't help making the contrast to Jack, who'd been tall and whipcord lean. Sure, Jack had been muscled, but not with Ignatius's breadth.

Sue paused by the counter and eyed the bouquet. "When's the last time someone brought you flowers?"

Miri tried to recall and couldn't. Jack had always brought her things he'd found, like pretty shells, unusual pieces of driftwood or paintings. "It's just a thank-you for setting up the meal with his daughter."

"He'd be a perfect place to start over—unless you don't like handsome, well-dressed, polite men with good teeth and a full head of hair."

She needed to turn up the air-conditioning. It was hot in here. "I need to get a vase."

She hustled to the kitchen, putting thoughts of Sue and the pushy PI behind her. She didn't want a man in her life. She had the Fisherman's Widow, and keeping it open took all her time and energy. And she was not burying herself in her work. She was doing what she loved.

JESSIE SCANNED THE ominous sky beyond the outside dining area. The sunny morning was becoming a stormy afternoon. Boat traffic had thinned out, and even the birds had taken cover elsewhere. Dark smudges of purples, blacks and charcoals encroached on the horizon. Her fingers itched for a brush. She'd use watercolors to achieve that layered effect. Maybe she'd have time to paint it tomorrow.

Only one fortyish man remained seated in her section. She laid his bill on the table. "Can I get you anything else, sir?"

"Nah." He tilted his head and examined her through narrowed eyes. "Don't I know you from somewhere?"

She studied his unfamiliar face and shook her head. Was that a pickup line? If so, it was an old one. "I don't think so."

"I'm sure I do. I've been trying to place you."

His conviction sent prickles of uneasiness up her spine. She forgot names but never faces. Had he seen her in the news when her lottery win had been announced? Surely he couldn't recognize her with dark hair and brown contacts? "Sorry. I guess I just have one of those faces."

"Where are you from?"

Trying to conceal her growing discomfort, she glanced toward the open dining room windows. Logan was close enough to hear her if she needed help. Battling the urge to retreat, she scrambled for an answer. "I live down the road."

"But you're not a local," he pressed.

"There aren't many of those in Key West," she said, trying to make light of his remark. She edged toward the door.

"Yeah, but I know you from somewhere other than here. I just can't figure out where."

"Jessie." She jumped at the sound of Logan's voice immediately behind her. Although she'd been doing her best to avoid him today, she was relieved by the interruption. She angled herself so she could keep an eye on both threats—Logan and the customer.

"Take your break *now*," he ordered with slight emphasis on the last word. "I'll cover for you until you return."

She didn't want to be beholden to him, but she needed to escape before the customer placed her and blew her cover. "Thank you. Have a good day, sir."

She hurried inside and hadn't gathered her composure when Logan joined her. "Who is he and how does he know you?"

"He doesn't. If you were listening, you heard me tell him I just have one of those familiar faces."

His blue gaze raked her features. "Hardly. Was he harassing you? Hitting on you?"

Was that a backhanded compliment? "No. He was just making conversation."

"Sue said he's been in three days straight, always sitting where he could watch you. Today, he specifically requested your section."

Panic slammed her like a rogue wave, knocking her off balance. Three days? And she hadn't noticed? When had she let her guard down? *When you became so focused on another threat—Logan.*

Wanting to race back to the safety of her compound, she glanced toward the front door. The bare wall behind the cash register hit her like a second swell. Her painting was gone. Had it fallen? Was it damaged?

"Where is it?" she asked Logan, pointing at the empty wall.

"It sold. For the asking price."

The bottom dropped out of her stomach. She was too shaken to care about Logan's smug I-told-you-so tone. "I—I never expected it to sell. When? Who?"

"An hour ago a local couple bought it for their daughter. She's accepted a job offer in Seattle. They want her to remember home."

First the stranger. Now this. Jessie's emotions were such a jumble she didn't know whether to laugh or cry. She certainly couldn't do the latter in front of Logan. Her throat and chest tightened.

"You said you didn't want to meet the buyers," he added when she remained mute.

"No. I—I—" She what? She'd sold her first painting. Someone had liked it enough to pay a chunk of money for it. She should be thrilled. And she was excited, but also a little...bereft? It was if she'd lost a dear friend without getting to say goodbye.

She needed to talk to her mother. But she couldn't. Not about this.

Logan's continued scrutiny made her uncomfortable. She forced a smile. "I'm glad. Really."

"Liar. But then we knew that, didn't we?"

Indignant, she clamped her molars tight on the urge to tell him to go to hell. Did he have to be such a jerk?

"Excuse me, I need to eat and then get back to work." Not that she was hungry. A three-course meal of the stranger, the sale and the surly accountant had decimated her appetite.

"Bring your second painting in tomorrow. With Miri's out for restoration, we have a bare wall."

Did she want to sell another one? Of course she did. But her paintings were sort of like pets or children. She'd invested so much into them that giving them up wasn't as easy or painless as she'd expected it to be.

"Do I need to pick it up?" he pressed.

"No. I'll...handle it."

Then the stranger approached the cash register. She made a hasty escape and prayed he didn't remember where he'd seen her—if he even had— and say something to Logan.

"LOGAN CHANCELLOR NASH!"

His full name, snapped out in that tone, echoed through the empty restaurant. Logan stopped just short of the Widow's front entrance and turned to face his aunt. "Yes, ma'am?"

"Don't you 'ma'am' me, trying to butter me up. Stop picking fights with Jessie."

"She's—"

She threw up a hand. "I don't want to hear it. I'm short staffed. Sue's threatening to quit. I can't afford to lose Jessie. You'd better make nice with her. You hear me?"

"I hear you. But aren't you concerned about her secretiveness?"

"No. Because sometimes a person's worth is here." She thumped her chest with a fist. "It can't be measured in black-and-white words and numbers on a page. If you'd spend more time concentrating on the people in your present instead of the ones who are long gone, you might figure that out."

The jab wasn't a new one. "Elizabeth and Trent need to pay for what they did."

"You were raised in a churchgoing family, son. I know the good book told you that vengeance isn't your job. But forgiveness *is*."

"Not going to happen." She didn't understand. He was searching for his exes as much for her as for himself. "If I find them soon, I might be able to recoup some of the money they stole—that includes the money to buy back Jack's boat. It's for sale again."

The corners of her mouth turned down. "Let it go, Logan. I have. The lost possessions of our past will never make us happy in the present. What would I do with a charter fishing boat, anyway?"

"Live on it, like you always planned to do when you retired."

"Not without Jack. Besides, I like my house."

"Miri—" Again she interrupted him with an upraised hand.

"Selling that boat allowed me to keep the Widow's doors open. Don't make me shut them now because I can't staff the place."

He wouldn't stop searching for the ones who'd betrayed him. But he couldn't handle the worry and exhaustion carving new wrinkles into his aunt's face. "Colleges are on break. See if you can rustle up some of your summer help to fill in."

A tired smile stretched her lips. "I knew there was a reason I let you hang around. You're pretty smart for a bean counter."

The familiar jab made him smile. He didn't want to be at war with Miri. And if that meant making nice with Jessie, then so be it. It was always easier to get information out of friends than enemies anyway.

JESSIE STARED AT the coffeepot with gritty eyes and cursed the contact lenses she was afraid to go without now that Logan had started showing up unexpectedly.

Willing the machine to brew faster, she bent over the sink and splashed cold water on her face, then dried off with a paper towel. She'd tossed and turned last night, dithering over whether to return to the restaurant. Going back meant *potentially* risking her safety if Sue was right about that man watching her for three days. But breaking her promise to Miri would *definitely* leave the woman in a really tough spot.

She was damned if she did and damned if she didn't, as her dad used to say. This was the kind of dilemma she'd always relied on her family to help her figure out. She didn't know what to do.

The pot's last gasp and the ringing of her phone filled the kitchen simultaneously. Staring at her brother's number on the screen, she stood frozen. She wasn't up for doom and gloom today. But if she didn't answer, she'd only be delaying the inevitable. A second peal jarred her into action.

"Hey," she said into it.

"Did I wake you?"

"No. I just haven't had coffee yet." She pinched the phone between her jaw and ear and reached for the biggest mug she could find in the cabinet. She'd never needed coffee to jump-start her day BTW.

Before the win.

"You all right, kiddo?"

"Sure. Just trying to decide what to do with another day in paradise."

"Sarcasm? That's not like you, Li'l Bit."

No. It wasn't. She yearned to tell Brandon

about the creepy customer. He needed to know. If something happened to her, the stranger would be where he needed to start his investigation. But, tangled in her web of lies, she didn't. Instead she asked, "What's new in peach country?"

"Mom bought her pistol yesterday. It's pink, for crying out loud."

The disgust in his tone made her smile. "Leave it to Mom to turn something she's going to hate carrying into a fashion statement."

"No criminal is going to take a pink gun seriously."

"The bullets will work the same way, right?"

Silent seconds ticked past. "Wake up on the wrong side of the bed, Grumpy?"

Jessie grimaced. "I'm sorry."

"I know you're frustrated with being away for the holidays, but try to be aware of how many thousands are flocking south and how many of them could have seen your face all over the news."

"I'm a brunette now and I'm wearing brown contacts. No one will recognize me." He needed to know that, too, if she went missing.

"Smart. But still, keep out of sight."

"Right," she mumbled then tuned out the rest of his familiar speech while she filled her mug then took a sip.

"Jessamine? Are you listening to me?"

She snapped to attention. "Of course." Another

lie. "I need to get started with my day. I'll talk to you tomorrow."

It was only after she'd hung up that she realized she hadn't asked if he'd changed his mind about her returning home. What was the point? She knew the answer.

She grabbed her mug and the thermal coffee carafe and shuffled outside. The Key deer scampered from beneath the deck and into the foliage as she descended the stairs. The crushed shells beneath her feet were neither cool nor warm on this balmy seventy-degree morning. Back home it would be at least forty degrees cooler now.

She made her way toward the pier, pausing to sip her brew and glance over her shoulder. The sun peeked above the rooftops across the street, spreading a sherbet glow of pinks and oranges across the sky. Pretty and very different from last night's stormy sky. At the moment, she didn't have the delicate touch needed to work on a watercolor. Later, if she felt human enough, she'd bring out her paints and attempt another picture of…something. What hadn't she sketched or painted yet?

She turned back toward the dock and spotted two sinister fowl squatting on her turf. Today, she was in no mood to let them get away with it.

"Shoo!" she shouted and stomped on the boards, spooking the creatures from their perches. She sank onto a lounge chair, ignoring the dew dampening her pants. Her goal: to sit, soak up the sun and drink coffee until she figured out her next move.

Should she go back to work or play it safe?

She'd made it halfway through her bucket-size mug and still hadn't made a decision when her cell phone rang again. She groaned. Brandon must have forgotten to issue one of his daily dire warnings. Reluctantly, she dug the phone out of her pocket, but she didn't recognize the number on the screen.

Her pulse hitched. What if yesterday's stranger had finagled her number from someone at the restaurant? Did anyone besides Miri have it?

Get a grip, girl. More likely, it's a wrong number. You're letting your brother's paranoia get to you.

Knowing she'd never relax if she didn't find out who was calling, she pushed the button. "Hello?"

"Jessamine, how is my baby girl?"

Her mother's voice made her sit up so quickly she sloshed coffee down the front of her shirt. She set down her mug and plucked the hot fabric from her skin. "Mama! This is a surprise."

"Brandon told us last night you weren't coming home for Christmas. I hate that he always calls when I can't speak to you and from somewhere other than home. You know your brother. He's afraid someone will track the call to a cell tower and place you if he calls from here. But I needed to hear your voice and make sure you were okay."

She hadn't spoken to her mother in weeks. A flood of emotion rushed over her. There was so much to tell her…and so much she couldn't say. "I'm…I'm good. Whose phone are you using?"

Her mom's chuckle filled Jessie's ear. "You don't get to be my age and have a special agent son without learning a few tricks. I made Brandon give me your number—just for emergencies, I told him. Then I drove down to Columbia and bought a phone from a convenience store. I've driven over to the outlet mall to use it." Her mother sounded quite proud of herself. "So how are you? Be honest, Jessamine. I'll know if you're not."

Honesty was an impossible order. Once she left this island behind, she would never tell another lie. Lies made life too complicated.

"I'm doing more painting and drawing than ever," she hedged. "I have time to concentrate fully on the details these days. I never realized I could be so…prolific. It's beautiful here, Mom. I wish you could see it…but I miss home."

"We miss you, too, honey. You don't know how much."

"Brandon's freaking out over your pink pistol."

"He can complain all he wants, but after—"

The abrupt stop jarred her. Ten seconds ticked

past, each one making Jessie more ill at ease. "Mom, what aren't you telling me?"

More silence. "Someone broke into your house again last week. Brandon didn't want you to know. Your new alarm worked and scared the criminal away. He didn't take anything, and he got away before the police arrived. But we have a picture of him from your security camera, so they'll catch him. And your daddy fixed the door-jamb and reinforced it. It's better than new."

The crook hadn't taken anything—except Jessie's sense of security. Loss and a feeling of violation welled up inside her. She dropped her head into her hand. Damn this lottery win. Would she ever get her old life back? Would she ever feel safe in her own home again?

"That's why Brandon insisted I stay longer, isn't it?"

"Yes. None of us like it, but it is for the best."

"Thanks for letting me know, Mom. I don't like being kept in the dark."

"I told Brandon you wouldn't, but he insisted there was nothing you could do from there except worry. Jessamine, this period of trials will pass, and we'll all be better off than before. You'll see a big difference in your dad, too, when you get back. He's responding to his medications."

Her mom could always find a cloud's silver lining. "That makes it all worth it."

"Do you need anything? Whatever it is, I'll find a way to get it to you."

She needed to get back to normal: to her family, her home and her job. But those were the very things her mom couldn't deliver. "Thanks, Mom, but I'm all right."

"What about money? Do you have some of those cards left?"

She couldn't tell her mother how low she'd allowed her funds to get because she'd thought she'd be home by now. "I'm good. Thanks."

"If you're sure? Then tell me about your paintings."

"They're all of local stuff. The birds, Key deer and plants."

"I wish I could see them."

Her mother would never see the one she'd sold. The realization filled her with sadness. "Me, too."

A splash nearby startled her. She twisted in her chair, expecting to see that the pushy cormorants had returned. Instead, Logan, paddling a kayak, was five yards from her dock. Her heart lurched. How had she missed his approach? She didn't want to talk to him, but short of retreating to the house where he'd likely follow, she didn't have a choice but to stand her ground.

"Good morning," he called out.

"Do you have company?" her mother asked.

Jessie winced, then ducked her head and reached

for her sunglasses. She'd have to hang up on her mother—something she hated doing—and tell another white lie. "Someone's paddling by in a kayak. There's a lot of that down here."

"Jessamine Martin, are you telling a fib?"

Apparently, her mother's uncanny ability to tell when one of her children wasn't being truthful worked long-distance.

"Sorry, I didn't know you were on the phone," Logan said holding on to a cleat at her feet.

"Have you met someone? It's very early. Did he stay the night? Does your brother know? Should Brandon check him out?" Her mother's voice rose with each question.

"No to all of the above."

"I hope this means you've put Aaron behind you," her mother continued, ignoring Jessie's comment. "But, baby, don't rush into anything. Especially now. I know you're lonely, far away from home, and at the holidays, too, but you're also vulner—"

"It's nothing like that. Not even close. I'm glad you called, but I have to go."

"I can take a not-so-subtle hint. I won't even ask his name or if he's tall, dark and handsome, but I do want to hear all the juicy details soon. Very soon. Please, Jessamine, *please* be careful. A rebound romance—"

"It's not that. I promise." She walked a few

yards away from Logan, covered the phone and whispered, "Love you. I'm glad you called."

"Love you more. And one day when you're a mother, you'll understand how much. Don't tell your brother I have this phone. Call me back when you can. If I can't answer safely, then I'll skedaddle to somewhere I can. And when you discard your current phone, you'd better send me your new number." The line went dead.

Jessie's heart sank. She was turning her mother into a liar. She stared at the phone and loneliness expanded to fill every crevice of her being. Then she spun and confronted Logan. His dark glasses reflected her angry glare.

"Don't you ever work?"

He shrugged then rested his paddle across the front of the kayak, bringing her attention to the well-defined creases between his deltoids and triceps. Again, the urge to sketch him hit her from out of the blue.

"It's early. I'll be in the office by nine. Coffee smells good." He offered a hopeful smile.

The flutter in her belly was a hunger pang. Nothing more. "I only have one mug."

"I brought my own." He dug around in the front compartment and produced a travel mug.

"Coffee's black. No cream or sugar."

"Just the way I like it." He reached into the hole in the hull again, retrieving a white paper bag. "It will go well with these. Fresh bear claws from the best bakery on the island."

Her stomach betrayed her by growling loudly. She'd skipped breakfast. "What do you want, Logan?"

"I'm just being friendly. Here."

He offered her the bag. She took it. Their fingers bumped. So did her pulse.

"Why?"

He laughed—a low rumble that would have been appealing from anyone else. "Are you always suspicious when people are nice to you?"

"Only with you. You've made it clear you don't like or trust me. So why are you really here?"

"Because Miri's important to me, and she likes you."

He tied off the kayak then climbed onto the dock. His legs were long and tanned and lightly swirled with dark hair. Even his bare feet were sexy. No. Not sexy. Just…sketchable. He had good feet from an artist's perspective—bone and sinew clearly defined.

So he was attractive. Big deal. That didn't mean she was attracted to him. She just appreciated— purely from an aesthetic standpoint—a nice body. Warmth climbed her cheeks. She hoped her line of thought didn't show on her hot face.

"Jessie, I'm sorry. We got off on the wrong foot because, as Miri says, I'm a rule-following bean counter. And you're breaking a few. But I can't deny that you're working as hard—if not harder—than every other Widow employee." He extended a hand.

Shocked by his apology, she returned the gesture automatically. The heat of his palm seared hers and stole her breath. She snatched her hand back, ducked her head and opened the bag, gulping air. The pastries' mouthwatering, sugary scent filled her nostrils.

How could she refuse to share her coffee? She nudged the pot with her toe. "Help yourself. It's probably cold by now."

"Not working on your tan today?" he asked as he poured.

"No." Thank heavens she'd pulled on yoga pants and a long-sleeve T-shirt. They might be old and nearly worn-out, but at least she was covered.

"Will you paint today?"

"Maybe later." Hoping to avoid talking to him, she shoved the pastry into her mouth and took a big bite. The flaky confection practically melted on her tongue.

"Have you finished the cormorant painting?"

She shook her head.

"Was the island your background?"

She nodded.

"Have you paddled over there yet?"

Wary of his curiosity, she swallowed and weighed her answer. "No."

"Why not?"

She avoided answering by taking another bite and shrugged.

"The kayaks hanging under the house are part of your rental agreement. All safety equipment is included."

Suspicion intensified. "You've been checking up on me?"

"I was curious about the house. I looked it up on the agent's webpage. So why haven't you been paddling?"

"I don't know how to use a kayak, and going out on the water alone with no one to check up on me doesn't seem smart." She instantly regretted volunteering that information. "Buddy system and all that."

"I'll teach you the basics. But not today. Tomorrow."

"What's in it for you?" Her mother would be ashamed by Jessie's lack of gratitude.

"Like I said, you're working hard for Miri." He dug into his pocket then extended his hand. "You disappeared last night before I could give you the cash from your painting."

The thick wad of bills in his palm made her gulp. Money. For her art. It seemed surreal. Her hands shook as she took the roll, careful to avoid touching him again. She counted the twenties with sticky fingers. Five hundred dollars.

"Checking to see if I cheated you?"

"No. I—I just can't understand why someone paid this much for my work. I'm not an artist."

He shoved back his glasses and searched her face. "Are you serious?"

His disbelief was flattering. "Even if I were one, I'm an unknown."

"Exactly. An unknown with exceptional talent. When you gain recognition, these folks can say they snapped up one of your earliest works."

She stared at the cash, her fingers growing clammy around the bills. She was an art teacher—that was what she was. She couldn't wait to get back to her students, and once she did, there wouldn't be time for the intricate work she'd done here. Admittedly, the pieces were her best work, but she'd never be good enough to give up her day job.

She blurted her biggest fear. "I think the first sale was a fluke."

"The sale wasn't a fluke, Jessie. Trust me on that. Bring the second painting tonight. Better yet, bring two. Unless you're really not interested in marketing your work."

The old dream refused to die. "I am. But…"

She was terrified. Of making a mistake. Of humiliating herself. Of having her secret heart's desire crushed once and for all.

He polished off his doughnut then his coffee. "There is no but. Do you want me to help you choose which ones?"

That meant letting him back inside. "No!"

"Then thanks for the coffee. And I'll see you later." He climbed into his kayak and paddled off, leaving her more tormented than she'd been before his arrival.

She should have told him she wasn't returning to the restaurant. But if she didn't, not only would she be breaking her promise to Miri, but she also wouldn't get to display more paintings. And if she didn't display her paintings, then how would she ever know if the first sale had been a fluke or if she actually had a marketable talent? Could she live with always wondering *what if...*?

The money in her hand gave her the answer. Because of the sale she could afford not only groceries but also Christmas presents for her family and a birthday present for her mom.

How could she not go back to work?

CHAPTER SIX

LOGAN PACED THE length of I's boat, but twenty-four feet wasn't enough to work out his tension. Jessie was a puzzle he couldn't figure out.

The awe on her face when he'd given her the cash had unsettled him. She honestly didn't believe she had talent. Had no one ever told her? Then the hope in her eyes when he had told her had hit him like a punch in the gut.

And clearly she had no idea how hot she looked in her threadbare workout gear. Where the hell had she been living? In a cave? In solitary confinement? That possibility concerned him. Could she have been in prison? Was that why she refused to allow the background check?

He paused in front of I. "I need you to find out who Jessie is and what she's running from."

I tipped back his beer, swallowed then wiped his mouth with the back of his hand. "Can't. Not without something to work with. A first name—a nickname, at that—and no last name will get me nowhere. You need fingerprints or something."

"Did you run her car tag?"

"Since you insisted, yes. It's a rental. And I don't have a connection who can tell me whose name's on the contract or where the lease originated."

"Can you get something out of her landlord?"

"Not going to happen. The woman who owns the agency cheated on her husband a few years back. I worked for the husband. My evidence against her cost her a lot of alimony. If I show up at her office, I'll probably get shot. You could try, but since you're already borderline stalking the waitress, I wouldn't recommend it. Sit down. Your pacing is getting on my nerves."

Logan perched on the edge of a cooler.

"What makes you so sure Jessie's trouble?"

"C'mon, I. You've seen how jumpy she is. That guy from yesterday freaked her out. She got so pale I thought she'd bolt."

"She should be worried if the old broad's right and he's been watching her three days. Did you ask the guy how he knew her?"

"Yeah. He claims he can't remember. Says he's a truck driver who follows the I-95 corridor from here to Maine. That's a lot of territory, and he could have seen her anywhere. This morning when I paddled by Jessie's, I interrupted a phone call. She started whispering, then hung up fast."

"You went to her house again?"

"Yeah." And he'd wished he hadn't once he'd discovered she wasn't wearing underwear. Seeing the tight buds of her nipples and the curve of her butt beneath the thin, worn clothing had been ten times sexier than her bikini.

You are not turned on by that shyster.

"Nash, when you tail someone, you're supposed to stay out of sight."

"I'm befriending the enemy—at Miri's request. I have a plan. Jessie won't even know what I'm doing."

I shook his head. "I don't want to hear it. That'd make me an accessory."

"If you don't like my methods, you follow her. I'll pay you."

"No. You're paying me more than you can afford already."

"Forget Elizabeth and Trent for a minute. Jessie's more urgent." He couldn't believe he was saying it, but right now protecting Miri mattered more than finding his ex-wife and clearing his name. And, yes, he hated to admit, he was curious about Jessie.

"Now you're talking. Forgetting your exes is the smartest thing you've said in over a year. Get Jessie's info from Miri."

"She won't give it to me, and she hasn't left an employee file lying around where I can pick it up. You try."

I shook his head. "No way. I'm not crossing your aunt."

"Why?"

"Because Miri's fond of the girl, and both of them helped me make such a good impression on my daughter that Bethany wants to set up another dinner at the Fisherman's Widow next week. I'm not screwing that up. Have you done an internet search of 'Jessie' and 'artist' and see what you come up with?"

"I did. I found nothing."

"Maybe there's nothing to find except a bad breakup and a vengeful ex."

"You don't believe that."

"If I don't it's because I'm a distrustful SOB. Look, Nash, I'd hate to see you get charged with stalking. Back off. Give the girl some room. She'll show her hand sooner or later."

"Before or after she rips off Miri?" Frustrated, he checked his watch. Almost three. He wanted to avoid leaving Jessie alone with Miri whenever possible. "I have to go."

JESSIE STEERED INTO the restaurant parking lot. From the safety of her locked car, she scanned the surrounding area. She didn't see last night's stranger. If she was lucky, he'd had his fill of seafood and had moved on.

She didn't see Logan, either. For once, she wanted him near, but only because he made her feel like displaying her work wasn't tomfoolery, as her daddy would call it.

Still keeping an eye out for the stranger, she

checked to make sure her pepper spray was in her pocket, then exited the vehicle and extracted her canvases from the backseat. Warily, she made her way to the side door. Miri and two girls who looked eerily similar stood inside wearing the Fisherman's Widow uniform. They had to be twins, or at least siblings very close in age.

Jessie felt a rush of...disappointment? The emotion made no sense. She should be happy if Miri had hired help. That would allow Jessie to leave this job that was forcing her to lie to her family. But as ill-advised as it might be to keep this job, she enjoyed the work, liked Miri and Sue's company and felt a sense of purpose when she had somewhere she was supposed to be.

Miri waved her over. "Jessie, come in and meet Tara and Lara. They've worked for me the past two summers. Last night I texted them an SOS, and they've agreed to help out while they're on winter break from college. They'll be here through New Year's Eve."

Jessie said her hellos, trying to hide her disappointment over being reminded of yet another holiday she wouldn't celebrate with her family. She glanced around. "Is Sue in the back?"

"No. She was so exhausted I gave her the day off. You take tomorrow."

If she did, that would leave her without an excuse to avoid Logan's kayaking trip. *Just say no. You don't owe him an excuse.*

"Show me what you've brought," Miri insisted.

Jessie rotated the canvases. The chorus of oohs bolstered her ego but also made her self-conscious.

"Jessie, they're wonderful."

"Thank you, Miri. They're just scenes from behind the house."

"Where did you learn to paint like that?" the girl she thought was Tara asked, wide-eyed.

Jessie didn't consider the twins a threat but worried about what might be repeated to Logan. She edited her answer. "I've always dabbled."

"You're this good with no formal training?" Lara wailed in dismay. "I've been drawing for years, and I can't do anything close to this."

There was no way she could let the girl feel inferior. "I studied art in college with excellent teachers who helped me refine my skills."

"You took classes?" Lara asked.

"A lot of them. I min—" A footfall behind her made her pivot. Logan. She'd been so distracted by the girls she hadn't checked to see if he occupied his usual table.

How long had he been listening? Had she said too much? She searched his face. His gaze fell to her work, and she caught her breath, foolishly waiting for his approval. His opinion shouldn't matter. But it did. However, his expression gave nothing away. To hide her disappointment, she asked Miri, "Which one do you want behind the register?"

"Your great white heron looks so lifelike I want to feed him a fish. But I think I want the hibiscus up here. The colors pop."

Pam, the other waitress, joined the group. "You should have seen the one she just sold," she told the newcomers. "The Key deer looked so real I wanted to pet them."

"Do you have a picture of it?" Lara asked.

Jessie shook her head. "No. I don't have a camera."

"What about the one on your phone?"

"Mine's a basic model. No camera."

"You have no record of the one you sold?" Miri asked.

The pang of loss intensified. "None."

"That's a shame. Logan, would you hang this one, please?"

He did as asked then took a card from his pocket. "Title?"

"*Afternoon Perfume*?"

Logan wrote on the card then tacked it on the wall. She read another high price and gulped. "You're good for my ego, but are you sure…?"

"Was I right last time?" He took the canvas from her, scanned the dining room then started toward the opposite wall.

"Wait!" The word erupted from Jessie's mouth,

startling her. He looked down. She realized she'd grabbed his arm. His skin was warm against her palm, the muscles beneath it rock solid. She dropped her hand and tried to unglue her tongue from the roof of her mouth.

"Miri should decide which painting she'd like restored next." The words gushed out in a breathless rush.

He opened his mouth as if to argue.

"She's right," Miri said, then pointed to an acrylic of a fishing boat tied in its slip. "That one. Then I can have the memories of Jack's mistress without the expense of keeping her afloat."

Jessie thought she saw Logan flinch. But he pivoted too quickly for her to be sure. Eyebrows raised, she glanced at Miri. "His mistress?"

"Jack loved that boat. He spent more hours with her than he did me. I sold it after he died. Logan's almost convinced I want it back. But I don't. The memories we made on the *Holy Jackerel* are best kept right where they are." She tapped her temple.

Logan returned with the boat picture. "I'll drop this one off at the restorer's tomorrow." Then his blue gaze pinned Jessie. "Be ready for your kayaking lesson at 8:00 a.m."

He strode out the front door before she could protest that she had no intention of spending the morning with him.

LOGAN DELIBERATELY ARRIVED thirty minutes early, hoping to catch Jessie at whatever it was she did to fund her expensive accommodations. Bobbing in his kayak, he held on to a dock cleat and scanned the property from the water. The only sign of life was a trio of deer rustling in the vegetation growing alongside the fence—probably the ones in her painting. There were no lights on in the house, and the only car on the grounds was her rental.

He tied up then made his way down the length of the pier. If she was looking out a window there was no way she'd miss his approach, but he didn't see any movement behind the glass. Dew covered the sedan's paint and the hood was cool. It hadn't been driven recently. There were no other tire tracks in the crushed shells.

He climbed the stairs, his rubber-soled water shoes nearly silent on the treads, and looked through the windows as he traversed the long deck. No movement. No people. No Jessie. He knocked on the back door. She peeked warily out from the bedroom wing then slowly crossed the den and opened the door. The sight of her in her swimsuit hit him with a visceral punch that took him aback—he saw dozens of women in skimpier suits every day. Then he spotted the pepper spray in her fist.

He raised his hands and hit her with his most engaging smile. "Don't shoot. I'm unarmed."

Her gaze flicked to the manila envelope he held then returned to his eyes. "You're early."

"Current worked with me." He lowered his arms.

"I didn't have your number or I'd have called and told you I can't go. I have to run errands today."

"I'm taking you to No Name Key so you can get this kind of detail in your next picture." He offered his ticket to success. There was no way she'd refuse to accompany him when she saw what he'd done for her.

Brow pleated, she took the manila envelope, peered suspiciously inside then extracted the eight-by-ten photographs. Her breath caught. "My deer picture! How did you get this?"

"I kept the buyer's name and number. When I heard you tell Miri you hadn't made a copy of it, I asked them to let me take a photograph. They've also agreed to let you borrow the original and get it professionally scanned by a fine art printer if you'll do it before their daughter leaves town."

He'd prepared for several reactions, like quivering lips and eyes filling with gratitude, but tears hadn't made the list. She blinked furiously and ducked her head as she shuffled through the remaining photos of the art currently hanging at the Widow. A droplet splashed onto her chest and rolled down the slope of her breast. "Thank you."

Her choked-up voice pricked him with a twinge

of guilt. He hadn't done it for her. He forced his eyes away from that tear. "No problem. Let's go."

Refusal replaced her thankful expression. "Look, Logan, it's really nice of you to offer, but I have things I need to do today."

She couldn't say no. If she did, how would he find out more about her? He planned to get her to relax over the next couple of hours, then at some point she'd slip up like she had last night when she'd told the waitresses about college and given him something to utilize in a background search.

"If you're not going, then *you* have to call and tell Miri. She was in the kitchen at five concocting some new recipes she wants us to test on our outing."

She bit her lip and shifted from one bare foot to the other. "She was?"

"You should feel honored. I'm usually her only guinea pig."

Indecision flickered in her eyes. And that damned tear still glistened on the swell of her breast. He hoisted his gaze upward again and silently cursed his distraction.

"The picnic basket is loaded and waiting. Miri sent her life jacket for you, and you can borrow my camera. There are some pretty cool things to see on No Name."

"I could drive over there."

"The road doesn't go where we're going. You'd never see what I can show you from the kayak.

No Name's a cool key. There are only forty-four homes, and it wasn't on the power grid until 2013."

Her sigh and dipping shoulders signaled capitulation. Satisfaction flooded him—like it used to when he landed a big client back in his advising days. He couldn't protect Miri if he couldn't identify the threats against her.

"I guess I could spare an hour."

The tear had *almost* evaporated. "Put on a long-sleeved shirt. And water shoes."

From the way she stiffened he realized he'd barked the commands. "Unless you want me rubbing sunscreen on your back."

"Give me a minute." She shut the door in his face. Then the lock clicked. Why would she lock him out if she didn't have something to hide?

Moments later she returned wearing sunglasses, a ball cap and a loose buttoned-up white shirt. Her face glistened with sunscreen. She stepped outside. Her upper half was covered, but she'd left her legs bare.

"What's in the sack?" he asked to get himself back on track.

"My phone, insect repellent and a sketch pad. Photos are great, but sometimes I just have to..." The fingers of her right hand twitched. "I have to draw."

He waved her ahead and caught a whiff of strawberries and coconut as she passed. Keeping his gaze fixed on her thick braid, he descended the stairs. She paused, glancing up at the kayaks hanging from the underside of the house. "Which one should I use?"

"None of them. You're riding with me."

"I'm pretty coordinated. If you'll tell me how, I can paddle my own."

"Not this time."

Looking less than thrilled by the prospect of riding with him, she strolled down the dock, pausing to thread her hair through the back of the hat. "That isn't the same boat you had the other day."

"Kayak," he corrected automatically and jerked his attention from the curve of her butt, revealed when her shirt hiked up. "This one was Miri and Jack's. It's a tandem."

"When does she ever have time to go out? She's always working."

He handed her the pink life jacket then donned his own. "Before Jack died the Widow was closed on Wednesdays and Thursdays. Those were Miri and Jack's sacred together days. They spent them either paddling the backwaters or on *Holy Jackerel*."

Her expression turned wistful. "My parents swear couple's time is the only way to keep a marriage healthy."

He and Elizabeth had never gone out solo. She'd either invited her friends or they'd been wining and dining one of his clients. "What do your parents do when they go out?"

"Mom loves to—" The wariness returned. "Do different things. How do I get in that?"

He fought the need to push for more. Patience would tease more out of her than pressure. "You're sitting up front. Let me get in first, then you hand me your bag and I'll put it in the waterproof compartment." He put words into action.

"Sit down on the edge of the dock and slide in." He waited while she eyed the craft and looked over the edge of the planks into the water. "Come on, Jessie. It's not deep. I'm holding her steady."

"Don't rush me." She flashed him an irritated scowl as she eased down onto her bottom and very slowly, very cautiously stretched out a leg.

"Can't you swim?"

"Yes. But a shark hangs out under here sometimes."

He leaned over, spotted a four-foot nurse shark lurking by the crab pot. "She's harmless."

She snatched her leg back, banding her arms around her bent knees. "She's there now?"

"Yes. Waiting for a fish or a crab, not a human." He caught himself grinning and couldn't stifle it. But her cautiousness when she'd been so ferocious with him was interesting. "I promise she won't bite you. Not even a nibble on your toes."

"That's not funny." She took a bracing breath, then extended a long, smooth, tanned limb and his grin vanished. She had great legs—not something he needed to notice.

"How'd you get the scar by your knee?"

"I fell out of a tree." She scooted into the craft so quickly she almost overturned it. Squealing, she clutched the sides with a white-knuckled grip.

He braced himself against the dock. "I wouldn't have pegged you for a tree-climbing tomboy."

"Then you'd be wrong."

"Why were you climbing a tree?"

"Because my brother dared me," she said in a distracted tone.

"Is he older or younger?" he pressed, shamelessly using her distraction and fear to his advantage.

"Older."

"What does he do?"

She took a deep breath as if to reply then seemed to collect herself. He wished he could see her face. "Pester me. Like you're doing."

He battled frustration. He'd been getting somewhere. "Unsnap your paddle. We're going to scoop and pull our way across the water."

She did as he asked, hesitantly at first and then after a few hundred yards, more competently. They made it halfway across at a pretty good clip. She was stronger than he'd expected. "You've paddled before."

"A canoe, not a kayak. But…it's been a while."

"Are your shoulders getting tired?"

"I'm okay. The exercise feels good."

"We're coming up on a sunken sailboat. Keep your eyes on the water and you'll see it a little farther ahead." They reached the submerged craft. He dragged the paddle to hold them in place. "It's about ten feet deep here. Can you see fish and lobster swimming in and around it?"

She cautiously leaned to look. The kayak wobbled. She gasped, dropped the paddle and grabbed the sides. He caught the floating handle before it drifted away. "Relax. I won't let you turn us over. Even if you did, the kayak will float and so will you as long as you keep your vest on."

"How did the wreck get here? Did it run aground?"

"No. Storms and hurricanes break boats away from their moorings. Some sink and don't get salvaged because they aren't worth the recovery cost. There are several wrecks in the waterways and offshore. They make a natural reef—good for fishing and diving. Have you ever been diving?"

"No. I want to, but…" She shrugged. He again regretted that his position behind her kept him from seeing her face and gauging the emotion behind her guarded words.

"Why haven't you?"

"I wouldn't know how to go about it. How do you know where the wrecks are?"

He again had the feeling she was screening her words. "Jack was a certified diver. He used to take me out snorkeling for lobster. You can catch them by hand down here. No need for a trap."

"What about the claws?"

"Spiny lobsters don't have big claws like the American or Maine lobsters you see north of here."

"It must have been great growing up with this in your backyard."

"It was. What did you have in your backyard?"

"Grass."

"Where was that?"

"North of here." She threw his words back at him, upping his frustration.

"How far north?"

"Too far to walk. Have you dived in the Tortugas? I've been meaning to take the boat ride over there."

The finality of her tone told him he wouldn't get more right now. "I've dived there and several other places around the world."

But that had been in his previous life, when expensive vacations hadn't been unusual—before Elizabeth and Trent had screwed him. "I don't have a mask and snorkel with me today, but the water's pretty clear if you want to dive in and take a closer look."

"No!"

"You're perfectly safe. If you get a fishing and lobster license, I'll take you diving."

Her braid swung like a pendulum as she shook her head. "No, thanks. Can we go to the island now? I have things to do when we get back."

Derailed, he decided to bide his time and grill her more over their early lunch. He dug the paddle into the water, propelling them forward. "Do you like to fish?"

"I can take it or leave it. But I'm not here to fish. Tell me about Jack."

Another diversion. He let her get away with it. How could he describe the man who'd been more of a father to him than his own?

"Jack was a great guy and probably the smartest man I've ever known. He usually had either a book or a fishing rod in his hand. When the bite was slow he held both. He ran his house like he did his charters—with strict rules for safety and genuine enjoyment of every day and everyone. He was crazy about Miri and not afraid to show it or say it."

"She said he loved the *Holy Jackerel* more than her."

"Wrong. He pampered that boat *because* of Miri. Their goal after they retired was to sell the house and the Widow, then live onboard and travel. He maintained it like he did his wife—as if he intended to keep her forever."

Her shoulders dipped in a sigh. "That's sweet. Have you told Miri?"

Had he? "No."

"You should. She feels second best. No one likes that."

The defeat in her almost inaudible statement raised a dozen questions. He tried to find the right way to follow up while steering the craft into the creek mouth. Jessie shoved back her sunglasses and shrank into her seat as they entered the low canopy of mangroves.

"Are there snakes in here?"

"A few."

She hunched lower and scanned the branches. "Venomous?"

"Some are. But we probably won't encounter those." He beached the kayak in his usual spot. "Look. There's a yellow-crowned night heron."

She twisted to see where he was pointing then followed his finger. He dug out his camera and tapped her shoulder with it. She startled and turned in her seat. "Lord, I thought that was a snake dropping out of the trees."

He couldn't help chuckling. "Want this?"

"Yes. Thanks." After a quick once-over, she turned it on, adjusted the lens and snapped several shots. Her competency revealed a familiarity with high-end cameras—another remnant of his old life.

"Head ashore. There's a picnic table down the

path. I'll bring the basket. Take as many pictures as you want. I'll email them to you later."

Her shoulders stiffened. "Could you put them on a memory stick?"

"You don't want to give me your email address?"

"I'm not set up for email while I'm here."

That was hard to believe. Nobody survived without email and internet access anymore. "I'll download them onto your computer when we get back."

"I don't have one. I told you. I'm on sabbatical. No distractions."

Sure she was. "Right. Go ahead. I'm right behind you."

She rose carefully, shakily in the rocking craft, then stepped ashore. He handed over her bag. She scanned the area. "Where's the road?"

"Are you planning on walking back?"

"I need to be oriented," she stated with exaggerated patience.

He pointed. "That way. A few hundred yards past the picnic table."

She picked her way down the path, carefully watching her steps as if she expected a giant snake to jump out and bite her. Bringing her to an unfamiliar place was a strategy to keep her off balance while he questioned her. It had worked with clients when he'd wanted to know their true investment goals and not hear them parrot what they'd heard others say.

When he joined her, she was sitting on the bench spraying insect repellent on her legs. She popped to her feet, set the spray down and circled to the opposite side of the table but remained standing. The directness of her gaze nailed him in place.

"You said Jack was smart?"

Why did that sound like a leading question? "Yes."

"Do you think Miri isn't?"

Sensing a trap, he spoke carefully. "She is. But she's too trusting."

"Would you rather she be jaded and bitter and emotionally cut off?"

"Of course not. But she can't be a sucker for every sob story."

She shook her head. "You underestimate her. She's a very good judge of character."

"No. She isn't. The reason she's always looking for help is because she has a habit of hiring anyone who's down on their luck. She patches them up and they reward her by moving on."

"You used the word *reward*, but with a negative connotation. Do you believe giving someone a hand up is a bad thing?"

How had she put him on the defensive and made him feel as if he were failing some kind of test? "Having to repeatedly train new workers isn't cost-effective."

"Helping people is not only the right thing to

do. It's a satisfying endeavor. You need to trust her instincts more and stop trying to micromanage her."

The jab knocked his chin like an uppercut. "I don't micromanage. I promised Jack I'd look after her."

She leveled another one of those long-suffering looks on him again. "Logan, one of the reasons Miri asked for my help was to run interference with you."

The bald statement delivered a staggering blow. He and Miri needed to talk. "There are things you don't know."

"Tell me what I need to know to understand your viewpoint."

He set down the basket and opened the lid, trying to formulate his reply as he extracted the covered dishes containing their meal. How much would he have to give Jessie to regain the upper hand in this conversation?

"After Jack died Miri wouldn't come out of her bedroom. It took Sue and me days after the funeral to coax her out and get her to eat something. She wouldn't leave the house. The Widow stayed closed for two weeks."

She lifted the card Miri had taped to one lid and read, "'Amaretto shrimp, citrus coleslaw and jalapeño-cheddar hush puppies.' Sounds delicious."

His mouth moistened in anticipation. He distributed plates and utensils and handed her a bottle of water. He had a shrimp almost to his lips when he noticed her bowed head and paused. A churchgoer. That didn't necessarily mean she wouldn't swindle an older lady.

She lifted her head, pushed a hush puppy into her mouth and chewed, then fixed her gaze on him. "Logan, besides the great food, what do you think makes Fisherman's Widow such a successful restaurant? It's ranked highly by all the travel guides."

Thrown by the question and even more by the fact that he'd caught himself watching her eat, he tried to figure out where she was going with this. "Location."

"That's a good guess. But you're only partially right. There are a few vacant storefronts on the street, so the setting alone doesn't guarantee success of any venture. Right?"

She paused, eyebrows hiked, as if waiting for his response. "Right. The food's very good."

"Yes, it is. And it's reasonably priced. But the Widow's biggest asset is Miri herself—not just her cooking. Have you noticed how interactive she is with her customers?"

"Yes," he ventured, trying to follow her angle.

She flashed him a quick smile. "She feeds a lot of locals—not just tourists—and she treats her regulars like family. She knows all about them, their children, grandchildren and even their pets. They know the same about her. Correct?"

He nodded. This conversation felt familiar. Why, when he hadn't had it with Jessie or anyone else?

She ate another shrimp, biting the flesh from the tail. He couldn't help noticing her short nails, long fingers and white teeth. Then she dabbed her lips with a paper napkin. He blinked. What was wrong with him today? You'd think he'd never seen a person eat before.

"Have you ever considered how hard it would have been for Miri to pretend to be cheerful and play the gracious hostess just days after her husband's death while facing hour after hour of condolences from people who knew her and Jack so well? She would have been reminded of her worst pain over and over again."

The insight made him uncomfortable. "You can't run a business with closed doors."

"I suspect her regulars knew and understood the circumstances. I'd bet most even came to Jack's funeral."

"They did." Why hadn't he thought of this before?

"Did it hurt her bottom line any in the long run to take that time for herself?"

"No. What are you? A grief counselor?"

"No."

"A lawyer?"

She gurgled a laugh, a warm sound that washed over him in an unsettling way. In fact, this whole lunch was disturbing. He'd intended to grill her and yet she'd turned the tables on him. He was the one on the hot seat.

"I'm not a lawyer, either. What I am is someone who learns a lot from observing. For example, I saw my grandfather lose interest in everything after my grandmother died. We were afraid he would succumb to a broken heart."

"That's romantic babble. Nobody dies from a broken heart."

"Modern medicine says otherwise."

"Marriages end every day. People pick up the pieces and move on."

"Is that what you did?"

He would not discuss the failure of his marriage with her. "We're not talking about me."

"No, we're not. But you need to realize that your situation was very different from Miri's. The end of a good thirty-five-year marriage to your soul mate is not the same as voluntarily ending a shorter one. It takes longer for some to move on than others. My mom had to drag her father around like a dog on a leash and make him go through the motions of living until he found his footing. He, like Miri, needed to establish a new normal. He had to realize that he could survive without his life partner by his side—something he'd never expected to have to do."

He wasn't going to waste time with this conversation. He'd only half finished his lunch, but despite the food being delicious, his appetite was gone. He lifted the camera from the table. "Move closer to the palmetto. I'll get a picture of you for your family."

"No. Don't." She raised her hands to shield her face.

"You don't want memories of this trip?"

"Trust me, I won't ever forget it." She didn't sound as if her recollections would be fond ones.

Her panic over a simple photograph was suspicious. Tact and patience evaporated. "Who are you hiding from, Jessie? And is Miri at risk when he finds you?"

"I'm not running from anyone. I just hate having my picture taken—especially when I look like this." A hand swept up and down to indicate her makeup-free face. He bit his tongue on the urge to tell her that even with her hair pulled tightly back and her shiny skin she was a beautiful woman. "Like Miri did, all I need is time to establish a new normal."

More questions sprang to his tongue. Who had hurt her, and—

"Let's finish this feast before it's ruined," she interrupted, derailing his train of thought. "Miri will want a full report on the flavor palette."

A fact with which he couldn't argue. This outing wasn't going as he'd planned. Jessie was beating him at his own game. But he would come up with a way to salvage the morning and find out what made her tick and who had driven her into hiding.

CHAPTER SEVEN

"Look," Logan said.

Jessie scanned the area at which he pointed, and, as had happened a dozen times in the hour since lunch, she didn't see anything other than trees and leaves. "Where?"

He stepped behind her, cupping her shoulders. His torso pressed her back. Then he extended his arm. "There. On the branch. Watch for a flash of red."

Her heart sprinted. Struggling to regulate her breathing, she followed the line of his bicep, his forearm, his finger, but she didn't spot the small lizard until it puffed out the reddish flesh of its chin. "What is it?"

The tight whisper of her voice was barely recognizable. Under the guise of lifting the camera, she wiggled away from the heat of his skin. Her hands shook a little as she focused the lens. Her back and shoulders still burned with his imprint. Why did he affect her this way when she didn't trust him or even particularly like him?

"It's a green anole, or a Carolina anole. He's

a very aggressive little guy and he can change colors."

"Like a chameleon?"

"Yes. But he's not a chameleon."

After snapping several shots, she lowered the camera between them. "You've shown me so many birds and reptiles this morning. How do you find them in the foliage when most are well camouflaged?"

He shrugged. "I have Jack and Miri to thank for that. They taught me how to see and appreciate what's around me. I'm sure you're just as perceptive back home in…?"

She ignored the unspoken question. "I guess I am. They must have been great surrogate parents."

"They were. There wasn't much Jack didn't know about the outdoors."

"And Miri?"

"She taught me how to cook and clean up after myself."

The genuine love and loss in his face tugged at her heartstrings. "I heard you already knew how to do that."

"Not to her specifications." He spoke with tenderness rather than rancor. She suspected Logan might be a nice guy when he wasn't busy being a domineering jerk. And maybe he was nagging Miri because he loved her and wanted the best for her. Then she mentally yanked herself back in line. She couldn't afford to let down her guard with Logan, and if he continued being nice, she just might do that.

"I really should get back. We've already been gone much longer than I anticipated. Thank you…for everything. I have so many pictures and ideas."

That couldn't be disappointment on his face. A crease pleated his brows. "All right. We'll have to do it again."

"Um…maybe." But it wasn't a good idea.

THE FISHERMAN'S WIDOW was at the tail end of the lunch rush when Logan pushed through the kitchen's delivery entrance. Irritated by the lack of progress during what had actually been an otherwise enjoyable morning with Jessie, he sought out his aunt.

Miri stood at the stove beside her chief cook, Hal. She looked up. "Oh, good. You're back. I was just telling Hal about the shrimp. How was it?"

"Fine. Did you ask Jessie to run interference with me?"

"Damned with faint praise," she said to Hal, then took the picnic basket from Logan and set it aside. She tilted her head to indicate he join her in her office, where she sat behind her desk. "I asked for her help, yes."

He was too agitated to sit in the visitor's chair.

"Why didn't you tell me to back off instead of involving a stranger?"

"I have. Repeatedly. You won't listen."

"I listen."

She shook her head. "Logan, I love you. And I know Jack, the poor misguided fool, probably asked you to look out for me. But he didn't mean for you to second-guess every decision I make. Even he gave me free rein running my restaurant."

He expelled an exasperated breath. "It's not the same. Your cushion isn't as deep as it once was. You don't have his income to fall back on. You can't afford to take risks."

"You blame yourself. I get it. But you are not responsible for your exes' bad decisions. You need to get that through your thick head, but you can't seem to, no matter how many times I repeat myself."

Because it wasn't true. "They stole from you right under my nose. I should have realized what they were doing. I should have—"

He bit off the words. He should have realized that while he was out busting his ass trying to win new clients his wife and his former best friend were screwing each other sexually and him criminally.

"You'd known Trent since you were children and trusted him to keep your books. But that wife of yours…" She shook her head. "She might have been beautiful and a business asset, but she was always more interested in her possessions than anything or anyone. You can't keep beating yourself up because others betray you. People let us down, Logan. It happens."

"Especially the ones you hire."

She snapped upright in her chair. "You need to get a life and stay out of mine."

"I have a life," he protested.

"You don't date. You don't have friends—except for that leech of a private investigator. When was the last time you took a woman out for a meal or had a beer with friends?"

"Two hours ago."

She chided him with a stern look. "The meal I provided for you and Jessie is not what I meant and you know it."

"I don't need a woman or friends."

"Yes, you do. Everybody needs friends. And love. And at your age, sex. Although I can see why you're a bit gun-shy, you can't seal your heart off forever. It's unhealthy."

His face and ears burned at her frankness. "I'm fine."

"No, you're not. Also, you preach to me about investing, but how much are you socking away for your retirement when you're throwing away all of your money chasing Elizabeth and Trent?"

"That's an investment in my future."

"You won't have a pot to pee in in your future if you keep wasting money on the past."

They were treading the same ol' territory. But something Jessie had said this morning about her grandfather had struck a chord. "I'll make you a deal. I'll start dating if you'll close the Widow one day a week. You need the break and so does your staff."

She shook her head. "I can't do that. My customers want me open."

"Your customers survived when you were closed two days per week and you cleared just as much money working fewer hours. Wednesdays and Thursdays are slow days. Just think— you could take out the kayak or spend a day in your kitchen at home playing with food."

He could tell from her squinty-eyed appraisal that she was considering the sincerity of his plan. He wasn't the least bit interested in dating. Sex, sure. He obviously needed to get laid if his sudden fascination with Jessie was anything to go by. He'd watched her all morning as if he'd never seen anybody doodle before. And touching her... had been a mistake. But trust a woman again? Be snookered by a pretty face and a good lay? Not gonna happen.

Then Miri nodded. "I will if you will. You first. Now, let's discuss something more pleasant. How did your morning paddle go?"

She didn't give him time to enjoy his victory.

"Good. Jessie did several sketches, made charcoal rubs of some of the leaves and took hundreds of pictures with my camera. She claims she doesn't have an email address or even a computer for me to send her the files."

Miri shrugged. "She hasn't given me one, either, if that's what you're hinting at."

"I'm not. But it's odd for someone of her age and obvious affluence not to use the internet."

"She said she's on a sabbatical. That means taking a break from all the things that keep you from being productive. Email and social media are time sucks. Everybody says so."

He wasn't getting anywhere. "I'll bring the pictures by on a memory stick tomorrow."

"You're not hanging out here with your friend to bug me tonight?"

He fought a wince. "No. I's working and I'm going to try to put together a little black book of possible date material. And you have to figure out which day you're closing. We'll need to have the door signs and webpage adjusted."

He wasn't going to date anybody—at least not seriously. He had nothing to offer. Not anymore. But letting Miri believe he was would get her off his back.

JESSIE SAT ON the dock Tuesday afternoon, letting the sun dry her hair and staring at the scrap of paper in her hand. Upon their return from No

Name Key, Logan had given her the name and phone number of the buyer. She was supposed to call and schedule a time to borrow her Key deer painting and take it to the printer's.

Overwhelmed by the thought of making that call, she'd stalled by taking a shower, then going through the phone book and calling three printers who advertised they made the kind of copies she needed. One had impressed her more than the others, and the hundred-dollar price tag was doable with her tip money.

Her heart raced faster as she pulled her phone from her pocket, but she didn't dial. Meeting the person who'd bought her work and identifying herself filled her with apprehension on so many levels. One, interacting with anyone on a personal basis was risky. They might ask questions and she might slip up. She'd had a hard enough time dodging Logan's sly inquiries today.

Two, if she didn't do it, she'd have no record of the work she'd poured her heart into. Could she just let it go? The emptiness of that thought told her she needed to get her painting copied.

Three, the buyer had paid a lot of money for her work. What if he'd changed his mind after three days of looking at it and decided it wasn't worth it? Returning the cash wasn't an issue. She hadn't spent it. But her ego might never recover.

Four, Brandon would have a fit.

The paper crumpled in her fist. She let herself be distracted by the dive boat cruising past. When Logan had suggested she check out the sunken sailboat this morning, she'd been tempted, but she doubted her colored contacts would stay in if she opened her eyes underwater, and she couldn't risk losing one in front of Logan.

The lenses were nonprescription. She'd bought several sets on the drive down when she'd had the wild idea somewhere around Jacksonville of changing her coloring and going incognito so that she could have a little freedom. She was wearing the last set. Because of her job she could afford to buy more. But could she find them in the Keys?

The phone vibrated in her hand, startling her so badly she almost dropped it. Brandon's number flashed on the screen and she grimaced. He'd called twice this morning and she hadn't called him back. The idea of pretending all was well knotted her stomach. But she didn't have a choice except to answer.

"Hi," she chirped in her happiest voice.

"Where in the hell have you been? If you hadn't answered this time I was going to drive south."

"I'm sorry. I went out in a kayak. I had the phone in a waterproof compartment and didn't hear it ring." The truth. "I haven't been home long." A white lie—she'd been home an hour.

"You're all right then?"

"Yes. Peachy. Back in the safety of the walled compound."

"Jessamine, going kayaking alone isn't a good idea."

"Brandon, you sent me down here and said, 'Enjoy the Keys.' I can't do that locked in the house."

"I hear you. I'm just worried about you. You're a target."

"I'm not a target if no one knows who or where I am." She thought of the stranger from the restaurant and her stomach muscles clenched. "I can take care of myself."

"Yeah, right."

His sarcasm stung. Then she realized she never had before the win. She'd relied on her family too much. It had taken making her safety net inaccessible to force her to become more self-reliant. That was a sad, sobering fact for a twenty-six-year-old to admit.

"I'm fine. I promise. And as much as I hate to admit it…the distance has been good for me."

"Are you sure you're all right?"

Knowing she'd earned his skepticism wasn't easy to swallow. "Positive. Look, I need groceries and stuff. I've got to go."

"Be careful, Li'l Bit. And answer your phone next time." The line went dead.

She lowered her hand and stared across the water at No Name. How had her life come to this?

Her father had been diagnosed her junior year of high school. Wanting to be available to help him if he needed her, she'd enrolled in a college less than an hour from home, then taken a job in the school district she'd attended as a child. Even her little house was only a few minutes from her parents' orchard. But even before that she'd preferred home to partying with friends.

She'd built herself a nice little cocoon. But she'd never tried to metamorphose and fly. Maybe it was time she did.

THE MASSIVE KEY LARGO VILLA intimidated Jessie so much she debated driving past and forgetting about getting her painting scanned. But her new resolve made her follow the course. Heart pounding, she pulled up to the elaborate wrought-iron gates and pushed the button on the intercom system.

"Yes?" a male voice crackled through the speaker.

"I'm Jessie...the...painter of the Key deer picture, here to see Mr. or Mrs. Clark."

"Come in" preceded the mechanical sound of the iron gate smoothly opening.

She drove forward into a circular courtyard that looked like something out of a landscape magazine, but despite the beauty, her hands were shaking so badly she'd never be able to sketch it. Gulping down her anxiety, she stepped out onto the brick driveway. The people who owned this home could afford to buy anything—why *her* work?

The front door opened and a couple she guessed to be in their fifties stepped out and descended the circular stairs to meet her. The man extended his hand. "Jessie, I'm Roger Clark, and this is my wife, Meredith. Welcome."

"We're so happy to meet you," the woman added. "Our daughter fell in love with your painting."

To calm her nerves, she told herself to treat this like a parent-teacher conference. "Um...thank you."

"Come in," Mr. Clark added. "Mr. Nash said you hadn't made prints and that this was an original."

Jessie tried not to gawk at the palatial two-story circular foyer with its gleaming white marble floors and staircase clinging to the wall. The architecture was stunningly beautiful with its clean lines and arches, but this was not the time to act like a country bumpkin. "Yes, that's right."

"Then we're fortunate to have it. But you really should consider releasing it in a limited edition of signed and numbered prints. It's a good way to build an audience."

"I...um, hadn't considered that. You wouldn't mind?"

"Oh, no. We buy a lot of art—usually limited

art prints. It's something for you to think about—to help pay the bills. Once you get the painting scanned, you can decide later on if you'd like to do a print run. But remember, the smaller the run, the higher the price. Come this way."

The living room was larger than her classroom back home and decorated in the same monochromatic white as the foyer. The only color in the room came from the artwork on three walls. Her jaw dropped when she recognized the artists of the other two.

"We're hanging yours here until Reagan leaves so we can all enjoy it."

Jessie took a deep breath for courage before launching into her prepared speech that seemed doubly important now that they'd hung her with such superior and intimidating company.

"You're sure you don't mind me borrowing it? I can leave the money you paid for it with you until I bring it back, if you like." That way if they changed their minds about the impulsive purchase, they could tell her—preferably over the phone—to keep the canvas.

The woman shook her perfectly coiffed platinum-blond head. "Oh, no, that's not necessary. We love the Fisherman's Widow. If we can pick it up there once you're done with it, we'll have the perfect excuse to drive down for one more meal before Reagan flies west."

"But we do have one request," Mr. Clark stated

and Jessie braced herself. "We're hosting a going-away party for our daughter on Friday evening. We'd like it back before then."

"We want our guests to see it," his wife chimed in.

Adrenaline and nervousness pulsed through Jessie's veins, drying her mouth and dampening her palms. "I'll leave it with the printer today, then you can come Thursday evening for dinner or Friday for lunch."

Her hostess pressed manicured hands together. "Lovely. We'll come Thursday. Would you be able to attend our party?"

Floored, Jessie gaped at the woman. That would be almost like a gallery show—something she'd never have. "I...um... I'm working at the Widow that night. But thank you for the invitation."

"Where can we see more of your work?" Mr. Clark asked.

Surprise stole Jessie's breath. "I have two more hanging at the restaurant now."

"You're exclusive to Miri?"

Her, exclusive? "Yes."

"Then she's very fortunate," Mrs. Clark said. "Now I'm looking forward to dining there even more. Roger will carry the painting to your car for you. It was so nice to meet you, Jessie, and if you change your mind about Friday night, you have our number. I know our daughter and our guests would love to meet you."

Numbly, Jessie led the way to her car, said her goodbyes and drove out of the gate in a near stupor. She made it out of their neighborhood before pulling into a parking lot and pressing cold palms to her hot face. These people liked her work enough to want to share it, and her, with their friends. The idea filled her with so much excitement she did a little dance in her seat. She needed to tell someone. But who? Not her family. Nor her old friends or coworkers. Miri would probably want to know.

But Logan was the one who'd made this happen.

She had to thank him for arranging this meeting. But she didn't have his number. The only way to voice her gratitude was face-to-face.

LOGAN STARED AT the attractive redhead across the table from him and tried to feign interest in her descriptions of places she'd been to, but after a morning watching Jessie's nearly silent appreciation of nature, his date's chatter was too much noise. But if dating was the only way to get Miri to take some time for herself, then he'd man up and do it.

His attention kept drifting to his aunt. Logan watched her work the dining room and realized Jessie was right. Miri knew most of her patrons.

And the ones she didn't know, she took the time to engage, leaving smiling faces in her wake.

"Logan, am I boring you?"

He snapped back to his guest. "No. I'm sorry. You've visited some great places. I was just watching my aunt."

"Your aunt?"

"She owns this place."

Alarm filled the woman's hazel eyes. "You brought me here to introduce me to family? I thought we were just...having a good time."

His collar felt tight. "Right. That's the plan. But the Fisherman's Widow serves the best seafood in town. I couldn't take a travel agent somewhere inferior on her first trip to Key West, could I?"

She looked slightly pacified. "I have to admit the food and setting are fabulous, but I don't want you to get the wrong idea. I'm leaving in the morning and don't plan to return any time soon."

Miri ducked back into the kitchen. She'd left him alone thus far, and he'd like to keep it that way. But before he could signal Sue to bring his check, his aunt returned, carrying a small tray. With her gaze trained on him, she headed straight for their table. Damn.

"We didn't order dessert," he told her when he spotted two slices of pie.

"It's on the house. I know how much you love my piña colada pie." Her expectant smile swung to his date. He blanked on the woman's name. Completely. Totally. Forgot it. He'd never done that before. He'd always been great with names and faces. It had been one of his assets back in Charleston.

After a beat, Miri extended her hand. "I'm Miri, Logan's aunt."

"Angelina Jones," his date responded.

"How do you know Logan?"

Cautious eyes flashed his way. "We met on Duval Street this afternoon."

Miri's eyebrows lifted. "Really? And where are you from, hon?"

"Knoxville. I'm in town for a conference."

"Pretty city. But far away. I hope you enjoy your visit to Key West, Angelina, and thanks for stopping by." Miri pivoted and returned to the kitchen.

Busted. Logan gritted his teeth. His charade had been fruitless. Unless he found a way to convince Miri otherwise, he'd have to repeat it—with better success next time. He searched again for Sue. The front door opened, and Jessie, wearing jeans and a pink shirt, walked in. His gut muscles clenched. With her windblown dark hair draping her shoulders and her cheeks flushed from this morning's sun, she made the woman across from him, with her perfectly styled hair and immaculate makeup, look artificial.

Jessie surveyed the room, spotted him and headed in his direction, then saw his date, U-turned and departed. What had she wanted? He had the urge to go after her and ask.

"Girlfriend?" Angelina asked.

"No. A waitress who works here."

"Why'd she turn around and leave?"

"I don't know." He threw some bills on the table. "Let me walk you back to your hotel."

"But…" Her gaze flicked to her untouched dessert, then she smiled. "Okay. I'm too full for dessert anyway."

He cringed inwardly. "Let me grab a takeout box."

He retrieved one from behind the bar, slid both pieces of pie into it and offered his hand. She took it. Holding her hand did nothing for him, whereas touching Jessie this morning had been like grabbing a live electrical wire.

Not liking that realization, he led Angelina from the Widow. Outside, he searched the sidewalks and parking lots for Jessie but didn't see her. Neither he nor his date spoke as they covered the two blocks to her hotel. He halted outside the entrance and released her.

She tilted her head back. "Would you like to come up for drinks and dessert?"

The invitation for more than a good-night kiss lit her eyes and curved her lips. And he reacted no differently than he would looking at a parking meter. Maybe Elizabeth had killed more than his ability to trust women. But he wasn't interested in investigating that possibility tonight.

"You have an early start tomorrow. Thanks for keeping me company this evening. Good night." Ignoring her frown, he handed her the dessert box and walked away.

He ought to regret turning down a sure thing. But he didn't. Angelina's cool composure had nothing on Jessie's childlike wonder, the ready smiles, quick gasps and quiet chuckles when something impressed her.

And he was out of his mind to be thinking like that about a woman who could be a crook in a girl-next-door disguise. And, he assured himself, the only reason he wanted to show her more of the local sights was to see what information he could get out of her.

In no time he was back at the Widow. He entered through the side door to the kitchen. Miri stood with Hal. She shot Logan a shrewd look and shook her head, then patted the cook on the shoulder and gestured for her office.

"Good try, but she was not marriage material," she stated baldly.

"You didn't say marriage. You said date and get laid."

"A wedding will follow those, I hope."

"Not going to happen."

"Why not?"

"All women are liars."

"Are you calling me a liar, Logan Chancellor Nash?"

Ouch. The full name. He grimaced. "Of course not."

"But I'm a woman, or at least I was last time I checked."

"I'm not getting married again, Miri."

"You won't as long as you're hung up on the past."

Old material. "What did Jessie want?"

Miri's brow puckered. "Jessie? When?"

"Ten minutes ago. She came in the front door then turned around and left."

"I haven't seen her today."

"She didn't come back here?"

"No."

He'd thought maybe she'd decided to use the employee entrance. If not, then had she wanted to talk to him? Why? "Let me have her number. I'll call her and ask."

"I'll call her myself. If she needs anything, I'll text you. Now shoo. I'm trying to work."

He recognized the stubborn cast of Miri's jaw and admitted defeat. Frustrated, he left.

Why had Jessie come in on her day off? And why had she turned around when she'd seen his date? He had to find out.

CHAPTER EIGHT

JESSIE DESCENDED THE back stairs, intent on working off her unexplained agitation by swimming laps in the pool.

What was wrong with her? She had no claim on Logan. Just because he'd been good company once he'd eased up on trying to pry information from her. And he'd been great at pointing out wildlife and interesting plants. And her pulse had skipped every time he touched. No, none of that made their morning together a date.

So why had seeing him with the beautiful redhead tonight disturbed her? It had to be the full moon. There was no other logical explanation.

She reached the pool, and following the caretaker's instructions, she flipped on the underwater lights to make sure no unexpected guests had invaded the heated water. When she didn't spot any, she dropped her towel and dipped in a toe. The water was a few degrees warmer than the balmy seventy-six-degree air. Swimming in the winter was a luxury she didn't have at home.

Poised on the edge, she prepared to dive in, then remembered she hadn't removed her contacts. If she wanted to burn off energy, she'd have to go back inside to do that. Then a car horn honked nearby. That in itself was remarkable on her quiet street. The blast sounded again. She peeked around the wall of the dressing room/bathroom that shielded the pool/hot tub area from the street. Bright headlights beamed through her gate.

"Jessie!"

Logan. The same swooping sensation hit her stomach that she'd experienced when she'd realized he was on a date. What did it mean? She wasn't interested in him *that* way even if his low-riding swim trunks had made it very difficult to concentrate on nature this morning.

"Open up," he shouted when she remained paralyzed in place.

She debated ignoring him. But he'd obviously seen her. And she needed to thank him. Backtracking, she grabbed her towel and bound it tightly over her swimsuit, then she cursed the fact that she'd left her sandals upstairs. If she hadn't she could have walked down the driveway and talked to him through the safety of the barrier. She'd learned in her first week here that the shells were sharp and a cut stayed sore for days. She couldn't risk needing medical attention for an infection.

Following the flagstone path back to the house, she hit the concealed button attached to one of the pylons. The iron gate opened. He drove his car into the courtyard and silenced the engine before climbing out.

"You got your light fixed," she observed aloud.

"Yes. Are you okay?" The low, rumbled question was barely audible over his shoes crunching on the crushed shell driveway.

She clutched the towel tighter to her breast. "I'm fine. Why?"

"Why'd you U-turn at the Widow?" he countered.

So much for hoping he hadn't seen her. "I was going to thank you for setting up the meeting with the Clarks. I picked up my painting this afternoon. But it wasn't important enough to interrupt your date."

"It wasn't a date."

She gave him the look she reserved for students she suspected of fibbing, and he grimaced.

"Okay, it was a date. But not that kind of date. It was just a hookup."

She flinched and wished he'd kept that unpalatable tidbit to himself. "And you took her to meet Miri!"

His frown deepened. "Not a sexual hookup."

"Is there any other kind?"

He shoved a hand through his hair. "I'm trying to get Miri to take some time off. She said she would if I would."

"Take time off? I never see you working." She bit her tongue. *If you can't say something nice...*

He looked even more uncomfortable than she felt. "I haven't dated since my divorce. She's pushing me into it. Tonight was for show."

Something coursed through her. It was *not* relief. But then what was it? She didn't know. "How long ago was your divorce?"

His jaw shifted. "We're not talking about me."

"You brought it up."

"We split close to five years ago," he offered grudgingly.

"That's a long time."

"I've had other things to deal with and a business to set up here."

"I see." But she didn't. She couldn't imagine being hung up on Aaron that long. But she hadn't been married to him. Thank goodness.

"Anyway, you started this."

She folded her arms and the knot of her towel broke free. His gaze dropped. She snatched the edges back together and retucked them, thankful the thick fabric hid her body's reaction. "And exactly how are you going to blame this on me, Mr. Nash?"

She hoped he missed her don't-bullshit-me teacher's voice.

"You said your mom had to force your grandfather back into life. That's what I'm doing with Miri. I'm trying to get her to think about something other than work."

"That makes sense. But what if she's not ready?"

"I'm worried about what will happen to her if she keeps going at this pace."

How sweet. "She does work a lot of hours."

"More than ninety each week."

And then she connected the dots. "You drove all the way out here to check on me?"

"Yes."

"I… Thank you. But I'm fine. Really."

The full moon highlighted his cheekbones and cast his eyes and the hollows of his cheeks into shadow. The combination of light and dark made his features even more interesting than usual. She'd only done a few portraits, but her fingers itched to try his. Maybe in oils. No. Charcoals.

"But…?" he prompted, jarring her out of her contemplation of gradients of gray.

She shook her head. "Nothing. They just—the Clarks, I mean—invited me to attend their daughter's going-away party and meet their friends. That was…unexpected."

"I told you buyers like to meet the artist."

He'd told her a lot of things that she hadn't been ready to hear. But she was starting to—*wanting to*—believe him now. Could her dad have been wrong about her not being able to make a living with her art? No. Her father was never wrong. He was the smartest man she knew, and he'd guided her on the right path every time she'd gone to him for advice.

But that was a moot point now anyway, since

she no longer *needed* her salary. But she needed the job, she realized. Not just because she loved sharing her knowledge with her students, but also because it forced her to interact with others so she wouldn't revert to being the introverted homebody she'd been in her youth, who'd been more interested in her art than people.

She blinked from that startling insight back to the present. "You did tell me. But I... I'm not ready for that. They're picking up the painting at the Widow Thursday evening and they want to see more of my work."

"Good."

"I suppose I should get the other two scanned, too."

"If you want a record of them before they sell."

"*If* they sell." She didn't want to get her hopes up any more than they already were.

"They will. Come in and get them early. Maybe the print shop can do it before we open. Bring more pieces in case they can't."

Excitement quickened her pulse. "I will."

"Do you want help choosing them?"

That meant inviting him in, and as off balance as she was today from her reaction to him and her recent self-discoveries, that was not a good idea. "Um. No. Thanks."

A gust blew her hair across her face. Before she could untangle her fingers from her towel to push it back, Logan's hand was there. She froze.

He captured the stray lock and tucked it behind her ear. The drag of his fingertip across her skin was unbearably erotic. Goose bumps lifted her skin and she struggled to suppress a shiver.

"You have beautiful hair. You never wear it down." Then he dropped his hand, seemingly discomfited by his remark.

A twinge of guilt squashed out the pleasure his statement elicited. Would he say the same about her much lighter natural color? Her dark hair was symbolic of the lies between them. And even if they had passed a few memorable hours together, trusting his Mr. Nice Guy persona was still out of the question. She had to remember that it hadn't been that long ago that he'd been out to expose her.

"It's not practical or hygienic to wear it loose at work."

"No. Guess not."

Standing here beside him felt intimate. The full moon was definitely messing with her equilibrium. She had to get rid of him. "Thanks for stopping by. I'll see you in the morning."

She didn't release her pent-up breath until the gate slid closed behind his vehicle.

"Good morning, Miriam Louise."

Miri startled and nearly dropped her spatula into the pot. She spun around. Logan's PI stood in the delivery door. "An ex-cop should know better than to barge uninvited into a business. You're likely to get shot."

"If you have a weapon, you're smart enough to keep it concealed in your office near your cash drawer. And if you don't want company, you should keep your door locked."

She did have a pistol beneath her desk. Not that she'd ever needed it. Oyster stew dripped across her fingertips. "My staff will be arriving soon. What do you want, Ignatius?"

The white paper bag in his hand crinkled in his fist. "Bethany called and invited me to lunch. Just her and me. The girls are in school."

"And?"

He shrugged. If she hadn't seen the tension in his face, she might have fallen for the dismissive gesture. "And nothing. I'm just making a statement."

Lord, this man was a mess. But his awkwardness told her more than anything how much rebuilding his relationship with his daughter meant to him. "Where are you going to take her?"

"Here?"

"No. You've brought her here already. As much as I'd appreciate the business, you need to go somewhere different. Somewhere quieter. Is she squeezing you in on her lunch hour?"

He nodded.

She set aside her spatula and washed her hands while she mentally ticked through a list of her favorite places. "The deli by the butterfly garden is close and it has parking nearby."

"That sissy place? Real men don't eat quiche. Or haven't you seen that bumper sticker?"

"Who are you trying to impress? Your knuckle-dragging friends or your daughter? The deli's food is delicious."

"Right. Good idea." Then he seemed to remember the bag in his hand. "Brought you these. Lemon custard–filled doughnuts."

Her favorite. But how in the world did he know that? "Has Logan been talking?"

"He's the one who told me about the bakery, but I caught Sue coming out of the shop last week. She said she always brought you one when she was near there."

Miri was touched even though she didn't want to be. "If you brought enough for two, I'll pour you a cup of coffee."

"I did."

She filled two mugs and brought them to the work island. "Pull up a stool."

He joined her and for several moments silence reigned as she enjoyed the tart-sweet combination of her favorite confection. She'd been trying to pry the recipe from the baker for years with no luck, and she hadn't been successful in recreating the filling, either. He must have a secret ingredient.

She hated to pop the last bite into her mouth.

Once she did, she licked her sticky fingers. When she caught Ignatius watching her, her cheeks warmed. For pity's sake, she was too old for blushing. "Wipe that grin off your face and go wash your face and hands. You have glaze all around your mouth."

"Don't s'pose you'd take care of that for me?" He waggled his bushy brows.

The twinkle in his eyes fanned the warmth to fire. She wasn't about to kiss the big lug—or anyone else. "Not a chance."

"Shame." He washed up, dried his hands and wiped his face with the damp paper towel.

She didn't go near the sink until he moved away. "I need to get back to work. I'm sure lunch with your daughter will go well. Thanks for the treat."

He didn't take the hint and leave. "What can you tell me about Logan's ex?"

The delightful taste in her mouth turned bitter. "Is that why you brought me the doughnut? As a bribe so you could question me?"

His neck and face turned ruddy. "I was bringing the pastries anyway, but I thought while I was here I'd see if you could give me something fresh for my search. I've exhausted every avenue Logan's given me."

She thought of the letter she'd received several months back, but she wouldn't tell him or Logan about it. Logan needed to move on, and bringing his lying ex back into his life would hinder that. She didn't know if he still had feelings for the conniving bi—*witch*, but his lack of relationships made her fear that he did. And that would not do. Elizabeth had moved Logan to Charleston and turned him into a money-hungry machine that Miri and Jack hadn't recognized and didn't care for on the few occasions they'd seen him. She couldn't risk a repeat.

"The best thing you can do with your search is drop it."

"Your nephew insists otherwise. There's no deterring him."

"I wouldn't help you even if I could. Now get out of my kitchen and don't come bearing deceitful gifts again."

Disappointed, and angry because she was disappointed, she shut the door behind him and turned the lock. Ignatius Smith was bad news. For her. And for her nephew. Key West would be a better place if he moved on.

THE KNOB DIDN'T budge when Jessie tried to turn it. Miri never locked this door when she was here, and she was always in the kitchen long before nine. Had Logan convinced her to take some time off? Jessie knocked. The door whooshed open so quickly she jumped back a step.

"What do you wa— Oh, Jessie. Good morning, hon."

Miri's harassed then flustered response surprised Jessie. "Are you okay?"

"Yes. I had some unwanted company earlier. I thought he had returned."

"Logan?"

"No. That PI of his."

Jessie's throat closed. Had he been asking about her? She gulped down her nerves. "What did he want?"

"He's doing a job for Logan."

That knocked her off balance. "He is?"

"Yes. I've asked him to drop it, but he won't listen. What do you have there?"

Trepidation filled Jessie. "Is he investigating anybody I know?"

She tried to make a joke of it, but the words sounded flat.

"Logan's ex. What do you have there, hon?"

Relief washed over her, then she yanked herself up short. It was nothing to her if Logan was hung up on his ex-wife.

"I brought two more paintings. I'll swap them for the ones here and drop those off at the printer to get scanned when I pick up the deer picture. If that's okay?"

"Of course it is. Oh, Jessie, I love your sunrise. I didn't know you did watercolors, too."

"I like to experiment with different mediums. I probably should focus on one, but—"

"No, no. This is lovely. You couldn't achieve this blend of shades with any other paint."

"That's what I thought. So…is…um, Logan here?"

"No, but I'm sure he'll turn up. He always does." Both love and exasperation flavored the words.

Jessie wasn't disappointed. The emptiness in her tummy was just…hunger. She'd missed breakfast. Given last night's moonlight madness, doing what she'd come to do and getting out of here before Logan arrived seemed prudent. "I'll switch these and get to the printer's."

"Let me help. Are you having the copies framed?" Miri asked as she followed Jessie into the dining room.

"I'd rather not spend the money on that right now. Maybe later."

Miri touched her arm. "I could loan it to you."

She wanted to hug the woman. "Thank you. But no. I need to do this on my own."

"If you insist." Miri took down the hibiscus and propped it against the hostess stand. "Put the watercolor here. The muted colors are so different from the acrylics it'll look washed out beside them."

Jessie did as bidden and stood back. She really liked the piece. That made her even more determined to recreate the storm clouds from a few days back. They'd be complementary—one so bright with the promise of a new day and the other dark and gloomy. She crossed to the heron, removed it and replaced it with the cormorants.

"Creepy," Miri said. "That one's eyes follow everywhere I go."

Like Logan's. "My thoughts exactly."

Then Miri's attention shifted to Jessie. "A bargain's a bargain. I asked you to help me for two weeks. That ends this Monday. I hate to lose you, but I have monopolized your time and kept you from creating more of these. I called an employment agency this morning. They're going to send me some experienced help."

Jessie nibbled her bottom lip. This was a good thing. Repeated exposure to Logan or his PI wasn't wise. And then there was her family. She hated lying to them. "I'm glad."

"I hope you'll continue to display your art here even when you're not working here." Miri held out her arms and Jessie stepped into them. The hug was bittersweet.

"Thank you, Miri. Thank you for everything."

"No. Thank you, hon. And don't be a stranger after Monday, you hear?"

Six more days and Jessie could get back to solitude and her art. It was the right thing to do. So why did it feel wrong?

LOGAN TRIED TO hide his impatience with the client who'd monopolized his morning. Like most of the businesses who'd hired Logan when he moved to Key West, Tom had been a friend of Jack and Miri's. Without that familial connection, Logan never would have been successful starting over in Key West—not with the scandal tarnishing him.

"Tom, I've got this. We have every receipt and every deduction covered. Relax."

The man was shaky and pale beneath his tan, and no amount of reassurance had helped. "Relax? Are you nuts? It's the IRS," he protested. "A fishing guide without a boat is nothing. If they take the *Aqua-Haul*, I'm out of business. And I got nothing else for 'em to take."

"The IRS isn't going to take your boat. You were probably red-flagged because you made forty-nine percent less this year. You have your client logs and all your maintenance records, and we have your medical bills showing your hospital stay and your rehab. The audit's an aggravation, sure, but I'll be at the meeting with you. We'll prove income and expenditures and be done with it."

"You're sure? I don't need to hire a tax attorney?"

"No." Logan had faced bigger dragons than the IRS before. He'd get the man through this.

"Okay then." Tom rose slowly, favoring the new hip. The replacement had gone well until infection had set in and put him flat on his back.

He'd been unable to work for almost six months, and he didn't need this hassle.

"I'm going to review everything again before our meeting, and I'll call you if I have any questions. But I don't ever fudge anything. I stand by what we filed. Go home, or better yet, go fishing."

The client finally left. Logan checked his watch and admitted defeat—Jessie would have long since left the Widow. He hadn't asked which printer she'd chosen. So unless he wanted to drive around Key West looking for her car, he'd have to wait until tonight to ask her how it went.

He was becoming personally invested in her art.

No. He wasn't. His sole interest was in bringing it to the Widow and making sure nothing Jessie did backlashed on Miri.

Jessie's dig about him never working had struck a nerve. No, he hadn't logged as many hours since she'd come onto the scene, but that was only because her refusal to follow basic employment rules was suspicious.

It wasn't because she was attractive. Or because she was an interesting combination of bold, in-your-face and skittish as a feral cat. He sought out her company simply because of Miri.

So why had he pulled that idiot move of brushing her hair back last night? And why did he still recall the softness of her skin on his fingertips and the silkiness of the strands dragging across his knuckles? And why was he champing at the bit now because he'd missing seeing her at the Widow this morning?

Because Miri was right. He needed to get laid.

But not by Jessie.

Until Jessie had asked, he hadn't realized that he hadn't been with a woman in more than five years. Right after Elizabeth and Trent had vanished with his and their clients' cash, he'd been caught up in proving his innocence and keeping his ass out of jail, and then in finding the guilty parties. Lately, he'd been neck-deep in helping Miri after Jack's death. He'd accused Miri of not having a life, but she wasn't the only one guilty of that.

He'd been talking to a client who owned a bar on Duval Street when Angelina had approached him and asked which of the one hundred flavors of frozen drink she should try first. It had taken him several minutes and a wink from his client to realize she wasn't really interested in the drink, but in him. Even then he'd asked her out to dinner not because he desired her but because of Miri.

He wadded up a piece of paper and threw it in the trash. "Fool. If you'd taken Angelina up on her offer, you wouldn't have spent the night remembering how Jessie's towel had slipped and wishing she'd dropped it." His voice echoed in his empty office.

All right. So he was attracted to Jessie. And

ironically, the first woman he'd looked at twice since his divorce was one he couldn't fully trust.

But nothing could come of it, and not only because of his trust issues. Miri had an ironclad rule against dating her waitresses. "Don't sleep where you eat," she'd said a dozen times during his teenage years when he'd spent too much time chatting up one of her girls.

The best thing he could do to fight his fascination with Jessie was to find out what or whom she was running from. That meant spending more time with her to ferret out the facts. But he'd kept his zipper up for five years—continuing to do so a little while longer shouldn't be that difficult.

Since he had time to kill before his lunch appointment, he extracted the SD card from his camera and shoved it into his computer. With a couple of clicks, thumbnail images of the shots Jessie had taken filled the screen.

"Holy spit." He rocked forward, clicking on and enlarging one picture after another. The images on the screen were calendar quality. Jessie knew how to use his camera better than he did.

The door to his office opened, forcing him to pry his gaze from the screen. I stood on the threshold. "Your aunt didn't think much of your ex, did she?"

"No. Why?"

"I thought Miri might have something to help me find the disappearing duo, but I get the impression she wouldn't have spit on your former missus if Elizabeth had been on fire."

"That pretty much sums up how she and Jack felt. But when the prettiest girl on campus singles you out, you go along for the ride and don't ask questions—at least that's what I did. Like I said, let's forget Elizabeth and Trent for a while and focus on Jessie."

"Are you still riding that horse? Forget about it. I told you, I'm not pissing off your aunt. I need her in my corner."

"Take a look at these."

I stepped behind his desk. "Nice. Yours?"

"Jessie's."

"She knows what she's doing with the whole visual-spatial thing, know what I mean? Maybe she's a professional photographer. You tried searching for photographers recently in the news?"

"No. But that's a good suggestion. You ready for lunch?"

"Change of plans. I need to cancel. My daughter invited me out. I'm meeting her at some sissy place your aunt recommended. I need it to go well if I want to spend time with my granddaughters."

"Why wouldn't it?"

I wiped a hand across his face and shook his head. "I can think of a dozen reasons—number one being my big mouth. I'm not exactly Mr. Sunshine, and it's been a lot of years since I had to mind my manners in front of a female."

"No, but you know how to act with clients. You'll do fine."

"Hope you're right. By the way, I saw Jessie at the printer's down on Shrimp Road. I helped 'em track some illegal copies once. They're good, honest people. And they like to talk about art. They might answer questions, if you know what I mean."

Adrenaline spurted through Logan's veins. He shot to his feet and grabbed his keys. "Thanks."

CHAPTER NINE

JESSIE FLOATED FROM the printer's, her emotions sailing so high she felt like a kite ready to snap its string. Due to the other people on the sidewalk, she refrained from happy dancing all the way to her car. Barely.

In the parking lot, she slid her deer canvas into the backseat, closed the door and shoved her hand into her pocket. The roll of bills collected from her tips was substantially smaller, but she couldn't regret it. She released the money and curled her fingers around the USB drive containing the file the printer had scanned. This small plastic object held…her future? She gave it a squeeze then shuffled her feet and shook her tush just a little. She couldn't help it.

"Jessie?" a familiar voice called before she could check to see who'd witnessed her exuberant display between the parked vehicles.

She spun around. Logan, the one who'd brought her to this point, stood a car length away. Unable to contain her excitement any longer, she launched herself at him, banded her arms around him and hugged him.

"Thank you! Thank you! Thank you!" She bounced up and down. His hands grasped her waist. The heat of his palms then his rigidity penetrated her enthusiasm, rocking her euphoric cloud.

She sank from her toes to her heels and looked up into his intense blue eyes. He stared back with dilated pupils, flared nostrils and a clenched jaw. The hard length of his body pressed hers from thigh to breast, abrading tender places beneath her clothing and making them spring to life. Another form of excitement showered over her, and her breath caught. Hugging Logan was a no-no. Her face flamed. She staggered back a step.

"I'm sorry. I didn't mean—my family—we're huggers. I didn't think. I just—" Her tongue tied.

"Whoa. Slow down. What happened?"

Forcing air into and then out of her lungs, she endeavored to form coherent sentences in her head before blurting out more nonsense. "The print shop owners love my work. They said I should run LEs—limited edition, signed and numbered prints of everything I've brought them. They want to see my whole collection, and they invited me to display and sell my work in their gallery. *Me*," she squealed, then slapped a hand over her mouth and struggled to rein in her excitement. "Me, in a gallery! I can't wait to tell M—" She couldn't tell her mom. Excitement leaked out like a slowly deflating balloon. "Miri," she amended. "I can't wait to tell Miri."

His slow, slightly lopsided grin was contagious. And sexy. No. Definitely *not* sexy. "I told you your work was good. Why are you surprised?"

She shook her head. "You don't understand. I've been told my whole life that I couldn't support myself as an artist. But the shop owners are professionals and they believe otherwise. They suggested I set up a webpage and an online store. They talked about licensing and copyrights and...so much stuff my head is spinning. And the prices they suggested I ask for each piece are impressive."

His eyebrows flatlined. "Who told you that you couldn't be an artist?"

Reality crashed over her. The lies between them meant filtering the truth. "A job with benefits and a retirement plan is a wiser choice."

"And that's what you have?"

That's what she'd *had*. "That's the choice I made."

"The person who misdirected you is a fool."

His declaration hit her like a head charge to the belly. Her defensive hackles rose. "No. He isn't. He just wanted the best for me. And rejections and poverty weren't it."

"Has he seen your work?"

How long had it been since she'd shown her family any of her creations? "Not recently."

"Then show him. It'll shut him up. I'll talk to the idiot with you, if you want backup."

Logan meeting her father? She fought a recoil. That would take some explaining and reveal the tangled web of lies she'd woven.

"Thanks. But I can handle it." She had to change the subject. "I have something for you."

She ducked into the car, retrieved the other USB drive from the passenger seat and offered it to him. A breeze teased his hair and carried the scent of his cologne. She endeavored to ignore both. "If you could download the photographs I took with your camera onto this, I'd appreciate it."

"Are you a professional photographer?"

"No. Oh, no. But I've taken several photography classes at the community college. It's kind of a hobby."

"Like painting and drawing."

His dark tone made her toes curl with trepidation. "Yes."

"And yet you don't have a camera or a computer."

She should have known he wouldn't give up. "They were stolen, and I haven't had a chance to replace them."

Skepticism clouded his eyes. "From the beach house?"

Her brain sifted for safe-to-share information. "No. Before I came here. Anyway, what brings you to Shrimp Road? You're not following me, are you?"

She threw out the last as a joke, but he didn't laugh. Instead, he lifted his sunglasses from the V-neck of his T-shirt and dropped them over his eyes.

"I'm headed to the grill in the marina village for lunch. It's an open-air food truck concept with chow almost as good as Miri's. Have you eaten?"

She saw where this was going. "No. I need to head home and get ready for work."

"The Widow doesn't open for hours. Let me buy you a celebratory lunch, then we'll go back to my office and download your pictures."

"You don't need to do that."

"I insist."

Could she refuse and still get her pictures? Not without seeming ungracious. "Okay. Tell me where and I'll meet you."

"It's not far. We'll walk."

He waited for her to lock her car, then gestured to the sidewalk. She fell into step beside him. Their knuckles bumped and she felt the jolt deep inside. Unfortunately expanding the gap between them was impossible due to the narrowness of the concrete strip and oncoming pedestrians. She folded her arms. Their upper arms brushed. Again her pulse skipped. Not good.

When they reached the grill's parking lot,

she heard a familiar sound and searched for the source. "Do they have guinea hens?"

He stopped, his attention beamed on her. "Yes. They nest on the property and provide insect control. How do you know about guinea hens?"

She had to be more careful, and she definitely couldn't tell him that they'd had them in the orchard—until the coyotes got them. "Like peacocks, theirs is a sound you don't forget."

"Where have you seen peacocks?"

They'd had those, too. "Too many places to count. They're the watchdogs of the South. What an incredible view of the harbor!" She bolted ahead, leaving him and his questions behind.

He caught up with her and, with a hand on her waist, steered her toward the line at the food truck. She quickened her pace to escape the electric charge. She had to get over this craziness around him.

"A burger?" he asked after they placed their orders.

She nodded toward the flat grill outside the food truck and shrugged. "The one he's cooking smells delicious, and I haven't had a burger in months. It was either that or a good pizza."

"I can tell you where to get that, too."

She took in her surroundings as she followed him to a picnic table. White paper lanterns shaped like jellyfish hung beneath the tiki hut shelter housing an outdoor bar, billiard tables and swinging hammock chairs. In the open area facing the water, she spotted cornhole boards and rectangular pits that could be used for horseshoes. Another thatched roof covered a stage with a brick dance floor out front.

"I've never been anywhere like this."

"Traditional old Key West outdoor dining. Wait until you taste the food. Sure you don't want a margarita? Theirs are top-notch."

She couldn't afford to loosen her tongue. "Too early for me, and I don't think your aunt would appreciate me coming to work under the influence."

"You wouldn't be the first." He paused as they both sat down. "Are you using the chef that's available with your rental house?"

"No. But sometimes it's more trouble than it's worth to cook for one. So I keep it simple."

"We'll come back after we go lobster diving. They'll grill our catch for us."

That sounded fun and almost like a date, which of course it would not—*could* not—be. Regardless, she'd have to pass. Even if she located replacement contacts and they passed the test of diving with a mask in the pool, the entire excursion would be too risky. She made a mental note to duck into the library before work tomorrow and use their computer to locate stores selling colored contacts. "I'll keep that in mind."

"Bands play on weekends. Do you and your boyfriend like to dance?"

"He doesn't." She was so caught up in watching the loose dogs cavorting in the grass that she'd answered before realizing he'd tripped her up. But the answer wasn't anything he could use to connect her to her past. "Didn't," she corrected. "He— We aren't together anymore. Isn't there a leash law here?"

"No. But the dogs won't bother you. How long ago did you split?"

So much for redirecting him. Again she weighed her response and saw no harm. "A couple of months ago."

"Fairly recent. Nasty break?"

Was he prying or just making conversation? It was hard to read him when he wore his sunglasses. "Breakups are never easy—even if they are for the best."

"But you claim he's not the reason you're hiding in Florida."

"I never said I was hiding. You did. And no, he's not the reason I'm here. I'm on sabbatical. The timing is coincidental."

"But convenient."

"Definitely. It keeps me from having to deal with all my friends' awkward questions. I'm sure you dealt with those when you and your wife separated."

"There were definitely a lot of questions after we split. Did your family like him?"

Despite the unique setting and mouthwatering smells, she was beginning to regret accepting his invitation. "No. Could we talk about something that isn't likely to ruin my appetite?"

"Miri and Jack didn't like my ex, either. Why didn't your family like yours?"

The tidbit piqued her curiosity. She'd have to play this Twenty Questions game if she wanted answers. "They said he didn't have my best interests at heart. Why didn't Miri like yours?"

The corners of his mouth turned down. "She claims Elizabeth turned me into someone she didn't recognize."

"How so?"

He hesitated, his gaze focused on a yacht cruising into the harbor. "You'll have to ask her. Food's here."

Good timing for Logan, but bad for her. She said her blessing and when she lifted her head caught him watching her. He lifted his beer. *"Santé."*

The French toast surprised her. "Have you been to France?"

"Yes." He picked up his hogfish sandwich and took a big bite.

Jessie had a thousand questions about where he'd been, but she stifled her curiosity. "I've always wanted to see the museums of Europe."

And then it hit her. Once this initial lottery fall-out was straightened out, she could afford to go anywhere she wanted—even Paris. The realization both excited and terrified her. But who would go with her? Her mother refused to fly. And her friends… Who were the real ones? She didn't know anymore. That meant traveling alone. BF—Before Florida—she never would have considered a solo trip. But now she might not have a choice.

"You'd better have deep pockets—or tap into some—if you plan on going."

His harsh tone popped the bubble of joy she'd been floating in. For a few moments she'd forgotten Logan was not her friend. He was her adversary.

LOGAN WATCHED THE light leave Jessie's eyes and her wistful smile vanish. She ducked her head and picked at her homemade chips.

He wanted his comment back. He'd been making progress and easing information out of her, but he'd blown it, and he had no one but himself to blame. He didn't like opening old wounds, but if he wanted to regain ground, he'd have to give her something that would undo the damage.

"I'm sorry, Jessie. That was a knee-jerk reaction to some bad memories. My ex-wife loved Europe so much that she begged for an extra week at the end of our last vacation there together. I had to return for a VIP client meeting, and when I voiced my concerns about her staying alone, my best friend offered to stay and keep an eye on her. I had no idea when I left them that it would be the last time I saw either of them."

Her eyes widened. "What happened?"

He hadn't even had time to recover from jet lag before investigators had appeared on his doorstep with crazy tales of missing money. His life had become one hellish interrogation after another until the case had been dismissed weeks prior to Jack's death.

"We found signs that they'd been having an affair and planning their disappearance for a while." Shame drilled a familiar spot in his gut. He didn't talk about his humiliation to anyone.

"They never came back?"

"No."

"I'm sorry. How did you divorce her if she's missing?"

"I filed for divorce with abandonment for cause."

He hadn't expected compassion, but her face filled with it. "Do you want her back?"

"As a spouse, no. But I have questions."

Like how long had they been screwing behind his back? Hell, he and Elizabeth had made lov— *had sex* the night before he'd left Paris. Had she gone straight from his bed to Trent's? And did she have any regrets about leaving him to possibly do prison time for their dirty deeds? Had she ever loved him at all, or had he just been a meal ticket?

"Is that why you have the PI looking for her?"

That was only part of the story. He wasn't sharing the rest. "Yes."

"I'm sorry," she repeated. Sympathy softened her voice. She reached across the table and covered his hand. The warmth of her touch hit him square in the solar plexus. He wanted her.

Damn.

He yanked his hand free. "Finish your burger. We need to get those photos copied if you're going to make it to work on time."

She blushed then focused on her meal. Could an innocent woman blush like that? And could someone with so little confidence in her artistic abilities be a con artist when the very nature of flimflamming required a bold assumption of success in such endeavors?

He wanted to say no, but he'd been completely fooled by two people he'd thought he knew better than anyone. He couldn't trust his judgment.

He took a swig of beer, but the now tepid brew didn't wash away the bitter taste in his mouth. "Are you going to scan all of your paintings so that you can release the LEs?"

"Eventually, I think. I hate to spend so much at one time."

"You have the five hundred from the painting sale. That should cover several scans."

"Oh, I won't spend that until I'm sure the buyers don't want it back."

Was she for real? "You think they're going to ask for a refund?"

She squirmed in her chair and lowered her chin. "They might. Until they pick up the Key deer, I still consider that money theirs."

Whoever had discouraged her had done a number on her confidence. If he ever met the culprit, he'd set them straight. Who was he kidding? Jessie's future was no concern of his—as long as it didn't involve harming Miri.

Thirty minutes later she'd followed him to his office and parked beside him. He unlocked the door and led her in. His one-room workspace was a far cry from the fancy digs he and Trent had shared in a historic Charleston building. The furniture was used but in good shape, a big contrast to the pricy antiques Elizabeth had bought to furnish his former workspace. Those, like his house and their expensive cars, had been sold to pay the debts his exes had dumped on him. He supposed he'd been fortunate Elizabeth had left him so many valuable assets to pawn.

Jessie perched on the edge of a visitor chair. Her opinion of his space didn't show on her face. Then he kicked himself for even checking for a response. He didn't need her approval. This place was temporary. He'd get back to nicer digs once Elizabeth was found and his reputation restored.

"Are you going to do anything with the photographs?" he asked Jessie.

"I...um...don't know. Like what?"

"Submit them to magazines? Sell them? Run some of your LEs?"

"I hadn't thought about that. If they're any good, I guess I can ask at the gallery if there's a market for them."

Her uncertainty twisted something inside him. She nibbled her bottom lip. It was a...distracting habit.

"You should. They're excellent." He opened the file and rose, then motioned her to come behind his desk. "Sit here."

She took his chair. He leaned over her to use the mouse and smelled strawberries. It was her shampoo, he realized. He filled his lungs with the scent then cursed his stupidity. She leaned left to give him room and tilted her head to the side, grazing his groin and making him suck in another breath. The contact sent a bolt of electricity through him. She abruptly scooted the chair forward, but it was too late. The damage had been done. Awareness crackled along his nerves. Clamping his teeth together, he looked down at the pulse fluttering beneath the tautly stretched skin of her neck, and the urge to taste her there hit him hard and fast.

Damn. He straightened and backed away from temptation. Long, dark, silky strands clung to his clothes. "You know how to drag and drop the files from this folder to your memory stick, right?"

"Yes." Her voice sounded as unsteady as he felt.

After tossing the stick onto his blotter, he shoved his hands into his pockets to cover his embarrassing reaction and crossed to the windows overlooking the street. He counted cars, red ones then blue ones, four-door, two-door, trying to get himself under control.

He definitely needed to get back in the singles circuit. Not an idea he relished, but like taking a dose of medicine to cure what ailed him, he'd do it.

"Logan?" Jessie touched his arm like a brand then snatched her hand back. She stood beside him—only inches away—with wary gratitude in her eyes, biting that lip. Damn, he wished she'd quit doing that. "You seemed miles away. I— Thanks again, for loaning me your camera and everything. Your...encouragement means a lot."

"No problem." He wasn't doing it for her. All he wanted was answers, and Elizabeth had taught him that everything and everyone had a price and an agenda. All he had to do was find Jessie's. But how was he going to do that when he could no longer afford to be alone with her without risking giving in to the hunger she'd managed to awaken in his dead soul?

THE DELIVERY DOOR blasted open at two thirty Wednesday afternoon. Miri turned to scold her employee. But it wasn't one of her people. Ignatius swaggered into her kitchen as if he had every right to be there.

"She kissed me," he stated, his face moony.

Something twisted inside Miri. Anger, she decided. Why had he returned? "You should have taken her to a hotel room."

His blissful expression turned sour. "My daughter, Miriam Louise. Not some floozy. She kissed my cheek, said she loved the deli and thanked me for taking her there. Says I'm two for two on winning restaurant choices, and she can't wait to see what I come up with next time."

She shouldn't gloat, but being right with this know-it-all felt very good. "What did I tell you? Now go away."

"Can't leave without delivering a message. The owner, Nell, asked how I heard about the place. When I told her, she said to tell you she has a new recipe for you to try. I promised I'd bring you for lunch tomorrow."

She backed away from the big goon so quickly she nearly fell out of her new work clogs. "You'll do no such thing."

"You're not open for lunch on Thursdays. You have no excuse."

"I'm fifty-seven years old. If I don't want to go, I don't have to. You can't make me." She heard snickers from her prep staff and her cheeks burned. She evil-eyed the culprits into silence. Good grief. Ignatius brought out the worst in her.

"Get out of my kitchen. I've warned you about coming into my work space. I can't have you getting me in trouble with the health inspector. And don't *ever* use that door when we're cooking."

"I made Nell promise not to give you the recipe until I brought you in." His smug tone raised her hackles.

"The devil you did."

He hit her with a beatific smile. "I'm a man of my word."

"I am not going to lunch with you."

Those broad shoulders lifted. "Your loss. She said she'd figured out the bakery's lemon custard thing. But if you don't want to know…"

No one but Nell knew how hard Miri had been working on recreating that recipe. "She did not."

"Tasted like it to me." He brought a small take-out box from behind his back. "Nell sent some for you, but since you're not interested, maybe I should eat 'em myself."

The scalawag! She ripped off her plastic gloves, hurled them in the trash and lunged for the box. He held it out of reach. "You dirty, stinking, Dumpster-diving dog! Give that to me."

He laughed, a low, rumbling sound that shook her like a long line of Harleys cruising past.

"You do have a way with words. Say please, Miriam Louise."

Gritting her teeth, she fought the urge to kick him in the shins. "*Please* give me the box, Ignatius."

With his face the picture of innocence—except for that roguish glint in his eyes—he placed the carton in her hands. She snatched it and opened it. But there was no doughnut. "It's tartlets."

"With lemon custard filling, which was quite delicious. I'll eat 'em if you don't want 'em."

"I want them." Lifting a quarter-size pastry, she sniffed it and then swirled her tongue in the filling. She rolled the creamy substance around in her mouth, letting it hit all of her taste buds.

"For Pete's sake, woman. Just eat it." Ignatius's growled order disrupted her contemplation of the flavor combinations. His pained grimace only made her slow the process even more.

"Don't rush me." She nibbled a tiny bit of crust with the next bite. The filling was as good as the bakery's—possibly even better, richer. Nell had discovered the secret ingredient! And the buttery tartlet shell was an ingenious touch.

The obnoxious PI made a choked sound. "Holy mother of marinara. Do you always have foreplay with your food?"

Shocked by his frank speech, she glared at him. "I'm trying to detect the ingredients—something you probably never do when you scarf down your meals whole. You're undoubtedly just as fast with your women."

She wanted to slap her hand over her mouth, but brazened through her embarrassment by concentrating on the morsel.

"Like the people who keep you in business, I enjoy my food. But when it's important, I know how to take my time." His supremely confident toothy mug made her skin steam.

Fighting an urge to fan herself and unwilling to be drawn any deeper into this ridiculous topic, she finished the tartlet in silent appreciation. She had to have the recipe, and contrary to what the big ego in front of her said, Nell would give it to her. They'd been friends ever since Miri had taught the woman the basics of operating a restaurant kitchen twenty years ago.

She dug her phone out of her back pocket and hit the contact button. Her friend and former protégée answered immediately. "Nell, you've nailed the custard. Please share the recipe."

"Gladly, Miri. You've shared enough of yours with me. But I promised your handsome fella that I'd only give it to you in person when he brought you to lunch tomorrow. I'm cooking up a few other new items I'd like your opinion on, too."

Miri kept her phone's volume loud enough to hear over the kitchen noise. She regretted that now. She could tell from Ignatius's shit-eating grin that he'd overheard. "He is not my fella. He works for Logan."

"Wonderful. I'm glad Logan has already screened him. Saves me some work. Oops. Soufflé timer is ringing. Must go. See you tomorrow, love." Then the line went dead.

A waterspout of fury and irritation churned inside Miri. She opened her mouth to tell the man to go to hell then noticed her entire staff had stopped working to watch the show. Reining in her wrath took colossal effort. Lord help her, she wanted to throw her knife at the man. But that would be the ruin of a three-hundred-dollar tool.

"I will go to lunch with you. But it is *not* a date. Do you hear me, Ignatius?"

He winked. Only then did she realize she'd forgotten to eat today. She felt quite light-headed.

"I think everybody in the kitchen and maybe even the alley heard you, Miriam Louise. See you tomorrow. Eleven thirty. That gives you plenty of time to enjoy our meal before you're needed here. Bye, yous guys."

With a cocky wave, the bastard left her to face her very amused staff. "Wipe those smirks off your faces and quit loafing. We have food to prepare."

That man was a hemorrhoid. She had to get Logan to get rid of him. In the meantime, she'd think of a way to make darn sure he regretted forcing her to dine with him.

CHAPTER TEN

JESSIE WAS DRAGGING when she crossed to the far corner of the parking lot Wednesday night—so much so that she didn't even jog to avoid the rain dampening her hair and clothing. It had been a crazy, tense shift.

Miri had been in a cranky mood. Nothing had pleased her, and the usual snafus of food service had irritated her more than was warranted. Which was so unlike the upbeat woman Jessie had come to know that she wanted to ask what was wrong, but she hadn't dared for fear of getting her head bitten off. It had been that bad. Even Sue, who was usually as blunt and bold as anyone Jessie had ever met, had kept her head down and avoided crossing Miri's path.

Had Logan and Miri had an argument? He hadn't come in tonight. Jessie knew because she'd checked. Often. Too often. The back of her head tingled anew when she recalled bumping into something this afternoon at his office—something she hoped wasn't what she thought it was. He didn't trust her. So he couldn't have had an erection when he was standing behind her. Could he?

Digging her keys out of her pocket with one hand, she waved goodbye as Miri and Sue pulled out of the lot. Then she pushed the button to unlock the door. It didn't open. The interior light didn't come on. She must have hit the wrong button. Checking the fob in the streetlight, she tried again. Nothing. No click. No light. Strange.

Rain dripped down her forehead as she shoved the key into the lock and mechanically opened the door. She slid inside, put the key into the ignition and turned it. *Click.* Turning it off, she tried again. *Click.* She'd grown up in an orchard with machinery. She knew the basics. Rain trickled down the windshield as she ran through the list of possible causes. It had started right before she left for work and… She checked the on/off switch for her headlights. She'd left them on. Dead battery. How had she missed the alert chime before getting out of the car?

Because she'd been thinking about bumping into Logan's—

She severed the thought, but she couldn't stem the flicker of heat in her belly.

Groaning, she slouched against the headrest. At home she would have called her father or brother for help. But who could she call here? She didn't have a credit card, and thanks to the rain, it had been a slow night. Did she have enough cash in her pocket to call a tow truck for a jump start? How much did that cost, anyway? She dug out her tips and counted fifty-two bucks. Doubtful that would cover it.

Miri's taillights had long since disappeared. Jessie hated to call her back, but it was the best option. She dug her phone out of her back pocket and dialed. It rang and rang then went to voice mail. No help there. She left a message.

That left flagging down a stranger as her only option. Risky. But what choice did she have? Could she find someone with jumper cables or one of those jump-start boxes?

She scanned the area. The rain had kept most people off the sidewalks, and she hadn't yet picked up the local's ability to distinguish tourists from residents. A tourist wouldn't be likely to have cables. Someone wearing a yellow rain slicker stood beneath the awning across the street. He lifted his head, blew out a plume of smoke, and the light hit his face. *The stranger.*

Ice sluiced through her veins. Fear knotted in her throat. She hadn't seen him in the restaurant tonight. But she'd missed him all those other times, too. Had he remembered where he'd seen her? Was he going to blow her cover? Was he stalking her? Or was his appearance just an eerie coincidence? She wanted to believe the latter. But she couldn't be sure. Brandon's crazy horror stories flooded her brain.

The urge to run hit hard, but she'd be safer in her car, wouldn't she? With a shaking hand, she manually locked her door. Where was her pepper spray? She fumbled for it, closing her fingers around the small canister.

She couldn't call the police. Fortunately he hadn't made a threatening move. But if he did, she'd have no choice. She could hear her brother's "I told you so." She'd get a rant rather than sympathy from him. She was where she shouldn't be, doing something she shouldn't be doing. Police reports were public record. They'd reveal her location and identity.

What should she do?

Heart pounding like a frightened rabbit's, she clutched her phone and debated trying Miri again. But no, that would put the older woman at risk for harm, too.

Logan. She could call Logan. Miri had insisted Jessie put his number in her phone for emergencies. But Jessie didn't want to risk being alone with him—especially after this afternoon.

Looking in her direction, the stranger pushed off the wall. Her stomach plunged. He paused for traffic before stepping into the road. Maybe he just wanted to talk. Maybe he wanted *her*. Fear dried her mouth.

She'd have to call Logan. Her hands trembled so badly, scrolling down her contacts was difficult. She found his name and tapped it. The phone rang. Once. Twice. "Please, please, please pick u—"

"Logan Nash."

She heard music and voices in the background. "It's Jessie. I'm in the Widow's parking lot. My battery's dead. Miri's gone. That guy—the stranger from last week—is here."

"Call the cops."

Jessie gulped and watched the man cross the center line. Was she being stupid? "I—I don't want to do that."

A pause, then, "Lock your doors. Don't open them. I'm on my way."

"Okay." She hoped he hurried.

The man reached the sidewalk on her side of the street. She tried blowing her horn to draw attention from the few other pedestrians, but it was dead, too. He knocked on the window. She jumped and grabbed her spray.

"Need help?"

She shook her head. "No. My…friend is on his way," she shouted.

"I can jump you."

He meant the car. Didn't he? "Got it covered."

"You sure? I have cables in my truck." He didn't seem threatening. But she couldn't take the chance. *All serial killers are charming*, Brandon had said in one of his lectures.

"I'm good. But thanks." She forced the last out with a smile that quivered.

"I'll wait until your friend gets here."

She had to get rid of him. "That's not necessary. But thank you."

He didn't leave. Moments that felt like eons later, twin headlight beams swung across them. Logan's car jolted to a stop perpendicular to her front bumper. He jumped out and approached the guy. A mixture of relief and fear rolled through her. She didn't want Logan to get hurt. The men exchanged words, then the guy walked away. Logan watched him until he'd entered the building across the street.

Jessie threw open her door and launched herself at Logan, hitting his chest hard enough to make him stagger. His arms banded around her, steadying them. "Thank you! I didn't know who else to call."

Then the heat of his body seeped through her damp clothing and every cell in her body snapped to attention.

"Jessie." His voice was more warning growl than spoken word. The hairs on her nape rose. She tilted her head back. A muscle in his jaw pulsed. Their gazes met, and the hunger she saw reflected in his eyes took her breath. Desire curled in her belly. Then he lowered his head.

His warm mouth feathered across hers, lifted then descended again, harder, hotter. The stroke of his tongue seared her lower lip, making her gasp. He deepened the kiss, pressing her mouth open for the slick caress of his tongue. Dizziness swamped her. She dug her fingers into his back, held on and kissed him back.

His hands raked parallel trails of embers down her spine then he cupped her hips, pulling her closer to the thickening ridge behind his zipper. Need ignited like a brush fire inside her, sending sparks flying to every corner of her being. Then his palms skimmed upward, his thumbs coming to rest beneath her breasts. She stilled and held her breath, wanting him to brush her nipples. When he didn't she arched her back, giving him room and silent permission to do so.

Logan swung her around, propped her against his car and leaned into her. Lean, taut thigh muscles burned against hers, and his arms tightened, binding her so close to his torso that the moisture in their clothing acted like soldering flux.

A whistle followed by a shouted, "Get a room!" shocked her into stiffening.

Logan lowered his arms and moved back a step. Mouth clamped tight, his nostrils flared with each inhalation. Jessie covered her tender lips with her hand and hugged her suddenly chilled middle with her other arm. Hunger gnawed at her, and she realized she'd never wanted Aaron as badly as she did Logan in that moment—so much so that she'd been unaware of where they were and uncaring who might see her shameful behavior.

Shakily, she pushed off his car then side-stepped until she'd put two yards between them. "I-I'm sorry. That shouldn't have happened. My family...we're huggers. I didn't think—I didn't mean..."

Eyes still blazing, Logan fisted and released his hands by his sides. Then he yanked open his passenger door. "Get in. I don't have jumper cables. I'll bring some tomorrow. I'm taking you home."

He issued the statements like rapid bursts of gunfire. She bit her lip and tasted him. Her pulse thudded harder—especially down there—reminding her she and Aaron hadn't been intimate since the lottery win, when the battles over how the money was to be spent or invested had begun. Even before that their relationship had never been what her girlfriends had called passionate. It had been...comfortable, like changing into sweats on a Sunday afternoon after church.

The gentle rain dampened her arousal and sobered her. Being alone with Logan after that conflagration not a good idea. Meaningless affairs had never been her style. And she couldn't have a relationship in Florida. Not one based on lies and half truths. "I...um...could call a taxi."

Did she have enough cash?

"No arguments, Jessie. This is the way it's going to be."

She grabbed her gear and did as he ordered. She hoped she didn't regret it.

LOGAN CURSED HIS mental meltdown. When Jessie had thrown herself at him, and he'd felt her cool wet curves turning to steam against his skin, he'd lost control. The kiss had blinded him to his location and even the rain falling on them. It was like nothing he'd ever experienced. If not for the smart aleck's call, he'd have had her in the back of his car and been deep inside her like a damned high school kid on prom night.

The pressure behind his fly increased. He bit back a curse. Getting her home safely and on the opposite side of a locked door was imperative. He eased into the driver's seat. His jeans were almost tight enough in a critical area to castrate him. He shifted, found no relief and cranked up the air-conditioning, hoping the cold blast would deflate the problem and ease his discomfort.

His evening had been a bust. He'd spent four hours cruising local oyster bars' happy hours and chatting up blondes and redheads in an attempt to get one brunette out of his mind. He'd had plenty of offers, but he was honest enough to admit it was probably because he was fresh meat on the market and not because he was a hot property.

Jessie's call had yanked him from that fruitless endeavor. Afraid he wouldn't get to her before she was harmed, he'd broken every speed limit on his short drive to the Widow. Why was he so concerned about her—he didn't even know if he trusted her.

Because the more time he spent with her, the more he wanted to believe she was the real deal. But what was she hiding? Was it only a bad breakup as I had suggested? If so, why was she afraid to call the cops? There were too many unanswered questions surrounding her. But that didn't stop him from wanting her.

He glanced sideways, then wished he hadn't. The streetlights revealed her bare arms were covered in goose bumps, but it was her nipples, as hard as pencil erasers beneath the wet tank top, that shot his blood pressure into the stratosphere. He was freezing her, but she wasn't complaining. Elizabeth had complained about everything.

Clamping his molars, he flipped off the air and reached into the backseat to retrieve his jacket. He tossed it into her lap. She put it on without protest, and he said a silent thank-you. Even if he could forget all the mystery surrounding her, she was Miri's employee and, therefore, taboo. End of story.

"Are you okay?" he asked after she was safely covered.

"F-fine. He just…scared me, I guess. Since he's been hanging around."

"He's a trucker. Travels from here to Maine and back. He stays in the hotel across the street every time he hits Key West and eats at the Widow at least once every trip. He was outside taking a smoke break tonight when he saw you."

She looked more tense than reassured. Her hand trembled as she tucked a damp lock behind her ear.

"Are you sure you've never met him?"

"I'm positive." She sounded sincere. Either she was an exceptional liar or she truly didn't know the guy.

They passed a couple of mile markers in silence. "Logan, I know it's none of my business, but…did you and Miri have a fight?"

"No. Why?" He glanced at her and caught her biting her bottom lip—something he'd very much like to do. His little head bobbed south of the border, forcing him to admit the reason he'd left the bars tonight without company or even phone numbers was because he hadn't found anyone who interested him half as much as she did. Not liking that idea, he focused on the road.

"She was…not herself tonight. I've never seen her so grumpy."

"Did someone not show up for work?"

"No. We had everyone we needed. Business was slow with the rain."

Miri should be his primary concern. Not the woman beside him. "I'll call her."

"Thanks. I'm…worried." Again, her concern sounded genuine.

"When did you say you were leaving Florida?"

She averted her face to look out the window.

"I didn't. But my lease expires January twenty-second. I'm not renewing it."

She was telling the truth—or at least part of it. He'd asked the agent when the house would be available and had been told the twenty-third.

"Does Miri know you're leaving?"

"Our agreement was for me to work two weeks. That ends Monday."

Tuesday she wouldn't be an employee…and soon she'd be leaving the state. That meant anything physical between them would be temporary. Exactly what he needed—a quick fix. Until he had his life straightened out, he had nothing to offer a woman. And given the way she'd returned his kiss, Jessie might be receptive to something fast, intense and temporary. His pulse kicked up a notch as he headed down her street. All he had to do was wait a few days, then he'd ask her out and pick up where they left off in the parking lot.

He'd get over his fascination with Jessie, date another woman or two and finally get Miri to start taking days off. Mission accomplished.

He barely heard the crunch of the crushed shells in her driveway over the anticipation drumming in his ears. He stopped by the keypad and put down his window then looked at her. "Code?"

Her lips parted as if to tell him, then she shook her head, shrugged out of his jacket and thrust open her door. Her nipples weren't hard anymore.

He caught himself checking and jerked his gaze back to hers.

"I'll get out here. Thanks for coming tonight and for the ride. I appreciate it."

He recalled the kiss and couldn't stop the grin tweaking his lips. "I could tell."

She inhaled sharply and ducked her head. Her cheeks pinked in the dome light. "Sorry about that."

"Don't be. I'm attracted to you, Jessie. I won't deny that. Want me to come in and check things out?"

She shot a quick glance toward the house. "No. Thanks. I've got it from here."

"I'll pick you up at two tomorrow and we'll jump-start your car before your shift."

"Are you sure you don't want me to take a cab and meet you there?"

"No. Be ready."

"Thank you." She exited the car, shut the door and rounded the hood, slipping between him and the keypad. Her hips blocked his view of the digits. With her curves only inches away, he had to fight the urge to trace his palms over them. He tightened his grip on the steering wheel and resisted temptation. Then the strawberry scent drifted through his open window. His knuckles turned white. The gate opened.

She hurried through, waved once more, flashed a nervous smile, then walked up the driveway. Each hip-swinging step made him ache to follow her and pick up where they'd left off. Then she pushed a button under the house, and the gate blocked his path.

He tried to tell himself that he wasn't disappointed she hadn't invited him in. But who was he kidding? He was disappointed as hell. And if he'd stayed, he wouldn't have been a Boy Scout— employee or not.

MIRI GREETED IGNATIUS with the same enthusiasm as she would a colonoscopy. "You're early."

Despite her sour welcome, he smiled. "Bad habit."

"The sooner we get started, the sooner you can get me to work. Do not make me late."

"I'll do my best."

She noted that the goon had actually cleaned up. His mug was freshly shaven and even his thick hair had been trimmed and tamed. He wore all black: jean jacket, pressed jeans and a designerish V-neck T-shirt that revealed a tuft of salt-and-pepper hair above a broad chest and flat belly. He'd even polished his boots.

Her stomach fluttered. Hunger. She'd forgotten breakfast again. Her reaction had nothing to do with him. "Are you channeling Johnny Cash today?"

"Why? Want me to sing to you? 'Ring of Fire,' perhaps?"

A song about desire. "No. This isn't a date."

"Course not. You don't date." Green eyes roved her from head to toe, making her a little self-conscious that she'd made no effort at all to impress him. She hadn't even bothered with makeup. His grin widened into the smug variety. "I knew you wouldn't let me down."

"Because I didn't leave town to avoid you?"

His low chuckle surprised her—mainly because it rumbled along her nerves in an unsettling way. "Because you didn't dress up. Grab your sunglasses and a jacket."

"It's seventy-six degrees. I don't need a jacket."

"If you don't bring one of yours, you'll have to wear mine." He started to shrug out of the denim.

"I'm not wearing your jacket. It would swallow me. I'll get mine, but I'm telling you, it's unnecessary."

"If you still feel that way after lunch, you can tuck it in my bag."

His what? She didn't care enough to ask. She wanted Nell's recipe, and if suffering an hour of his company was the only way to get it, then so be it. It wouldn't kill her. With a lack of grace that would have earned her a paddling from her mama, she retrieved a windbreaker and joined him on the porch.

He took it from her and held it for her to put her arms in. Bonus points. The man was a gentleman. Not that she was taking notes. If he was trying to impress her, he was wasting his time.

He gestured for her to precede him down the stairs and sidewalk and around the garage to the driveway. A big, shiny motorcycle was parked where his car should be. She stopped in her tracks. He bumped into her, then grabbed her waist to keep from knocking her over. She registered the heat and strength of his big hands, but the black and red Harley held her attention. The bags he mentioned were black leather saddlebags with silver studs.

"You aren't scared of a bike, are you?"

She'd die before admitting she'd never ridden one. But she'd been on every kind of watercraft imaginable. How different could straddling this thing be from riding a Jet Ski? She and Jack had done that a bunch of times. "No."

"Good." He offered her a helmet—one of those beanie kinds that sat on top of your head and didn't cover your ears. "Isn't that called a brain bucket?"

"It's DOT certified. I wouldn't put you in anything less."

When she hesitated, he settled it on her. The scrape of his callused fingers along her jawbones made her shiver. She gritted her teeth and pretended it hadn't happened. And she definitely didn't look at him to see if he'd noticed.

"Chin up. I don't want to pinch your tender skin." After she complied, he snapped the buckle. His knuckle dragged downward with irritating slowness, stopping just above her collar. Her nipples tightened.

"Pinches in this skin hurt like a mother."

She jumped back. What was wrong with her? Thank heaven the jacket hid her body's betrayal.

"I'll get on first. You climb on behind me." He donned a matching helmet, swung his leg over the bike, grabbed both handlebars then looked at her.

He looked hot. The thought shot through her head like a meteor, so quick and unexpected it momentarily paralyzed her. She'd never looked twice at any of the bikers who flocked to Key West. Why him? Why now? Surely at fifty-seven she was too old for a midlife crisis.

"C'mon, Miri. Throw a leg over. Put your feet on the floorboards and wrap your arms around me."

She snorted. "You wish."

She didn't want to hold him. But falling off held even less appeal. Short of refusing and making him think she was a coward, she couldn't see any way to avoid it.

Think of the recipe.

Gingerly, she did as instructed, settling behind him with her knees bracketing his hips. She kept as much distance between them as the backrest allowed. But still, she was surprised to find herself shaking.

Fear of the unknown. That's all it was.

A big paw covered her knee and squeezed. She

felt the heat of his grip a good ten inches north of the point of contact. He turned to speak over his shoulder. "Relax, Miri. I wouldn't hurt you for nothing."

Her breath shuddered in then out again. The tingle working through her forced her to admit she wasn't scared. She was…excited. Dear Lord. She must be losing her mind. "How long have you been riding this thing?"

"Long enough, and I've taken every safety course the dealership offers."

He shifted and pushed a button. The engine growled to life. The bike vibrated beneath her. She felt it in places that had been happily dormant for years. The stimulation reminded her of the sex toy Jack had brought home for their tenth anniversary. "In case you miss me while I'm away," he'd said. She'd only used it once to see how it worked. Afterward, she'd stuffed it in a drawer, preferring a relationship with a man to one with a machine.

The bike rolled forward. Startled, she grabbed Ignatius's waist and held on for dear life as he coasted down her driveway. The leaning turn onto the street made her squeal.

She smelled lime and fresh linens and searched for the source, then she realized it was him—his aftershave. He accelerated. Wind whistled in her ears and stirred the hair of her nape. The road and houses raced past. He eased into traffic, but he was going the wrong way.

"This isn't the way to Nell's." She leaned forward to shout into his ear. The action flattened her breasts against his back. She instantly regretted the move and quickly restored the gap. But it was too late. Her breasts seemed magnetized by the contact. Hormonal. Definitely hormonal.

He turned his head. His helmet straps accentuated the strong line of his jaw. "Taking the scenic route. Relax. Enjoy."

He held her captive on the moving bike. She fumed and debated giving him an earful. But that would mean more front-to-back contact, and her traitorous body hadn't yet decided to behave.

He headed north and soon approached Seven-Mile Bridge. She gulped. The idea of riding a motorcycle over the often windy bridge made her heart race. Traffic was light. The weather was perfect. Every biker they passed, and even their passengers when they had them, stuck a hand out, an action Ignatius mirrored. The biker wave. She'd seen the gesture too many times to count. But she'd never been on the receiving end of it.

Ignatius, though irritating in the extreme, didn't weave in and out of traffic, and he didn't speed. Slowly, tension eased from her muscles. She relaxed against the backrest with her hands lightly anchored on his waist. She took in the boats and birds and caught herself smiling. Rid-

ing a Harley wasn't the same as riding in a boat—
it was smoother and dryer—but it was similar in
many ways.

When he reached Marathon, slowed and made
a wide U-turn, she was almost disappointed. No.
She couldn't be. Her only purpose today was to
get that recipe. He was a necessary evil.

They met another bike, this one with a shaggy,
goggle-wearing and obviously happy dog in the
sidecar. She laughed and waved. As much as she
hated to admit it, she was enjoying the outing.
Then she looked up and caught Ignatius watching
her in the side mirror. His wraparound sunglasses
shielded his eyes, but his approving smile and nod
were impossible to miss. Her cheeks warmed—
from the sun, not because she was embarrassed
by her earlier ungracious behavior.

They arrived at their destination too quickly.
He pulled into a parking spot by the deli and put
his big, booted feet on the ground. "Jump off,
babe."

"Babe? Don't you 'babe' me."

He shrugged. "Hard not to when you sit back
there looking adorable with that big grin on your
face. You have a beautiful smile, Miri. Wish I
saw it more often."

The compliment hit her with a jolt of pleasure—
and she experienced an immediate sense of disloyalty to Jack. Holding on to Ignatius's shoulders for

balance, she hustled to get her feet on the ground and distance between them. Terra firma felt...odd. "If you weren't such an interfering pain in the butt, you might see it more often."

He laughed and stood beside her. "Give yourself a second to find your land legs. You okay?"

"Of course."

He winked. "Knew you'd say that."

Before she could digest her stomach's swooping reaction to that wink, his fingers were beneath her chin, working the buckle. Each rasp tickled something low in her abdomen. Then he was done and not one squawk of protest had passed her lips. He hung both helmets on the handlebars, grasped her elbow and guided her inside.

Nell took one look at his hand on Miri and her eyebrows hit her hairline. She pointed to a table—one with a small bouquet of flowers on it. None of the other tables had flowers. Ignatius steered Miri to it. She sat because she didn't know what else to do—and because her shaky legs still hadn't recovered from the ride.

Nell joined them. Curiosity sparkled in her eyes. "How was the ride?"

Miri glared at Ignatius. "You told her you were bringing me on the bike?"

Nell put a hand on her shoulder. "No, hon, I saw you drive up. So...?"

Everybody in Nell's family rode, and Nell

knew Miri never had. But Miri wouldn't admit she'd enjoyed herself in front of the man who'd forced her into this dat—

"She loved it," the goon answered for her. "She even learned the biker salute."

"Attagirl."

"What's with the flowers?" Miri asked.

Nell's gaze swung to Ignatius. "Ask him."

Miri's chest hurt. She narrowed her eyes on Ignatius. "This isn't a—"

"Date. I know. What're we having, Nell?"

"The menu's a surprise. I'm testing new dishes on you today. And yes, Miri, I'll give you the lemon custard recipe when we're done. If you behave." Her gaze swung to Ignatius. "Think she can?"

"I hope not."

Chuckling, Nell sashayed back to the kitchen, leaving Miri fuming and alone with the man she didn't want to be with—the one wearing what Logan called a shit-eating-grin. These two had been cooking up something—and it wasn't lunch. And she was *not* touched that he'd made an effort. She refused to acknowledge the bouquet.

"Why a motorcycle?"

"My dad had pictures of Brando, McQueen and Eastwood on their bikes hanging in our garage. I grew up looking at them and wishing I could be that cool. But it was too cold in Jersey, and I was too broke to have one."

"Aren't detectives well paid?"

"I sent every dime I could down here to Eileen for Bethany. First thing I bought when I moved here was that baby outside."

So he hadn't been a deadbeat dad. "I'm sure you're more Evel Knievel than Hollywood heart-throb."

"You mean I'm not pretty enough for Hollywood? For the record, I'd rather enforce the rules than break 'em. You did good, Miri, especially for a first-timer."

"Who says it was my first time?"

"You did, with the way your thighs trembled against me."

The comment felt...*intimate* and made her heart turn over like the spinner she kept in her garden. A certain area between her legs tingled. She glanced around to make sure no one had overheard his comment.

He reached across the table and patted her hand. "We'll make a rider of you. Never know. You might end up wanting your own bike."

She snorted and snatched her hand away. "Hardly."

Then she looked up and caught Nell watching the exchange. But her friend said nothing of it as she slid a margarita glass rimmed in shrimp in front of each of them. "Moscato shrimp with apricot and jalapeño cocktail sauce."

She hustled back behind the counter before Miri could beg her to stay.

"I take it you two like to fool around in the kitchen?"

The twinkle in Ignatius's eyes made the question sound naughty. "Nell and I like to experiment with recipes. It keeps our menus fresh and exciting."

The prudish tone of her voice made her uncomfortable. But she wouldn't defend herself to the PI.

"I'm all for trying something new."

She frowned and searched his face for double entendre, but the man's green eyes looked guileless. Too guileless?

"Do you cook, Ignatius, or do you get most of your meals from bars that serve free hors d'oeuvres?"

Her bitchiness made his eyes glimmer with mischief. "I know my way around the kitchen. I'll prove it whenever you find the nerve to let me."

He was daring her, and she wanted to call his bluff so badly that she shoved a shrimp into her mouth to avoid his trap. It took several seconds for the food to capture her attention.

"Needs a little dill to cut the sweetness," he said and she stopped chewing. Because he was right. "But it's good. I'd eat it again."

Her thoughts exactly. She didn't like agreeing with him. Not even a little. She finished her appetizer, trying to determine the other flavors in the dish, but her focus kept drifting to her da— companion.

Nell appeared with their main course. "Halibut with tomato, orange and tarragon."

She left them again. Like synchronized swimmers, she and Ignatius lifted their forks, flaked off a piece of the fish and tasted. Their eyes met, and she knew what he was going to say before he said it. "Needs dill," they pronounced in unison.

She smiled and then tried to stop herself. She would *not* have fun on this forced outing. "I gather we both like dill."

"You betcha. What else do you like, Miri?"

She blinked. How long had it been since anyone had asked? Jack had known. "What do you mean? To eat?"

"Eat. Read. TV. Movies. Music. What do you do when you're not in the kitchen?"

"I—" She didn't have an answer. She was rarely out of the kitchen these days. When she was at home she either tested new recipes, slept or puttered in her garden. When had she become so boring?

"Didn't realize that was a hard question. What did you like to do before Jack died?"

Hearing her husband's name on Ignatius's lips was...oddly disconcerting and felt disloyal. "Back in the day I was a pretty avid photographer. I used to love kayaking the backwaters or fishing the flats, watching the wildlife."

"But not now?"

"It's not as much fun by yourself." The admission made her squirm in her chair.

"Amen to that. Solo sucks in a lot of ways. Ever white-water rafted?"

"No."

"You'd enjoy the challenge of the river and nature on both banks. If you ever decide to take a day off."

And just like that he made her feel like her life was missing something. But it wasn't. She loved her job. She was a dedicated foodie. That was why the Fisherman's Widow was so successful. "There's nowhere to do that around here."

"A few places, but the closest good ones are in Georgia and the Carolinas. You should consider it for your next vacation."

She hadn't taken a vacation since Jack passed. She hadn't realized how much she missed their excursions. Were Sue and Logan right? Had she fallen into a rut?

"Miri?"

"Jack and I each used to secretly plan one week's vacation and surprise the other during the slow season." She immediately wished she hadn't shared that private information with him.

Green eyes held hers. "He must have been a special guy."

She blinked at the unexpected response. "Did Logan tell you that?"

"No. You did."

"I did no such thing."

"Did I ever tell you I was an exceptional detective?"

"Your humility is impressive." Her sarcasm wasn't subtle.

"I was good because I see what isn't said. Your face, voice and body language told me what I needed to know about your husband. He had to have been pretty special to make you leave Charleston and your family and move here."

Speechless, Miri stared into Ignatius's somber, sincere eyes and realized he wasn't a dumb goon at all.

He leaned across the table, and her heart missed a beat. "And one day, Miri, when you're ready to try again, you might find a guy who'll treat you as well as he did. One who'll help you fill in all the gaps that losing him left in your life. If Jack loved you as much as you did him, he'd want that."

Emotion welled inside her. She was afraid she'd burst into tears. Luckily, Nell broke the moment by bringing out the lemon custard—this time in a meringue cloud. Miri barely tasted it. She'd lost her appetite. And she could only blame the man sitting opposite her.

He was wrong, though. There was nothing lacking from her life. Not one darned thing.

Except sex. The thought broke through her mind like porpoises leaping from the water. She pushed the errant idea back beneath the surface. Jack had been her one and only lover.

And she was okay with that.

She didn't need a man.

Especially not the one across the table.

CHAPTER ELEVEN

THE RETURN RIDE to her house was over all too soon. Miri sprang from the Harley before Ignatius had the kickstand down and quickly removed her own helmet. She didn't want a repeat of whatever it was that had happened when he'd taken it off for her earlier.

Standing awkwardly in her driveway, she admitted that, like it or not, she owed him an apology for her earlier rudeness. "Thank you for this morning. I'm sorry I was not the easiest person to deal with."

It was strangely hard to get the words past the tension banding her throat like a too-tight turtleneck. "I enjoyed the ride. And lunch." Except the part where he'd made her question herself.

"I did, too." He hung both helmets over the handlebars. "I'll walk you to the door."

"You don't need to do that."

"My mama raised me to always see a lady to her door."

"This wasn't a date."

"Doesn't matter."

The constriction around her vocal cords intensified, and she realized she was nervous. Silly, really, for a woman of her age, but there was no other name for the combination of stiffness and shakiness. She pivoted and stalked to her front door with the PI on her tail, then shoved her key into the lock. Facing him again, she parked herself like a barricade on the doormat and shrugged off her jacket, clutching it in folded arms.

She didn't know what she'd expected. But his big grin wasn't it. "Thanks for keeping me company, Miriam Louise. Any time you want a ride, give me a call." He reached out and dragged one callused fingertip along her jawbone. "But, Miri, next time it will be a date."

Then he touched two fingers to his forehead, turned and left. The audacity of the man. Her insides quivered. Her knees wobbled. She tried to scrub away the tingle his touch had left behind. She would not call him and would not go on a date with him. He'd bullied her into one outing. He would not get a second chance.

His engine growled to life then faded into the distance. A strange disquiet settled over her. She mentally kicked herself out of her stupor and entered her house. What had she expected? For the pushy baboon to try to kiss her?

Yes. That's exactly what she'd expected. And she'd been prepared to set him straight because she hadn't wanted him to. So why did she feel so...deflated?

As pushy as he was with everything else, why hadn't he tried?

He claimed he read body language. Well, so did she. It was the best way to know if customers were satisfied with their meals. And every twinkle in those watchful eyes of his had told her he'd enjoyed her company.

So why hadn't he tried to kiss her? The question reverberated in her head and doubts encroached. Wasn't she attractive enough? Admittedly, she hadn't made an effort to impress him. In fact, she'd done the opposite.

She shook her head. She didn't want to be attractive to him. So why was she wasting time dithering instead of getting back to her kitchen where she belonged?

LOGAN CHECKED HIS watch again. Miri was always at the Widow way before two o'clock. He hit Redial on his phone and circled the building to check the patio while Miri's home number rang until the answering machine picked up. Her cell phone did the same. He didn't bother leaving another message on either line.

Where was she and why wasn't she answering?

Her truck wasn't in the lot with Jessie's car. All the Widow's doors were locked. She hadn't answered his knock at home. He'd looked through all the windows and seen no sign of her or anything out of place. But he hadn't been able to see inside her garage. Was she in there? And hurt? Why hadn't he insisted on keys to the Widow and her house?

He tried Sue again, but she wasn't answering, either. Had the women gone somewhere together?

As he headed back to the parking lot he told himself not to panic, but Miri was as close to a parent as he had. His father didn't count. He should have called her last night, but he'd been too rattled by the encounter with Jessie to want to talk to anybody. He'd call 911 and ask an officer to meet him at Miri's house to do a well check.

But just as he headed back to his car, her truck turned in to the parking lot. She climbed from the cab as if nothing was wrong. He surveyed her to make sure she wasn't injured. When he saw nothing amiss, relief rushed over him, quickly followed by anger because she'd scared the hell out of him. "Where have you been?"

She startled at his raised voice then turned, squinty eyed. A frown puckered her brow. "What's it to you?"

Her defensiveness surprised him. "I've been calling all morning. You didn't answer."

"I can't find my cell phone. I think I left it here last night."

"You didn't answer at home, either, or return my messages."

She glanced down the street. "I've been out this morning."

"Are you okay?"

"Why wouldn't I be?"

He couldn't betray Jessie's confidence—not if he was considering breaking his dry spell with her. "I was worried when I couldn't reach you."

"I do have a life, Logan, even if some people don't think I do." There was a sharp edge to her voice. Jessie was right. Miri wasn't acting like Miri.

"All I said was you needed some time off."

"And I took it. Now you're giving me grief."

Right. He was. "I'm sorry."

He followed her inside. She went straight to her office. Her cell phone was on her desk. She clicked through it. "You called seven times?"

"I was worried. You always answer your phone."

Her sour expression softened. "I'm fine. And you're right. I do need to start taking some time off. Beginning next week I'll close on Wednesdays."

The about-face surprised him. "Great."

"Just because I'm giving in first doesn't get you out of your end of the deal. I'm taking time for me. That means you need to start dating."

He grimaced. "I'm working on that."

"Where's Jessie? Her car's outside."

He winced. "I need to pick her up."

She lowered her phone. "Why?"

His ears burned. "She has a dead battery. I gave her a ride home last night and promised I'd pick her up today and jump-start her car. I was so concerned about you I forgot. I'm late."

"Then get going. I need my best waitress to help open."

"She said Monday's her last day."

Miri sighed. "I hate it, but it's true. She only agreed to help me until I could hire new waitresses, but I couldn't find any who met my standards. I had to call an employment agency. The gals who're coming are experienced. They'll shadow with Jessie and Sue Monday to learn our system."

And then Jessie would be fair game. When he didn't move, Miri made a shooing motion. "Go get her."

His pulse picked up speed in anticipation of seeing Jessie again. He turned for the door then paused. "I'm glad you're okay and that you're going to start taking some time for yourself."

"Don't try to butter me up."

He smiled for the first time that day. Miri was back to her old sassy self—if anything had been wrong in the first place.

JESSIE PACED THE end of her driveway Thursday afternoon. Sweat trickled down her spine. If she'd known Logan was going to be late, she would have worn a hat and sunscreen. Yesterday's rain had given way to a cloudless blue sky and there was no shade by the gate. Maybe she should have waited inside, but she was trying to be smart and proactive by avoiding being alone with him in the house.

Where was he? He should have been here thirty minutes ago. Had he talked to Miri? Was she okay? Or was he late because something was wrong? She'd known the woman less than two weeks, but she cared about her.

She reached into her pocket for her phone and bumped the roll of bills. Anxiety returned full force. Would the buyers take the picture or ask for a refund?

She kicked a rock and released a pent-up breath. She'd spent the night tossing and turning—not just because of that kiss. And she'd decided that the world would not end if she lost this sale. If the buyers didn't pick up the painting, she'd mail it to her mother for her birthday gift.

Logan and the gallery owners had said she had talent. Strangers believed in her. It was time she believed in herself—and time to let her family know how important her art was to her. What better way than by sending them what she considered to be her best work yet?

One of her grandmother's favorite sayings had been that if anyone can discourage you from following your dream then your dream wasn't strong enough. Jessie's dream hadn't been strong enough before. Now it was, and because of the lottery win she could afford to pursue it. But she'd keep teaching...just in case.

A car turned down her road before she could dial Logan. She couldn't make out the model. She blinked her gritty eyes, vowing to find new contacts tomorrow. She had in her last pair and they were beginning to irritate her eyes. As the car neared, she recognized Logan's vehicle, and her heart rate accelerated.

Kissing him had been wrong. There would be no more of that.

He pulled to a stop at the end of the driveway. She opened the passenger door and slid in before he could get out. "Did you talk to Miri yet?"

"Not until a few minutes ago." He turned the car around and headed for the highway. "She didn't answer her cell or home phones this morning. I searched everywhere I knew to look for her and couldn't find her until she arrived at the Widow acting like nothing was wrong. That's why I'm late. I'm sorry."

Wow, a man who could apologize. Impressive. Not that she needed anything else to like about him. "I understand. Thanks for the ride. But I won't have time to deal with my car before clocking in."

"Give me the keys. I'll take care of it."

Did she have anything in her car that could reveal her identity? The lease agreement was in her brother's name. But could Logan use that to identify her? Did it really even matter if he did? She didn't think he was a threat. But what if he said something to someone else? Her brother had said this morning that her new security camera had caught someone snooping around her house, which was troubling to say the least. It was best to continue keeping her identity under wraps. She'd have to get the paperwork out before handing over her keys.

"Thanks."

A long line of oncoming traffic held them up at the stop sign. Nervously, she glanced at him and found him looking at her. Heat simmered in his eyes. Her breath caught and her mouth dried. The memory of the kiss sat between them like another passenger. She forced herself to look away.

"Are you all right? Your eyes are red."

She searched for an answer. None came. She'd have to tell the truth. "My contacts are bothering me."

He pulled onto the highway. "You wear glasses?"

She didn't, but she didn't want to tell yet another lie. "Not if I can help it."

He smiled. She gulped and tried to ignore the flutter in her tummy. *Focus on something besides how good he looks.* "Did Miri say what was bothering her?"

"No."

"I haven't known her long. Is she often moody?"

"Never. She's the most even-keeled person I know."

Jessie frowned. What could have caused her to be so irritable? "I'll try to talk to her today—not that she has any reason to tell me anything, but…"

She felt his gaze on her but kept her eyes on the blimp flying above Cudjoe Key. "I'd appreciate you making the effort. And I'll ask Sue if she knows what's going on."

Logan's cell phone rang, breaking the tense silence that had descended on the car. He hit a button on the steering wheel to answer. "Logan Nash."

He listened then disconnected. "That was Sue. Miri's fallen and hurt her knee bad enough to need an ambulance."

"Ms. EVANS, YOU have a comminuted fracture of your patella. I'll wire all four pieces of your knee-cap back together using a purse string–type technique and pins or screws, if necessary."

Miri tried to make sense of the doctor's words through the haze of pain medication and the throbbing of her knee. "Then I can return to work?"

The surgeon, who couldn't be more than forty, glanced at Logan before turning his attention back to Miri. She didn't like his extremely patient expression—like she was stupid or something.

"No, ma'am. You'll be totally immobile for six weeks post-op, then—"

"But I have a restaurant to run."

"Please let me finish. I'm afraid you won't be resuming your regular job duties for at least three months, possibly more, depending on your healing time and progress with physical therapy."

Frustration boiled over. "You're not listening. I *have* to work—I want my clothes and another doctor who understands my situation."

She threw back the thin sheet and tried to swing her legs off the emergency room gurney. A nauseating bolt of pain shot up her leg.

Logan blocked her escape. "Forget it, Miri. You're not leaving. Dr. Jenkins is the best orthopedic surgeon for a fractured patella, and he can do the surgery first thing in the morning. Sue, Hal, Jessie and I will handle the Widow."

"Jessie's leaving—"

"I spoke to her a little while ago. She's agreed to stay. Also, the doctor says you can return to work at six weeks *if* you agree to sit and direct from your wheelchair."

Wheelchair? "What if I refuse the surgery?"

"Then, Ms. Evans, your right leg will be permanently disabled. Your kneecap will become arthritic. You'd never be able to walk normally again, and being on your feet all day would definitely be impossible." He paused, letting his dire prediction sink in. "So…if you'll sign the con-

sent forms, we'll get you on the surgery schedule. If you'd prefer another doctor, then expect
to wait a few days for an appointment to discuss
surgery. And you can expect more delays while
you wait for an OR slot. It's up to you. Either you
start the mending process immediately or wait a
week or two."

She wanted to scream, to cry, to throw something. They didn't understand. She could not
lose the restaurant. It was all she had left. Logan
squeezed her shoulder.

"We'll take care of the Widow. I promise. And
I'll line up someone to take care of you at home
while you recover."

"I can't afford—"

"I'll take care of it."

"You can't afford it when you're funneling all
your money to the PI."

"That's on hold for now. Sign. Please."

He offered the clipboard and the pen. Reluctantly, she took the paperwork and scratched her
name on all the highlighted lines. The doctor nodded and left. Logan followed him out; the drone
of their voices faded. She sagged against the pil-
lows, angry tears pricking her eyes. One stupid
fall and she'd lost control of her life.

This was all Ignatius's fault. If she hadn't been
thinking about the pushy bastard and his cocky
surety that they would have a date in the future,
she wouldn't have fallen off her new work clogs.

But the damage was done. And just like she had when she'd lost Jack, she'd pick up the pieces and keep going.

The only upside was she wouldn't have to come up with an excuse to avoid Logan's PI.

"THAT'S IT! WE'RE DONE," Sue said, and the gathered employees emitted a cheer.

"We survived a night without the boss," Hal added. "Let's get out of here."

Jessie scanned the dozen tired faces in the kitchen. "Miri would be proud of you. You pulled together like a well-trained team."

After a series of high-fives, all but the cook, Sue and Jessie filed out the side door. Jessie turned to Sue. "Any updates?"

"Logan's last text said Miri will have surgery first thing in the morning." Sue grabbed the night deposit bag. "I'm beat. Can't wait to get home and soak my feet."

Now that the adrenaline of getting through the crisis had drained, they were all tired. It showed in the way they shuffled out the front door. Jessie looked into the parking lot and suddenly recalled her predicament—the same as last night. Stranded. But at least tonight she had a pocketful of cash. Not only had the buyers picked up the Key deer painting, another guest had bought her hibiscus. She'd been so busy trying to cover her job and Miri's she hadn't had time to bask in the glow of her second sale.

"Can either of you jump my car or recommend a tow company?" she asked as Sue locked up.

A dark figure rose from the outside bench. Jessie's heart skipped in panic, thinking they were about to be robbed, then she recognized Logan's PI friend.

"Logan told me your battery was dead. I brought cables. I'll get you running or drive you home."

Logan had thought of her even in the midst of Miri's emergency. But the PI made her nervous. "Thank you."

The man shrugged. "Least I can do. I'd want somebody to help my daughter." His gaze swung to Sue. "Any news on Miri?"

"She'll have surgery in the morning. But she'll be off her feet for six weeks, maybe more."

"How's she going to manage?"

Sue shook her head. "We'll take care of things here, but at home? I don't know. I'm hoping there's enough money to hire someone, but I doubt it. Things have been pretty tight since—" She raised her eyebrows. "You know."

"Gotcha. I might know someone," the PI said.

"If you do, please pass that on to Logan. Hal's driving me home. We're dropping the deposit at the bank on the way. Night, all."

Since what? Jessie wanted to ask what Sue

meant. But she didn't. If it was any of her business, they'd tell her.

The PI turned to Jessie. "All right, missy. Let's get your car running." They crossed the lot together. "I won't ask why you didn't call the rental company to demand a replacement car."

Jessie gulped. He knew her car was a rental. "I didn't know I could do that."

"Their local office would send someone to help."

"If you'd rather I do that, I will."

"No need. I'm here. And for future reference, the person on the lease agreement needs to call and be here."

Her heart skipped a beat. Did he know the car wasn't in her name or was he fishing for information? "Right."

He climbed in the American-made SUV parked grille to grille with her car and started the engine, then raised the hood and returned to her side. "Jump in and pop the hood."

She did as he asked then joined him up front. He hooked up the cables then faced her, his expression somber. "As long as you don't try to pull any funny business on Miri or Logan, you got nothing to fear from me, Miss Martin."

The bottom dropped out of her stomach. He knew. Her fight-or-flight instincts kicked in. Should she leave Florida?

"Have you told Logan?"

"Nope. I read enough to know why you're hiding out down here, and you're entitled to your privacy. By the way, you're prettier as a blue-eyed blonde. You look just like your mama."

Yes, she did. He'd done his research. Fear tightened her throat.

He nodded toward her car. "Get in and see if she'll start."

Mouth dry with panic, she complied. After two failed attempts the engine turned over and purred. "Let 'er run a minute," the PI called out.

Jessie sat behind the wheel, her fingers clenching until they hurt. Should she tell Brandon about being discovered? If she did she'd have to explain the whole convoluted situation and he'd demand she come home. And as much as she'd longed for home a week ago, she didn't want to leave now. How could she when Miri needed her more now than before?

Ignatius unhooked the cables, shut both hoods and stopped by her open door. "She should run fine now, but I'll follow you home if it'll make you feel better."

"I-I'm good. Thanks."

"You gonna bolt?"

It would be the smart thing to do. But she shook her head. "I can't do that to Miri."

"Does your family know where you are and that you're safe?"

"Yes. I talk to my brother every day. And some-times my mom."

"Secure line?"

"Yes."

"Good. Smart. But I'm surprised a law enforce-ment guy would let you take a waitressing job if you're in hiding."

She ducked her head, heat stinging her cheeks.

"Ah. He doesn't know, eh?"

"You don't miss much, do you?"

"Not when it concerns folks I care about. Lo-gan's more than a client. He's a friend. And Miri's mighty special, too. So your family doesn't know what you're up to?"

She shook her head.

"Want to let 'em know I'm looking out for you?"

"No. That would…require a lot of explaining."

Ignatius pulled a card from his wallet. "My info. Cell number's on it. Call if you need me— any time. Now get on back to your hideaway. This is going to be a long weekend without the li'l general to keep everybody in line."

She was shaking as she drove out of the lot. Her secret was out. But was it safe with the man in her rearview mirror?

CHAPTER TWELVE

"WHAT DAY IS IT?" Miri's groggy voice pulled Logan's attention from the client file on his laptop.

He shifted in the hospital visitor's chair, trying to find a more comfortable position. "Friday."

"Our busiest night. Why are you here instead of at the Widow?"

"Because you just came out of surgery four hours ago. Sue will run things."

"She's great with the front of the house, but she can't handle the back."

"Then Hal will do it."

"Hal, God love him, is a fabulous cook. But he needs somebody to keep him on task. You have to do it, Logan."

"Miri, it's been a lot of years since I worked the kitchen line."

"It's been a long time since you waited tables, too, but you picked that right back up."

"Somebody needs to stay here with you. You've been sick to your stomach and—"

"That was from the anesthesia. I'm fine now that the antinausea medicine has kicked in, and I have a call button for the nurses' station."

He didn't want to leave her. Stupid, but he didn't. Seeing the ambulance pull away with her in the back had reminded him of the last time he'd seen his mother alive.

"I'm not leaving. I'll call Sue and check on things." He checked his phone. "I don't have a signal in here. I'll step outside."

"Fine. Whatever. But I need you at the Widow. I don't need a babysitter."

He left a message with the nurse and headed downstairs. Text tones lit up his phone as soon as he cleared the entrance doors. I's said, "Call me. ASAP."

But Logan called the Widow first. Gin, the bartender, answered and put him through to Sue. "How's it going?"

"All good. The team's pulling together. How's Miri?"

"Worried about keeping Hal on task. Otherwise, as good as expected."

"Tell her to rest easy. Jessie's stepped into Miri's role and she's keeping things moving. She's also taken over totaling the receipts every night."

A prickle of uneasiness ran through him. He was attracted to Jessie. That didn't mean he blindly trusted her with the restaurant's money. "Does she know how?"

"Says she did it in college."

Truth? Or a way to scam them? "I'd feel better if I did it."

"Suit yourself."

"I'll be there tomorrow night. Lock tonight's take in the safe."

He ended the call then punched I's contact button. He picked up on the first ring. "How's Miri?"

"Good. They'll release her tomorrow. She'll be in a wheelchair and completely non–weight bearing for a minimum of six weeks. Then she's allowed limited mobility after a few more months."

"Are they sending her to rehab?"

"The surgeon suggested it, but most of the places don't accept that crappy insurance company she uses."

That was his fault. She'd reduced costs by moving to a cheaper company after his fiasco.

"Then she'll be at home?"

"That's the plan...if I can make it work."

"You gonna hire somebody to stay with her?"

"I've been checking into prices. They want a minimum of sixteen dollars an hour. Multiply that times twenty-four hours, five days a week and six weeks, and she can't afford that and neither can I. It's a hell of a mess."

"I'll stay with her. Hire a nursing assistant to check on her and bathe her and I'll do the rest— feed her, get her to physical therapy, shop for her groceries and all that jazz."

"I can't ask you to do that. And if I did, Miri would probably kill me."

I laughed. "Or me. But she needs help and I'm

available. I do most of my work on the computer. I can take care of her and never miss a beat. I want to help."

"I appreciate your offer. And I'll take you up on it until I can find someone we can afford."

"Deal. Get me a key, and I'll take care of the rest. Oh, and you might not want to mention the arrangements to Miri just yet."

Understatement of the year. "Roger that. I'd spell you in the evenings and on weekends, but I'll have to spend that time working at the Widow."

"What's up?"

"Sue just told me Jessie's handling the deposits. We've never run a background check on her, and I'm not comfortable putting all the cash and credit card info in her hands."

"Forget about it. Jessie's okay."

Hearing that from I, a self-professed skeptic, was unusual. "Is that your personal opinion or your professional one?"

"It's a twofer. Jessie shouldn't be a problem."

"You checked her out, didn't you? What did you learn?"

"That she's unlikely to be a problem."

Too vague. "Unlikely?"

"I don't offer guarantees. But I wouldn't worry about Jessie."

"What can you tell me, I?"

"That there's nothing you need to know."

More ambiguity. But he knew I well enough to

know the man wouldn't talk if pushed. He said his goodbyes and headed back inside.

He'd confront I later and try to pry more information out of him. But for now, like it or not, Miri was stuck with Logan watching out for her at least until he got her home.

SATURDAY AFTERNOON MIRI eyed the brand-new handicap ramp leading to her front door with distaste. It reminded her how long she'd be banned from her life and the doctor's threat that her knee would never fully recover if she didn't stay off it as ordered. "Who built that monstrosity?"

Logan pushed her wheelchair toward the ramp. "I."

That single letter filled her with a volatile cocktail of emotions. "We don't need his help."

"Sorry to hear that, Miriam Louise." Only when she heard his voice did she notice Ignatius Smith sitting in *her* front porch rocking chair.

She jerked upright, sending a dagger of pain slicing through her leg beneath the heavy plaster cast. Hating for him to see her weakness, she tried to suppress her grimace, but the sympathy clouding his eagle eyes told her he hadn't missed anything.

"I, this looks great," Logan said. "I had no idea you were going to build it. Thank you."

"No problem. I enjoyed sharpening my rusty carpentry skills. And we need to be able to get

Her Majesty into the house and out here to her garden."

"What are you doing here?" Miri demanded, interrupting the men's chitchat.

"I'm here to serve." He bowed.

"You're what?"

"I'm going to be your nurse. Logan can't be here 24/7. I can."

"That is not funny." She looked over her shoulder at Logan. His cagey expression sent alarm slithering through her. "You said you'd hired someone."

"I did. A nursing assistant will come by every morning to give you baths and get you dressed. I volunteered to stay the rest of the time, including overnight."

This man in her house? Sleeping here? Seeing her at her worst? "No. No. Absolutely not. I need a woman to help me with…things. Hire someone else."

"That's what the aide is for, plus Sue and Jessie will take turns coming by before and after work every day. I have client meetings I can't miss in the mornings. Evenings I'll oversee the Widow. I will help you in any way he can, Miri. All you have to do is ask."

She grabbed the wheels and spun the chair around to face her nephew. He jumped back to avoid her slamming into him with her upraised leg. "Logan, I don't want that man here."

"That's tough, Miriam Louise," the cocky rascal in question replied from directly behind her. She hadn't even heard him descend the ramp. His big paws landed on her shoulders and squeezed, then he leaned down and whispered into her ear, "Because like a tattoo, I'm going to be hard to get rid of. Whether or not you're willing to admit it, you need me. Let's get you into the house."

The distracting tickle of his breath on her ear was the only reason he was able to wrestle control of the chair from her. He pushed her up the ramp. He'd built a smaller second incline from the porch into the house.

Anger whipped through her like hurricane-force winds. The man had taken over and made changes to her house without her permission. She opened her mouth to let rip a blistering rant, but finding her living room fully decorated for Christmas stole the wind from her sails. A tree adorned with twinkling lights and familiar ornaments stood in the bay window. Greenery, candles and bows she hadn't used in years decorated tabletops. She hadn't had time to decorate.

"Who did this?"

"I did," Ignatius said. Carefully, she twisted to look at the culprit. His ears and neck were a blotchy red.

"You snooped in my attic?"

"Christmas is only seven days away, woman. Your place needed a little holiday cheer. I figured you had stuff somewhere, so I looked. Anyway, I'll bet you could use some real food after two days of hospital swill. I've laid in enough grub for a good, long hurricane party. Looks like you'll get to sample my culinary masterpieces after all."

As the idea of being trapped with him for an extended period was freaking her out, a heavenly smell registered. Something Italian. "I don't need you cooking for me."

Her ungracious tone embarrassed her, but the man had overstepped too many boundaries to count. She felt as if she'd lost control of her life—to him.

"Too bad. You can't reach the stove. I like to cook and I gotta eat, too. I'm not much on fast food or delivery junk. So you'll get Grandma Smith's best recipes, like it or not."

His grandmother had taught him to cook?

He shoved her toward the kitchen table. The chair facing the window to the backyard had been removed. He positioned her very carefully so that her leg didn't hit the table. A snow globe with a Harley in it sat in the center of the glass oval. It wasn't hers.

"What is that?"

"Your bike until you decide to buy one. Figured it's the only one you can handle for a while."

His actions...disarmed her. But him living here? She scowled at Logan. "He cannot stay."

Her nephew's stubborn face didn't bode well.

"You can't be alone. Doctor's orders. Either I stays or you go to a rehab facility. The closest one with an opening that will accept your insurance is in Homestead."

"I can't keep an eye on the Widow from almost three hours away. When will the one in Key West have a spot?"

"They weren't sure. What's it going to be? I have to notify the doctor if you refuse to accept these arrangements."

She glared at Logan. How dare he put her in this position? Then she scowled at Ignatius. "If this is your way of trying to finagle a date, then you're wasting your time. I will not go out with you again."

"Not for at least six weeks. You'll have to resist my manly charms. Think you can handle that?" His dark brows waggled and his eyes twinkled with mischief. "My money says no."

Her stomach flipped—in disgust, she assured herself. She wanted to throw the snow globe at him—doubly so when she heard a cough that sounded suspiciously like a chuckle from her nephew.

"I'm staying here. But you—" She pointed at Ignatius. "You'd better behave yourself or my Ruger will be doing the talking."

"If you can find it. My mama didn't raise a dummy, and my granddaddy taught me how to handle volatile women. I already put your firearm and all the sharp knives out of reach."

She gripped the arms of the wheelchair and struggled to calm herself. He'd been in her nightstand drawer. She inhaled, long and slow, then exhaled the same way, praying for patience.

Lord, please get me through the next six weeks without killing the man.

JESSIE HUSTLED THROUGH the Widow's employee entrance Sunday morning. The prep staff had beat her to work.

"Good morning! Y'all are impressive. Everybody's early." She turned for the locker room to put away her keys and wallet and barely avoided colliding with someone who'd been behind her. Strong arms clamped her biceps. Her body recognized Logan's scent and touch before she looked into his intensely blue eyes.

"Sorry." The word whooshed out as her lungs emptied. The last time she'd been this close to him he'd kissed her. The memory sent her pulse rate out of control, and her whole body flushed, making her uniform feel clingy and hot. Despite everything, as much as she hated to admit it, she was attracted to him. And if her life weren't a lie—

She wiggled free and put a yard between them. "I didn't see you. How's Miri?"

"Home. Cranky. But surgery went well." Logan

searched Jessie's face. "Did you do something different?"

The bottom of her stomach dropped out. She'd bought replacement contacts Saturday morning, but she hadn't been able to find the same brand. While her new contacts were still brown, they were tricolored instead of bicolored. She hadn't thought anyone would notice a few additional flecks of gold.

She lowered her gaze. "Must be my makeup. Thanks for asking your friend to jump-start my car. He must be a good guy if he offered to help Miri."

"He is. I'd trust I with anything. And you're welcome." He remained in her path as if he had something more to say. Apprehension trickled through her. Had the PI revealed what he'd discovered despite his assurance that he wouldn't?

"I've already notified everyone else. We're reverting to the Widow's old hours, and we'll be closed on Wednesdays and Thursdays while Miri's out. I hope she'll keep those hours once she returns."

She nodded, avoiding eye contact and needing to escape. "I'm glad you could stop by with updates. We're all thinking about Miri, and I'm keeping her in my prayers."

"I didn't just stop by, Jessie. I'll be running the Widow until Miri's back on her feet."

Logan would be her boss. How could she see

him every day and keep her secrets and her distance?

"I want to start by looking at Thursday, Friday and Saturday's receipts and deposits."

He didn't trust her. And maybe he shouldn't. It had been years since she'd handled the money for her godmother's barbecue restaurant. What if she'd made a mistake? Would he label her a thief and call the police?

She could see the headlines now: South Carolina's Biggest Lottery Winner Caught Embezzling from Restaurant. And the media frenzy would start anew. Even if she wasn't guilty, her family would be humiliated.

She gulped her nervousness. "Let me put my stuff away and I'll join you in the office."

THE NUMBERS LOOKED RIGHT, Logan concluded an hour later, but something was off. Jessie was jumpy and wouldn't look at him. Why, if she had nothing to hide?

Maybe he was too distracted by her proximity, her scent, the long braid draping over her shoulder, to focus and he'd missed something. He wanted her—a fact that, even with him now being her temporary boss, hadn't diminished. Not even the open door to the noisy kitchen could dispel the sexual awareness.

Focus.

"Where did you learn to handle restaurant accounting?"

He noted her hesitation. "My godmother has a restaurant. I worked there throughout high school and summers during college. When my godfather had bypass surgery, she taught me the financial side so she could be with him during his recovery."

A plausible story. But was it true? She'd never lifted her gaze higher than his chin. Staring at her downcast head meant being sidetracked by the hint of cleavage her uniform tank top displayed. His body reacted predictably.

He forced his attention back to the column listing her tips. She'd claimed she would turn the number in to her accountant. He hadn't believed her then. But there it was on the screen. And it looked accurate.

He realized he wanted to trust her. He wanted to believe that this woman who'd taken on extra duties for someone she'd known only three weeks—and for no pay—was genuine and not an opportunist. But such generosity seemed too good to be true. And he'd been suckered by a pretty face before.

Elizabeth had been the most beautiful woman he'd ever seen, and she'd used her looks and wiles to wrap him around her finger and shut down his brain.

A tap on the door pulled his attention from the past. "Yes?"

Pam stood outside. "The dining room's filling up. We need Jessie out front."

Jessie straightened, her relief palpable. "May I go?"

"In a minute." He searched her face, noting her averted eyes. Something was definitely different. But what? *Not* her makeup. She barely wore any. "Look at me."

Her reluctance obvious in the slow lifting of her dense lashes, she complied. And then he got it. Her eyes weren't sparkling from excitement. The gold flecks in her irises were different, and her eyes weren't red like they'd been the other day when she'd complained about her contacts irritating them. "You got new contacts."

She swallowed. "Yes."

"You wear colored contacts?"

She inhaled, exhaled then shifted on her feet. "Yes."

"And these are different from your old ones."

"Yes," she replied through a clenched jaw.

"What color are your eyes when you don't wear them?"

Her gaze flicked to the calendar on the wall behind him. He thought she'd refuse to answer, then resignation settled over her features. "Blue."

He tried to picture her with blue eyes and

couldn't. "Why choose brown? That's an atypical choice."

She shrugged, but the movement was stiff. "I just wanted a change."

"Tables are full," Sue shouted as she passed the office door.

"You can go. But Jessie, I want to see you—the real you."

Her deer-in-the-headlights expression before she hustled out filled him with questions.

What else wasn't real about Jessie? He was determined to find out. Because a woman with secrets was never good news. He could thank his ex for that painful lesson.

"Two days and I haven't killed him. I deserve a medal." Miri fumed to Sue on Monday over vegetable lo mein. Her friend had brought lunch from Miri's favorite Chinese restaurant.

Sue looked through the window at the man in question currently mowing Miri's small backyard. "Is Ignatius being a pain in the tail?"

"No, he's being *nice*. Too nice. He waits on me hand and foot. I can't even pee without him standing outside the door listening. He claims it's because he's afraid I'll fall transferring from the wheelchair to the toilet. I think he's just kinky." She was being a grumpy bitch and she knew it. But Sue didn't seem to take offense.

She blotted her mouth with a napkin, but the

smile crinkles beside her eyes gave her away. "No wonder you were happy to see me—and for me to take you to the restroom."

"It's not funny. He cooks and cleans, and he sings. All the time. He's singing now."

"How can you tell?"

"His lips are moving." Then her cheeks burned at the revealing comment. She watched him. Too much. "I'm sorry. The pain pills are making me crazy. Try as I might, I can't even forget he's here when he makes all that racket."

"Is he any good?"

"He could sing in a church choir for all I care. You're missing the point. How's work?"

"Surprisingly good. Logan is going to come in every night to close out the books. I think he has the hots for Jessie. He can't keep his eyes off her. She watches him, too."

Miri scowled. "He'd better not run off my waitress."

"I don't think that'll be a problem."

"I'm just saying, until he lets go of the past he's no good for any woman—especially one as sweet as Jessie."

"He's not the only one holding on to the past."

"I am *not*." An electronic sound chirped nearby. Miri searched for the source and spotted a cell phone. Ignatius's phone.

Sue picked it up. "Should we answer it? The screen says Bethany's calling."

"That's his daughter. Might be something wrong. Pass it to me." Sue handed her the phone. "Hello? Bethany?"

"Um...yes, who is this?"

"Miri Evans. We met when your father brought you to the Fisherman's Widow. Ignatius is outside. Should I call him in?"

"Oh...no. He... I...didn't realize you were dating."

"We're not. I had surgery. He's helping me for a few days. What did you need?"

"I was going to ask him if he'd watch the girls tomorrow. They're out of school on Christmas break, and my boss just called an urgent meeting. But I can try to make other arrangements."

Kids in the house would keep her from being alone with Ignatius. "If you don't mind dropping them off at my place, your father and I could watch them. They'd be welcome."

"Are you sure?"

"I'd love the company. I have some ornaments I bought to paint and haven't done so yet. They could help."

"If you're sure...and Dad won't mind?"

"I am positive." She relayed her address. "We'll see you in the morning." Then she disconnected.

Sue leveled a look on her. "What have you done?"

"Found a buffer."

The back door opened. Ignatius did a double take when he spotted his phone in her hand. "Snooping, Miriam Louise?"

"Your daughter called. I thought it might be an emergency, so I answered. She needs you to watch the girls tomorrow."

He paled. "No can do."

"Oh, yes, you can. She's dropping them off at eight."

His jaw went slack then tightened up. He looked as if he might be sick to his stomach. "I'll call her back and tell her to make other arrangements for Sydney and Chloe."

"You'll do no such thing. They'll be good company. I even have crafts to keep them occupied. And if you can take directions, we'll bake cookies with them."

She shouldn't take such delight in the horror on his face. "Have you ever kept the girls before, Ignatius?"

"No."

"Then it's time you did. You said you wanted to get to know them, and this is the perfect way to do so."

Tomorrow would be fun—if only because he looked like he thought it would be torture.

CHAPTER THIRTEEN

JESSIE HEADED INTO the Widow Monday afternoon with a sense of accomplishment. They'd survived their first weekend without Miri, and this morning she'd checked everything on her to-do list.

Her good mood bubble burst when Logan's was the first face she saw. The kitchen was empty save him. Tension invaded her limbs and tummy. "How's Miri?"

"Adjusting."

"I promised her I'd stop by after work tonight and help her get ready for bed."

"She'll enjoy the company."

As always, his unwavering gaze made her antsy and a little breathless. Why did she have to be attracted to someone *now*? "Where is everybody?"

"We're the first ones here. Where were you this morning? I stopped by your place."

Her pulse skipped. "I had errands to run and Christmas and birthday gifts to buy and ship. And I also had the photographs printed. I want to put them in an album for my—for future reference." Why was she babbling like a fool? She'd almost said "students." She was getting too comfortable around him.

"You're not going home for the holiday?"

She tried to conceal her sadness. "No."

"Is your family coming here?"

Why had she said anything? She didn't want his pity. "No."

"Does Miri know?"

"She has enough on her plate. I'd rather she didn't worry about me. I'll be fine. Why did you stop by my place?"

He hesitated, searching her face. "I wanted to make sure your car was running okay."

Why didn't she believe him? He could have called. "It is."

"The cormorant picture's missing."

She'd experienced a pang of loss when the creepy birds she'd christened after the man in front of her had been carried from the restaurant. But she'd vanquished that emotion by celebrating her third sale and having the images she'd taken with Logan's camera downloaded onto an SD card that fit a digital picture frame. Her mother would love it. "It sold last night."

"Congratulations."

Hal walked in, dispelling the strained atmosphere. Jessie heaved a sigh of relief. What was it about this man that held her spellbound when she knew nothing could come from their relationship?

Logan's expression turned all business. "The

waitresses from the employment agency start today. They'll be shadowing you and Sue."

"Got it."

Then he returned to Miri's office. But he left the door open. She could feel his eyes watching every move she made until she escaped the kitchen. But because of that kiss, the way he watched her had changed. His eyes were no longer filled with distrust. They were filled with something she had to ignore. Something that hummed through her like the music teacher's tuning fork.

Desire. But she could resist that...as long as she didn't start to really like him.

MIRI'S HOUSE WAS a delightful surprise. Jessie stopped at the base of a ramp that still smelled of fresh wood to admire the tiny Victorian storybook cottage.

Its steep, gabled metal roof glimmered like sheets of silver under a bright half moon. The bric-a-brac trim resembled icing on a gingerbread house, and the front porch wrapped around the side like a lacy white garland. At the far end, a porch swing drifted gently in the evening breeze. The windows glowed with welcome.

She immediately wanted to see the place in the daytime, to take in the garden filled with sunlight and colors instead of shadows and shades of gray. Her fingers itched to paint a likeness of it for Miri. She followed a crushed stone path toward a birdbath to gauge the best angle.

The front door opened, and the PI stood in the gap. He studied Jessie a moment and her heart skipped with alarm, then he moved aside and Miri wheeled into sight. "Jessie, I'm glad you're here. Come in."

Jessie returned to the ramp and ascended. "I love your house."

Miri's smile turned wistful. "The historic architecture of the Keys has always fascinated me. Jack built this place for me. I knew nothing about it until he brought me here and handed me the key—it was the day after Logan went away to college. He was trying to ease my empty-nest syndrome."

That was the thoughtful kind of love Jessie dreamed of finding. It was the kind her parents shared. Would she ever find it? Would she ever be brave enough to look again? She'd been so wrong about Aaron. Did she dare trust her judgment?

"The monstrosity of a garage came later out of necessity," Miri added dismissively. "The best I can say about it is that it gives us privacy by blocking the house from the road. Our lot was too narrow to build it beside the house, and it would have blocked the view from the bedrooms."

Keeping a wary eye on the man who knew her secrets, Jessie pointed at the Christmas wreath made from native seashells hanging on the door. "This is beautiful."

"Jack found that on one of his trips. That man never said he loved me. Words were not his thing. But he showed it in a thousand ways. He was always bringing me some little trinket."

"He should have told you," Ignatius grumbled.

"Words are empty. Actions tell the truth," Miri insisted.

The two glared at each other, locked in silent combat. Fearing an argument, Jessie jumped in. "Actually, I think you need both. Actions prove your words are sincere. My parents do that. And none of us have ever doubted their love for each other or for us."

A sound from behind her drew her gaze. Logan stood at the top of the ramp. She hadn't heard his approach. Her stomach dive-bombed like a pelican hitting the water. She'd left him doing some bookkeeping and hadn't expected to see him here.

She moved farther into the room and away from Logan. Her gaze scanned the festive decor and her heart ached with emptiness. While others flocked to the mall for Black Friday sales, she, her mother and sister had always banded together the day after Thanksgiving, traveling from house to house to help decorate one another's homes. She'd missed that ritual this year. Her little house would be empty and dark with no twinkling tree in her front window. Worse, she'd been so focused on missing home that she hadn't bothered decorating here.

She shook off the gloom. "Your Christmas decorations are lovely."

Miri frowned at the PI. "Kris Kringle's responsible for that."

These two definitely had negativity between them. "What can I help you with, Miri? You mentioned painting something?"

"Ignatius's granddaughters are coming over tomorrow. I have miniature birdhouse ornaments for them to decorate. I could use your help getting all the craft supplies together. I have an assortment of brushes and paints and embellishments, but I need to choose the ones that are age appropriate. You'll be better at that than I."

"I'm sure they'll enjoy it. I didn't realize you like to do crafts."

Miri went silent, staring at her hands. "I used to in the evenings to wind down. I hope my paints and brushes are still good."

"We'll check. If not, I can pick some up in the morning. Do you want me to come by and help tomorrow?"

"Oh, no. Ignatius will be here. He needs to spend time with his granddaughters."

The man looked less than thrilled about the prospect. No, Jessie realized as she studied him closer, that wasn't dread in his eyes—it was fear of failure. She'd seen it in students' faces many times.

"You'll do fine," she told him, but he didn't appear reassured. "It's just paint, and any mistake can always be painted over."

"Has Jessie told you she's going to be alone for Christmas?" Logan asked, and Jessie's stomach sank lower. So much for pretending he wasn't here.

Miri's gaze swung her way. "Why didn't you say something?"

She didn't want the pity she saw on the woman's face. "It's okay. I'm planning to cook all my favorite recipes and listen to Christmas music, and—"

"Come here and cook those recipes," Miri insisted. "Sue and I always put on a big feast and—"

"This year, you'll delegate," Ignatius interrupted.

Miri's spine went rigid, and her cheeks reddened. "Jessie can be my hands and feet. She'll do what I tell her and not improvise the way you do."

"I haven't heard you complaining about my cooking. In fact, you clean your plate. Every time." The air crackled between them.

Miri's gaze swung to Logan. "Couldn't you have found a better jailer?"

Logan laughed. "I is the first person I've ever seen who can make you listen. You heard the doc. Follow orders or you'll never heal."

Miri's scowl could curdle milk. "Jessie, let's

go through my art supplies. They're in my bedroom closet."

"Let Jessie get them down," Ignatius ordered.

Miri swung the wheelchair around and rolled it away. Jessie glanced from one man to the other, trying to figure out what was going on. She felt as if she'd been dropped in the middle of a war zone, but she didn't dare complain for fear that the PI would reveal what he knew to Logan.

Anxious to escape, she followed Miri. The woman was so on edge she barely resembled the kindhearted person Jessie had come to know and care for. Tension lined her face and pulled a purse string of wrinkles around her mouth.

Jessie closed the bedroom door. "Are you in pain?"

Miri sighed. "Yes, but I can handle that. It's that man in there that's getting under my skin. He's smothering me. Tries to do everything. I'm used to my independence. Even before Jack passed, he was gone most of the time. I did for myself. Ignatius won't let me. Between his and Logan's hovering, I'm ready to run away from home."

The familiar refrain made Jessie smile. "You sound like my dad. He has Parkinson's. We all try to keep him from overdoing it by jumping in to help. He feels like we're robbing him of the things he *can* still do for himself. He has to keep reminding us that one day he will need our help,

but now he doesn't. Your situation's the opposite.
Try to keep in mind that you'll only need help for
a few more weeks."

Miri's face softened. "You miss your family."

"Of course."

"Jessie, I'm going to be blunt. Sue told me you
and Logan are dancing around each other. Don't
let loneliness drive you into a relationship with
Logan."

Jessie's face burned. She'd had no idea others
had noticed the chemical storm between them.

"I think you're wonderful, and because I don't
want you to get hurt, I'll tell you that Logan's
heart was broken. Badly. He's not over it yet.
Ignatius's continued presence in his life proves
that."

A warning she needed to hear. "You don't have
to worry. Until my life is…settled, I can't afford
any entanglements. Now let's look at your supplies and see if you have everything you need."

If she was lucky, Logan would be gone when
she finished helping his aunt.

JESSIE'S STALLING HAD been in vain. Logan was
still there when she came out of Miri's bedroom.
"Miri's gone to bed, so I'll head home."

He rose. "I'll walk you to your car."

"That's not necessary."

"I'm leaving, too."

She glanced at Ignatius. "Good night. Call if

you need help tomorrow. I know Miri said you could handle it, but I don't mind. Your grand-daughters seem very sweet."

He nodded. "Thanks. I appreciate that."

Then with no other way to delay being alone with Logan, she preceded him out the door.

He paused on the porch. "What you said in there about actions and words...did your ex do that?"

Her breath caught as his question hit home. "No. He said all the pretty words. But his actions showed the opposite. I just wasn't smart enough to see it."

Everyone around her had been, though.

"Jack taught me a lot of life lessons on that swing. When I'd come home from college, we'd sit and talk about what I'd learned. He acted like he had all the time in the world for me. It was enough. I knew how he felt about me," he said defensively. "I didn't need the words."

With Miri's warning fresh in her mind, she resumed her trek down the ramp instead of ask-ing questions about his past. "From what you and Miri have said, Jack sounds like a great guy."

"He was."

She heard loss in his voice and had to fight the urge to reach out and comfort him. "I thought you would've come to see Miri earlier today."

"I can't visit during the day now. I have a cli-ent going through an audit."

She grimaced. "I'm sorry."

"So am I."

Logan cared about his client. She saw it in the lines etched on his face. "Is he a friend of yours?"

"He was a friend of Jack's and is a genuinely nice guy who's had some bad breaks. This should have been an open-and-shut case, but the IRS agent is going over every single receipt. We'll prevail in the end, but this guy's losing prime fishing charter days, which he can't afford."

"It sounds like you enjoy your work."

"I do. If you'd asked me ten years ago if I'd enjoy doing taxes for small businesses, I'd have adamantly said no. But what I do matters. These guys aren't high rollers who won't miss a few thousand bucks here and there. They're good people, like Miri, who need every dime they make. It's my job to help them hold on to it."

Logan's impassioned speech made her realize he was a good guy, too. She hadn't seen that early on when he'd been antagonistic toward her, but little by little she'd been catching glimpses of the man behind the protective armor. She didn't need to think about that right now when she was trying to resist the physical pull between them.

She stopped at the curve in the sidewalk. Their elbows brushed. A tingle shot up her arm. He was close—too close—in the moonlit garden. She looked up at him and felt the tug of attraction. Her mouth dried and her pulse accelerated.

"You can go ahead. I'd, um…like a minute to

look at the house. I want to paint a picture of it for Miri."

"She'd like that."

"Do you think she'd mind if I came back in the daylight?"

"Not at all. But if you'd rather surprise her, I have some pictures on my computer of the house before the ramp was built. I can find them and get them to you."

His thoughtfulness chipped at her resistance. "A surprise would be great."

He glanced away, then back at her. "I apologize for the ambush in there. But nobody needs to be alone on Christmas. I've done a few holidays solo and it sucks."

Another chip fell away. "After your wife left?"

A muscle in his jaw knotted. "Yeah, and a few times when I was out of town on business and didn't make it home."

"That must've been tough. We always have the whole clan present. It's noisy and chaotic."

"But you love it."

"Yes." A gust of wind blew her hair across her face. Before she could brush it back, Logan's warm fingertip scraped across her cheek and tucked the lock behind her ear. He kept his fingers just below her ear. If he moved them forward an inch he'd feel her pulse racing.

Then he used his thumb to lift her chin. "If your eyes are naturally blue, then what's the real color of your hair? I know it's politically incorrect to ask, but I've been trying to guess. Blue-eyed blonde or blue-eyed brunette? I'd bet the first. You don't have the skin tone for the second. And I can't see you as a redhead."

Her mouth dried. She should have realized he was smart enough to put the puzzle together. "You guessed correctly."

He scanned her face then nodded. "You're beautiful, Jessie. I can only imagine your natural coloring is even prettier. Why?"

She'd shared too much already. Forcing a shrug and a comical face, she said, "I just wanted a change. You know. People are never satisfied with what they have."

She had been, she realized. Before the lottery she'd been very content with her life, her family, her job, her friends. She hadn't wanted anything to change. But now…

She dropped her gaze as the uncomfortable insight slithered through her. She'd been denying her art, something that now filled her with pride, pleasure and a sense of accomplishment. She'd been happy with a mediocre fiancé whose only thought after her win was what he could buy for himself with her money. And she'd surrounded herself with so-called friends who'd turned on her—or away from her—with envy. She still remembered her shock when her best friend had suggested Jessie pay for a cruise for five teachers in their little group and how she'd thrown an irrational tantrum when Jessie refused. And then there was her family… She'd allowed them to make all of her important decisions.

How had she not seen that she'd made a mess of her life before now? How could she ever go back to that state of being?

"Jessie?"

She blinked, trying to dispel her disquiet. His touch burned along her jaw. She backed away to dislodge his hand, then glanced toward the house. The investigator stood watching from the window.

Panic surged. She gulped it down. "It's late. I need to go."

She hustled toward her car, running from Logan and her painful realizations. The moonlight was shining on more than Miri's roof. It was beaming on the very bad choices Jessie had made. And she didn't like what she saw.

Logan blocked the door with his hand before she could open it. His proximity reminded her of the night he'd kissed her. A few inches and she could be in his arms. Her body's electric reaction told her she wanted that. But she couldn't have it.

"You all right? Do I need to follow you home?"

She swallowed the knot in her throat. "I'm good."

"You went somewhere very dark back there. Jessie, whoever hurt you, I'm not him."

She gave him points for being perceptive. "I know. You seem like a really nice guy, Logan. But I'm not in the market for a guy right now. Nice or otherwise. This...thing between us... can't happen. Not now. We both have...stuff to work out."

His eyes were in shadow. She couldn't read them, but she could feel his probing gaze. And she could feel her resistance crumbling.

She jerked the door from him, ducked into her vehicle and backed out of the driveway. When she risked a glance in the rearview mirror, Logan was where she'd left him, staring after her.

She meant what she'd said about bad timing. She had to find the willpower to stick by her decision.

"A NICE GUY," Logan groused as he drove home. Jessie didn't know him very well.

How many times had Elizabeth called him the opposite of nice? Driven. Ruthless. Power hungry. Single-minded. Willing to sacrifice anything in pursuit of a new client.

Why hadn't his ex understood that he'd been doing what Jack had taught him—trying to show her he loved her by working his ass off so she could have the big house, nice car, designer clothes and luxurious trips that seemed to make her happy? And the jewelry? He'd spent more than most of his current clients made in a year on Elizabeth's bling alone.

But had he ever said the *L* word? Not that he could recall. Not even when he'd proposed. He'd told her how beautiful she was, what a great team they made, how much he enjoyed her company. Even though he'd loved her with every fiber of his being, he'd never declared it.

Miri had been satisfied with Jack's brand of love, and Logan had never doubted his uncle loved him. How could Elizabeth not have known how Logan felt? He'd shown her in every way he knew.

He wiped a hand across his face. Maybe Elizabeth was one of those women like Jessie who needed both words and deeds. If so, then he'd failed at the first. Did that excuse her thievery and deceit? No. But it helped him understand how a relationship that had once burned hot with passion had turned into cold ashes.

What he felt for Jessie was anything but cold. He couldn't keep his eyes—or his hands—off her. His fingertips still tingled with the memory of her soft skin. And the only thing that had kept Logan from kissing her tonight was I watching from the window.

As a financial adviser, Logan had been at the top of his game and able to charm clients into investing not just more, but more often. His fancy dinners at sought-after restaurants, his special gifts at Christmas had made his clients feel important and valued. But when it came to matters of the heart, he'd kept his mouth shut and let his deeds do the talking.

Given his history and his nature, he was incapable of giving Jessie what she needed. But he still wanted her.

She'd claimed their attraction couldn't go further. But he would convince her otherwise. He had to.

CHAPTER FOURTEEN

JESSIE SAT ON the dock Tuesday morning contemplating the colors of the sunrise. A sketch pad lay neglected on her lap. She couldn't seem to focus on anything.

Her cell phone rang, startling her. Her mother's new number filled the screen. Answering meant risking her mother guessing Jessie had a bad case of homesickness. But not answering would cause an even bigger problem. And she did need to give her a heads-up. "Hi, Mom."

"Good morning, love. What are you up to today?"

"Sitting on the dock contemplating what I'll paint next. I'm glad you called. I wanted to warn you to be on the lookout for packages on Friday. I've shipped all the Christmas gifts to your house so you'll have them to open with all the others."

"Oh." Silence filled her ear. "That's sweet, dear. We didn't expect you to do that."

"I may not be there to celebrate with you, but I have been thinking about you all."

"What will you do with yourself on Christmas Day?"

She bit her lip, mentally editing her reply. "I'm

going to cook our favorites and eat till my stomach hurts."

Her mother chuckled. "Sounds familiar. So you'll be staying home?"

It wasn't home. "Food, Christmas music, sappy TV shows…what more could a girl need?"

"Have you put up a tree?"

"Not yet."

"You should. I hate that you'll be there all alone, but it might make you feel a little better."

"I might." She wouldn't.

"Jessamine…" Jessie braced herself when she heard her mother's tone. "When you get home, we need to discuss your house. Your father, Brandon and I have been talking. There continue to be random people knocking on your door at all hours of the day despite the No Trespassing signs. We have them all on security video. We've looked into property in a gated community, and we feel you would be safer if you moved there."

The idea repulsed her on many levels, the first of which was having her house on continued video surveillance. The second was leaving the little cottage she'd loved simply because someone else insisted. Funny, a month ago she would have blindly followed their suggestion. "That's a month away. No need to worry about it now."

"You need to think about it."

"I will. So what else is new?"

"You received a letter from the school board

yesterday." Jessie's stomach muscles clenched. "Would you like me to open it and read it to you?"

"Please," she croaked.

She heard the tearing and crackling of paper. "'Dear Ms. Martin, upon further review of your excellent teaching record, we would like you to return to work at the beginning of the spring semester.' Well, isn't that nice?"

Elation filled her like a helium balloon. She rose and danced on the dock. She could return to work in two weeks. Then reality hit and her feet stilled. "Brandon wouldn't like me coming home early or returning to work."

"No. Probably not. But I'm sure he'll relent if you move to a more secure place."

Move to a place he and her parents had chosen without regard to her tastes or opinion? Even if her brother agreed, could she go back to work knowing she didn't need the money and she'd be taking the job from someone who did? Would her fellow teachers resent her and give her the cold shoulder the way they had after the win? But what about her students? She missed them, missed their eagerness to learn and create and watching them discover hidden talents.

But returning to work meant leaving before Miri was back on her feet. While she debated her new options, she focused on a boat near the wreck that Logan had shown her. A dive flag flapped in the wind. Before she went home she wanted to do some of the things on her list—things she hadn't done for fear of being recognized.

"Let me think about it, Mom. I might wait to return to work in the fall when things have settled down. That'll give me time to figure out if I want to move."

Empty air greeted her and filled her with discomfort. A part of her wanted to blurt that she'd do as her mother had suggested. But she bit her tongue. Last night's realizations had been painful— her life was a mess and it was her fault. She needed to come to grips with her mistakes before she made any more.

The wind carried a whoop from the dive boat. She scooped up the binoculars and zeroed in on a diver in the water holding a lobster in his hand.

She would definitely go diving before she left Florida—even if it meant going without her contacts.

"Jessamine, you know we only want what's best for you."

"I know, Mom. Look, I have to run. I, um... have something in the oven." She winced at the lie. "I'll talk to you soon. Be on the lookout for those packages. My love to you and everyone else. Bye."

Then she did something she'd never done to her mother before. She disconnected—for fear she'd let herself get talked into something she didn't

want to do. Because she wasn't sure she had the
strength to resist a full Martin press.

"ARIN'T YOU GOING to paint one, Grandpa?" Chloe,
the ten-year-old with eyes the same green as Ignatius's asked.

Miri looked at the tough former detective almost cowering against the kitchen counter. The
poor man was terrified of his own grandchildren.
He'd been a nervous wreck since his daughter
dropped them off thirty minutes ago.

"Yes, Ignatius, come and sit between Sydney
and me and decorate an ornament." Her saccha-
rine words drew a scowl.

"I'm not much of a painter."

"Have you ever painted a house or a room?"

The pleat in his brow deepened, and his eyes
narrowed suspiciously. "Yeah."

"This is a little house." She lifted her ornament
then her brush. "And this is a little brush. Same
process. Smaller strokes."

The girls snickered.

"You're a funny girl, Miriam Louise."

Sydney patted the chair. "Come on, Grandpa.
You can do it. We'll help. Then we'll hang it on
our tree. Mom says stuff like this makes memories that last forever."

Miri watched his resistance buckle at the
child's words. He inched forward, as wary as a
man preparing to wrestle a hungry gator, and

wedged his big body into the too-small space. His gargantuan paw shook as he picked up a tiny house from the pile and set it on the craft paper she'd spread across the table.

"What color, Grandpa?" Chloe asked.

"Uh…"

"You should do blue like your uniform in the picture Mom has," Sydney suggested.

His head whipped toward the girl. "She has a picture of me?"

"In her bedroom. You can do a cop ornament. Blue and gold. Maybe you could paint your badge on it."

"Yeah. Okay." His voice sounded choked. Miri searched his face. His eyes were damp. The big goon had teared up over the idea of his daughter having his picture in her room? Suddenly she realized, he wasn't just her jailer—he was a man who genuinely loved his child and wanted to make amends but didn't know how. She could show him.

She handed him a brush and the blue paint. "Use a fat, flat brush for the base coat. Cover the wood well like we're doing. The girls can play in the backyard while this layer dries. Then after lunch we'll do the details with a smaller brush."

"Right."

"I want to decorate mine with these," Chloe said, grabbing a handful of red cabochons then promptly dropping them under the table. She dived for them. Moments later she popped up with her treasure. "Your leg's really hairy, Miss Miri."

Heat climbed from Miri's neckline to the roots of her hair. Children were brutally honest. She didn't blame the girl. But she wished her poor hygiene hadn't come up in front of Ignatius. It was bad enough that she was stuck wearing the frumpy housedresses Sue had loaned her instead of her usual pants, but pants wouldn't fit over the cast covering her from ankle to upper thigh.

"I know. I can't get in the tub to shave it while I have the cast on."

"You don't take baths?" Sydney sounded appalled.

"I have a nurse who gives me what they call a bed bath every day. She soaps me up and dries me off, but it's not the same as an honest to goodness soaking. The first thing I'm going to do once I get this cast off is take a very long, very hot shower."

"I don't blame you," Sydney said. Then, thankfully, talk turned back to decorations and the cookies they'd bake later.

Miri didn't dare look at Ignatius again until after the girls had gone outside. The empathy in his eyes was hard to stomach.

"Got shot once. I couldn't shower or shave for a while. Miserable feeling."

Alarm raced through her—more than was warranted for a man she barely knew and didn't particularly like. "You were shot? When?"

"About five years ago."

His dismissive tone irked her. "Does Bethany know?"

"Nah. Didn't want to worry her. She had two babies and a husband to look after. She couldn't have come to Jersey."

"Who took care of you?"

He shrugged. "I got by."

"Where did you get shot?"

"Right shoulder." He tapped a spot level with his armpit.

"Weren't you wearing a vest?"

"Bullet got me at an angle through the armhole. Known risk. It comes with the job."

Her breath caught. If it had been on his left side he might not be here today. "Is that why you got out of police work?"

"You're pretty perceptive, Miriam Louise. Yeah. I realized how close I came to never knowing the girls. So I retired and moved south."

"Then you know how much I hate this." She gestured to the wheelchair and her leg.

"Yes, I do. I know how much it sucks to have to rely on other people and how bad you want to get back to a job you love. Even the clothes..." He shook his head. "I had to wear wifebeaters under shirts I couldn't button and sweatpants because I couldn't work a zipper. So no matter what you say or do, I understand that it's coming from a place of deep frustration. All I can tell you is to hang in there. It'll pass, Miri."

Her chest hurt—not just because he'd called her by her real name, but because he got it. He got *her* and this crazy helplessness. She just nodded because she was too choked up to speak.

"Now I need to get cooking. The girls are gonna want their lunch when they get through playing with your cat."

"I don't have a cat." She followed his pointing finger and spotted a fluffy butterscotch-colored feline basking in the girls' attention. It was small, three months old at the most.

"Thought it was yours. I've been feeding it."

Who was this man who considered taking a bullet routine but was petrified of two preteens and fed stray kittens? She didn't know, but she was suddenly more than a little interested in finding out.

MIRI NICKED HERSELF again and threw the razor down in disgust. She'd decided to try to shave her leg while Ignatius was taking the girls home. She'd wheeled to the bathroom sink and propped the offending leg on the toilet lid. With her casted leg straight out, she couldn't bend far enough to reach the bottom half of her leg.

"Miri?"

She grimaced. Ignatius was back.

"Where are you?" She heard something rattling as he approached. "Everything okay?"

"Just peachy."

"You decent?" he called from outside the bathroom.

She yanked down the hem of the ugly dress. "Close enough."

He stuck his head around the corner and took in her precarious position. "You're bleeding."

"I'm not as flexible as I used to be, nor as skilled with a razor, apparently."

He set the bag he carried in her lap. "Where's your first aid kit?"

She pointed to the cabinet. He retrieved it and surveyed the contents, then pointed at the bag. "Open that while I clean up these cuts."

She looked inside. "An electric razor?"

"Merry Christmas early. My beard itched like a mother—uh, real bad when I couldn't shave. I didn't want you that miserable."

Touched beyond words, Miri stared at his broad back while he laid out items in a neat line on her counter.

"Gonna sting. Ready?" He daubed antiseptic on the first cut without waiting for her response. It burned like fire. She gasped and jerked. "Sorry."

She gritted her teeth while he efficiently cleaned each nick. Then he turned to her, took the bag she'd been stupidly holding and hadn't opened, extracted the razor and plugged it in, then lifted her foot and plopped down on the toilet lid.

She stiffened. "What are you doing?"

His warm fingers grasped her instep, then a buzz filled the air. "Shaving the parts you can't reach."

"I can—" She swallowed her automatic protest. No, she couldn't. It was humbling to have to accept help with such a personal procedure. "I'm sorry. I should have asked the nurse to do it. Thank you."

"No problem." Starting at her ankle, he pushed the razor to her knee. His big, warm, slightly callused palm followed, checking for missed hairs. She felt his touch in places that shouldn't be excited about getting her legs shaved. The vibration combined with the caresses was exceedingly erotic. He repeated the action again and again. Each pass made her private parts more sensitive than the last, even though he didn't come anywhere near them. If he didn't hurry and finish, she'd be moaning soon. Thank heaven she'd handled the top half of her leg or she might have had an orgasm.

Good Lord, pull yourself together.

"You have runner's legs."

"I never run. From anything."

He chuckled. "I don't doubt that. What I meant was your muscle tone's good. Better than some of the gym rats I see."

The compliment flustered her. "I'm on my feet all day."

He set the razor on the counter. "All done. Feel better?"

What she felt was frustrated. Sexually frustrated. It might have been years since she'd experienced sexual arousal, but that didn't mean she didn't recognize it. She hoped he didn't notice her response. Her mouth and lips were as dry as the desert. "Yes. Thank you, Ignatius."

His gaze paused at her breasts. Her nipples were as hard as the cabochons the girls had used earlier. His face flushed—probably not as much as hers—and his chest expanded with a deep breath. Then he stood, carefully placing her foot back on the cool metal footrest of her chair.

"I'm going to take a walk and see if that cat belongs to one of your neighbors. When I get back I'll start dinner."

Then he was gone.

She leaned back in her chair and exhaled. It was going to be a *long* six weeks. And she definitely could not get the hots for her jailer.

WEDNESDAY MORNING DAWNED bright and clear and perfect for painting, but Jessie didn't carry her sketch pad to the dock. Yesterday's conversation with her mother had left her antsy and itching to check items off her list before she ran out of time.

Satisfied with her decision to do something

productive with her days off, she sank onto her chair, sipped her coffee and soaked up the colors while debating her options. Today she even appreciated the contrast of the black birds on the white pier next door against the backdrop of a peach- and watermelon-colored sky.

Should she take diving lessons? Tour the Dry Tortugas National Park? Go deep-sea fishing? Not that she was much of a fisherman, but her father, brother and brother-in-law could live vicariously through her stories about going. The park had the most to offer. She could snorkel the coral reef, enjoy wildlife and see the old fort. It was less than seventy miles south of the Keys in the Gulf of Mexico. She could catch a tour boat out of Key West to get there. As soon as she finished her coffee, she'd drive south.

The drone of a boat motor in the distance caught her attention. The craft came closer, startling the cormorants. She recognized the driver instantly. Logan. Her pulse skipped like a stone across a pond's surface. She couldn't blame that or her jittery hands on the dark brew she'd consumed. Like her, Logan wore sunglasses and a hat and had bare legs beneath shorts. Today he wore a loose-fitting pale yellow long-sleeved button-up shirt—the kind the men in her family wore when spending a day on her brother's bass boat.

"Morning," he called out as he drifted closer.

She set down her mug, rose and reached for a line to help him secure the boat.

"I'm celebrating the IRS finally cutting my client loose by fishing at the trestle bridge today. The old Overseas Railway track has historic value. You should see it up close before you leave the Keys. Come with me, Jessie."

Considering how attracted she was to him and her promise not to let that go anywhere, she should refuse. But not today. Today, seeing something unique to the area with someone who knew it as well as a native made it worth the risk. The national park could wait.

"I'd love to. What can I bring? Should I pack sandwiches?"

"Put on a swimsuit and sunscreen and wear your hat. I already have drinks and snacks. There's a waterfront restaurant where we can dock and eat lunch outside."

She raced into the house, put on her suit, added a cover-up then reached for her contacts and paused. Logan knew her eyes were blue, and he might be willing to teach her to dive for lobsters, which she couldn't do wearing the contacts. She left them on the counter, slathered on sunscreen, donned her hat and shades and threw her wallet and a towel into her beach bag. Eager for her day of adventure, she practically skipped to the boat.

He offered his hand to help her board. His grip

was firm but gentle. A sizzle of sensation bubbled through her veins. She remembered Miri's warning but dismissed it. What she felt for Logan wasn't due to loneliness.

"Sit there."

She perched on the end of the bench he indicated. "Did you bring your cell phone?"

"Yes."

He dug into a duffel bag and extracted a plastic box. "Put it in here. It's waterproof."

He cast off the lines while she did as he'd instructed, then joined her but remained standing. When he throttled up the engine, the bow rose and the craft surged forward, tipping her against the seat. She grabbed the cushion seconds before their momentum carried him backward. The back of his thigh pressed her hand. Her skin burned even after he shifted away.

The engine noise made talking difficult and left her time to enjoy the sea breeze and sights. Logan said nothing until he pulled into a small marina and tied up. "I need to buy bait. If you want to fish, you'll need to come in and get a license."

Her automatic rejection of the idea died on her tongue. She'd been overly careful and even afraid to do anything because that's what she'd been told to do. But the likelihood of getting caught for fishing without a license seemed greater than someone in the bait shop recognizing her name months after the win. So why not?

She followed him inside. He headed toward the bait side of the shop. She pushed up her sunglasses and went straight to a register beneath a Fishing Licenses Sold Here sign. "I'd like to get a license, please."

The man flipped out a form. "Need your ID, miss. You want to add a lobster stamp to that? It's only five dollars more."

"Yes, I do," she added without hesitation.

By the time Logan came up behind her, she was tucking her new permits into her wallet. Proud that she was that much closer to ticking items off her list, she turned and smiled at him. His eyes widened and his lips parted. A slow smile curved his mouth. "Nice."

Confused, she blinked, then realized he was seeing her without the contacts for the first time. Pleasure filled her.

"Help you, sir?" The cashier's voice severed the moment.

Logan paid for his items and escorted her back to the boat. Again, he offered his hand to assist her in boarding, but this time he didn't release her. With his other hand, he lifted her sunglasses and studied her eyes. "You should never wear those brown contacts again. You have beautiful eyes."

Her heart thumped harder. She couldn't explain to him why she wore them. Not yet. Maybe never. "Thanks."

The moment stretched. Before she could do something stupid, like follow her urge to lean into him, she blurted, "I bought a lobster permit, too. Yesterday, I saw someone diving at the wreck you showed me. He caught one."

"If we have time this afternoon I'll take you to Jack's secret lobster honey hole."

"I'd like that." Logan released her and set them underway.

Anticipation and excitement skittered through her. As the wind tugged at her braid, she couldn't help feeling like she was living for the first time. Crazy, but she didn't know how else to describe the feeling. She only hoped her taste of freedom didn't turn bitter.

LOGAN KEPT THE hooks baited and the lines in the water. But he wasn't interested in catching anything for himself. Watching Jessie's excitement each time she fought a fish into the boat was like watching a kid on their first fishing excursion. He couldn't remember when he'd had this much fun.

The end of the rod bobbed hard and she squealed and popped off her seat.

"Reel it in."

The rod bent and her biceps and deltoids flexed. The woman had been doing more than carrying canvases to develop those. But what? He still knew next to nothing about her. The reel sang as the fish pulled. Her stomach, thigh and calf muscles strained, and not for the first time, he caught himself admiring her body and saying a silent thank-you that she'd shed her cover-up.

"I think this is a big one," she grunted as she battled, then she staggered forward a few steps. "Help!"

He jumped behind her, reached around her to grasp the rod and keep it and her from going overboard. The sun-warmed flesh of her back pressed into his chest, creating a weld strong enough to fuse them together. She bent forward as the fish pulled harder. The action tucked her bottom into his groin. Fire ignited at the point of contact. He gritted his teeth to hold back a groan and hoped she wouldn't guess what she was doing to him.

"Pull back," he grated into her ear. "Then reel as you lower the tip." His tip was currently aching to get out of his pants and into hers.

"I'm trying." She did as he'd taught her, lowering the rod then lifting again, slowly gaining ground but then losing it as the fish made a run. For the next fifteen minutes, he endured the pleasure/pain/torture of her rocking against him. He felt the quiver of her arms as she tired but continued fighting without any sign of giving up.

"This had better be something we can eat. And I'll bet it's bigger than your last one."

Her breathless but determined words made him laugh. His last catch was the day's record holder. Jessie's competitive nature had been a pleasant surprise. For the past three hours they—mostly, she—had been keeping score. Inches. Pounds. Keepers. Throwbacks. Their wager—the one who caught the biggest fish got a free dessert—had been her idea.

He dipped his head to fill his lungs with her strawberry and coconut scent and said into her ear, "Feels big. But you haven't landed it yet, so don't start salivating over your free dessert."

Eventually she fatigued her catch enough to get it close to the boat. It flipped its tail in a last-ditch effort to escape as it surfaced, and she peered over the side.

"What is it?"

"A cobia."

"Is it a keeper?"

"Absolutely, and good eating. Let me get the gaff." Using the long-handled hook, he brought the fish aboard.

"It's our biggest fish of the day. Right?"

Her excited gaze flicked to his, stopping him in his tracks. He couldn't get used to her bright eyes. Her excitement was contagious. He grinned.

"Congratulations, Jessie. You're going to get your banana split."

She fist-pumped and did a victory dance on the deck, and he didn't give a flip about losing. Seeing her have this much fun was worth whatever it cost him. "Want a picture with your winner?"

She stilled, hesitated. "Yes. Yes, I do. But I don't have a camera."

"I have my cell phone." He showed her how to hold the yard-long fish then wiped his hands on a towel and pulled out his phone to snap the picture. He took the fish and put it in the cooler then leaned over the side to rinse his hands. He didn't know what made him do it, but he jumped, squawked and scrambled his feet, acting as if he were falling overboard. Jessie screamed and grabbed the waistband of his trunks with one hand and banded her opposite arm around him.

That's when his teasing backfired.

The brush of her fingers against his belly and butt nearly made him fall over the gunwale for real. Battling for control, he straightened then turned.

"You scared me."

He felt like an ass when he saw the pallor of her face and genuine concern in her eyes. "I'm sorry. I was messing with you."

He reached out to brush a rivulet of sweat from her cheek. Then he did what he'd been wanting to do all afternoon. He threaded his fingers into her hair and pulled her forward.

Their mouths and torsos met like the crackle of oil in a hot skillet. Her lips parted without hesitation and her tongue sought his. He slicked his hands down her back, savoring the soft skin her bikini left bare and pulling her closer. Her arms encircled him and her fingers dug into his waist, kneading and releasing with such sensuality that his knees nearly buckled.

He wanted her ten times more today than he had that night in the parking lot. But a boat in sight of the pedestrian walkway of the old Bahia Honda Rail Bridge was not the place for what he had in mind. Slowly, reluctantly, he forced himself to release her inch by torturous inch. His labored breathing mirrored hers. Her heavy lids lifted and the hunger burning in her pale blue eyes made him want to say to hell with public indecency laws. But he stepped back, letting the ocean breeze cool the fire on his skin.

"Your—" he croaked then cleared his throat. "Your dessert awaits. Afterward we'll add a few bugs to the live well before we head in."

"Bugs?"

"That's what locals call spiny lobster."

He needed a cooling dunk in the water now. He hobbled as quickly as his erection would allow to pull in the anchor line.

Making love to Jessie was the only antidote to what ailed him. But would a few weeks of her be enough?

CHAPTER FIFTEEN

THE DAY COULDN'T have been more perfect, Jessie concluded from her waterside table at the restaurant. The shade of an umbrella blocked the sun's afternoon rays but didn't dispel the warmth suffusing her that had nothing to do with the weather.

Logan sat across from her, his white teeth gleaming against his tanned face between bites as he devoured his hot fudge sundae with the enthusiasm of a boy. People in various forms of dress from work clothes to bikinis ate at nearby tables.

"How did you find this place?" she asked.

"It's a locals' secret. Stick with me and I'll show you a few more." He winked.

Her stomach dropped like a boat anchor. She wasn't just attracted to Logan. She genuinely liked him. She even had a bit of a crush on him. Given the secrets between them and the temporary nature of her stay, she knew she shouldn't become intimate with him, but she suspected that intimacy was as inevitable as the coming sunset.

She wanted to kiss him again, to touch him, and have him touch her so that she could enjoy that rush of sensation. But she didn't think either of them would be happy stopping at kisses.

Nervousness decimated her appetite, making it impossible to finish her ice cream. "I've never seen most of the fish on the Widow's menu whole before today. And I didn't know restaurants would cook your catch for you. Our mangrove snapper was delicious."

"Back when Jack ran fishing charters, the Widow would clean and cook the catch for Jack's customers. Many of them were like you in that respect. They'd never eaten anything they'd just pulled from the water."

"What will we do with the rest of our fish? The cooler's almost full."

He pushed his empty dish aside. "When we get back to your place I'll fillet them. I can teach you how if you want. If not, I'll do it. That's what the table at the end of your dock is for. The scraps go in the crab pot to catch a future meal. Then I'll cook for us. We'll freeze what we won't eat within the next couple of days."

"You can cook?"

"Jack's not the only one who taught me invaluable skills." He twisted an imaginary mustache and waggled his eyebrows. This playful side of him melted her heart.

"Are you ready for part two of your adventure?" He rose and pulled out her chair.

She sprang to her feet. "Bring on Jack's honey

hole. I'm going to learn to catch bugs and check something else off my list."

"You have a list?"

"Yes, of things I want to do while I'm here." She recited the items as they walked back toward the boat.

"I can help you, but you'll need two days to do the Tortugas right. If you can wait until next week I'll go with you and, weather permitting, we can camp there Wednesday night."

Did that mean sharing a tent with him? "I've never been camping."

"One more thing for your list."

She smiled. "I like the way you think. I can wait, and I'd love your company."

And she meant it. She couldn't have chosen a better companion for the day. Logan knew the area, knew how to have fun and was an excellent, patient teacher. Not once had he made her feel stupid for not knowing how to do something. Not to mention he was sexy.

"Unless you brought a long-sleeved T-shirt, you need to apply more sunscreen before we dive," he said as they arrived at their boat.

"I...um...just brought this." She pointed at her cover-up.

"You can't snorkel in that. You've already had a lot of sun today, and I don't want you to burn. I'll do your back if you'll do mine." He held out his hand.

Knowing he'd soon be touching her gave her a better cardio workout than her coworkers' after-school spin class. She dug the tube from her bag and gave it to him. He squirted a blob into his palm then rubbed his hands together. "Take off your cover-up and turn around."

She did as instructed, then holding her braid out of the way, braced herself, but nothing could prepare her for the electrifying contact of his hands on her shoulders. Inch by inch, he massaged in the lotion, spreading heat and hunger through her. His hands descended from her shoulder blades to the hypersensitive skin above the side straps of her top, down her spine to her waist and then low on her hips above her bikini bottom. There was no way she could hide the goose bumps pebbling her skin.

She focused on one of the restaurant's brightly colored umbrellas and tried not to moan or hyperventilate. She had never been so aroused in her life, and having it happen in public was shocking. They weren't doing anything illicit, she told herself. So why did she feel so wicked?

And then he lifted his hands, leaving her both thankful and disappointed. Afraid he'd see how much he'd excited her, she struggled to find composure. But there was nothing she could do to hide her hard nipples, which the clingy knit of her top clearly revealed. When she finally turned he was wiping his hands on a towel, which he then tied low on his waist—but not before she noticed his tented trunks. She wasn't the only one affected. The knowledge only excited her more.

He offered her his bottle of sunscreen. Her hands shook as she accepted it and filled her palm with lotion. He presented his back, giving her an opportunity to drag air into her deflated lungs—air that whooshed out again the moment she touched his sun-warmed skin.

The eroticism of caressing his smooth, tanned flesh and feeling his muscles bunch and flex beneath her fingertips was beyond her experience. Mimicking him, she started at the top and worked her way down, relishing each indention along the way.

She'd never had a massage. She'd definitely never given one. But she now knew the appeal of both. Her breaths came quickly. Her mouth dried. And then she reached the waistband of his trunks and had no excuse to continue torturing herself. She'd hated having to take her hands off him to get more sunscreen and now she hated running out of back to rub even more.

He faced her, and she felt like an open book, as if he could see deep into her soul. She ached to remove his sunglasses to see if he was as strongly affected by her touch as she'd been by his, but she didn't. The tight line of his mouth and the rapid rise and fall of his chest were the only indicators she needed. His tiny little nipples were puckered and pebbled.

He nodded his thanks then busied himself casting off lines and getting them underway. By the time he cut the engine and drifted to a stop in the backwater thirty minutes later, she had herself under control. Mostly.

"We're beside another wreck. I'll throw out the anchor. Stay within three hundred feet of the boat after I raise the diver-down flag. Water's shallow. Depth of ten feet."

She looked over the side. The clarity of the water was unlike any of the bodies of water back home. Dozens of fish swam lazily around the hunks of broken, submerged boat. "It's beautiful."

"Wait until I take you to a coral reef. The colors of the fish there are like nothing you've ever seen. Photographs don't do them justice."

She liked that idea. "How did you ever leave here, Logan?"

When he didn't answer, she turned. He'd laid out an assortment of equipment. A frown pleated his brow. "Like you said, I thought I wanted something different."

He picked up a three-foot pole with a ninety-degree bent end. "This is a tickle stick. Gently tap your lobster's tail with this and he'll walk slowly forward. Then cover him with your net. I'll help you measure him, and if he's legal, we'll bag him. We wear gloves because our lobsters have spiny shells. Have you ever used a mask and snorkel?"

"Yes. Back home in the rock quarry."

"Good. Ready?"

"Are there any sharks?"

"Maybe. But they're not interested in you, I promise. If one comes close, just bump him with your tickle stick."

She believed him and trusted him. Excitement spread through her, making her as squirmy as her students the day before summer break. "Let's do it."

"Stay close to me and I'll show you how it's done, then you can catch your own. Look for their antennae in the grass or under the ledges."

They donned fins, masks, gloves and snorkels and slipped into the water carrying the sticks and nets. He touched her waist, and despite his gloves, she felt it deep in the pit of her stomach. He pointed down and she followed him underwater. The submerged hull was covered in plants and shells, but hints of the red stripes and blue underbody showed through. He swam to the edge of the wreck and pointed. It took her a few seconds to spot the antennae. Using the stick, he demonstrated what he'd explained and soon had the crustacean netted, measured and bagged. He gave her a thumbs-up and they surfaced. "Lobster dinner for you, ma'am."

She couldn't wait to try. "Let's go get some more!"

"Your turn."

She followed him down, swimming parallel to him. He touched her back. She almost sucked water through her snorkel. He pointed out another crustacean. She repeated what she'd seen him do. The lobster shot off. She surfaced for air, then tried again. The second lobster landed in her net. Breaking the water, she whooped with excitement. He high-fived her, then they dived again. After her third lobster, she grew brave enough to hunt solo—probably because she didn't see any sharks.

It seemed like only moments later he swam up beside her and pointed to the surface. She wasn't ready to go in. There were so many creatures in and around the wreck. She wished she had an underwater camera. Maybe on her next trip…

She wanted to come back, she realized. Back to the Keys. Back to the friends she'd made here who liked her without knowing about her money.

Back to Logan? Yes, definitely.

She swam beside him back to the boat and pulled out her snorkel. "That was fun."

He pushed up his mask and grinned. Her heart flip-flopped like a freshly landed fish. "You're a natural at this, Jessie. I'll dive with you any day."

The compliment buoyed her. "I hate to leave."

"We've reached our limit, and we need to head home and cook and clean our catch before it gets dark."

Only then did she notice the sun sitting low on the horizon and the fatigue of her muscles. They'd been in the water longer than she realized.

"Can't we clean them tomorrow?"

"Not game fish."

That meant it would be dark before they finished. Logan couldn't drive the boat in the dark. Could he?

But that shouldn't be a problem. She could take him home and pick him up in the morning.

Or she could let him stay. The prospect left her breathless.

"LOOKS LIKE YOU got yourself a cat," Ignatius said as he filled their plates with meat loaf, asparagus and small red potatoes. "The consensus is that it was dumped here the week before your fall."

"I don't need a cat." She wasn't a fan of meat loaf, but since she couldn't reach the stove to cook, she had to eat what was set in front of her.

"I'd take her, but I'm out of town too often. I'll ask Bethany if the girls can have her. If not... I hate to take her to the shelter. Too many cats there already."

She couldn't bear the thought of being responsible for it being destroyed. "If the girls can't keep her, I will."

"Good. You were great with Chloe and Sydney today, by the way. How did you learn to handle girls—or is it something you women are born knowing?"

She laughed. "Lord, no. It's trial and error— lots of error. I spent a lot of time with Sue's daughters, so I've had some experience. Keeping them busy keeps the peace."

"I'll remember that."

Miri stabbed the meat with her fork and shoved it into her mouth. A unique combination of flavors hit her tongue. She chewed, swallowed and ate a second bite, but she couldn't distinguish the seasoning. "What did you do to this?"

Face neutral, he paused with his fork shy of his mouth. "Why?"

"Because I like it, and I don't usually care for meat loaf."

A sly smile curled his lips. "My secret recipe. You'll never get it out of me. Though you're welcome to try any type of inducement you can think of."

Was he flirting with her? Her heart pitter-pattered like a young woman's. "You wish."

"Now that you mention it, yeah, I do. Give it your best shot."

The twinkle in his eyes caused her lungs to cease functioning. Her head spun. Moisture flooded her mouth. She gulped it down and searched for a safer subject. "How did you learn to cook?"

"Bachelors have two choices—eat fast food all the time or learn to cook. When I was laid up, there was nothing to watch but cooking shows. Figured I might as well learn something. That was before I decided to move south and make the switch to private investigator."

"What happened then?"

"I had to study my as—tail off, pass the tests, get the licenses and all that red tape."

"I didn't realize you had to be licensed."

"I ain't just a pretty face, Miriam Louise." He said it tongue in cheek. "The cooking shows are addictive. I still watch 'em sometimes."

A man after her own heart. She smiled against her will. "I watch them when I can't sleep."

She hated to ruin the truce between them but had to state her case. "I still want you to convince Logan to forget finding Elizabeth and Trent."

His smile fell. "Not much chance of that. He's convinced his life is in limbo until he finds them. What do you care anyway? It's not hurting you."

"He needs to date, to meet people, to live, like people his age are supposed to do. I want grand-nieces and nephews."

"Just because he's not living the way you want him to doesn't mean he's doing it wrong. Stop meddling, Miri."

"I'm not meddling," she protested and earned an are-you-kidding-me face.

"Moot point anyway. The trail's colder than a polar ice cap. I've never seen people disappear as cleanly as those two have. From what the previous investigators gleaned from Elizabeth's and Trent's computers, they'd spent months plotting and left a lot of red herrings. I've exhausted every lead."

She thought of the letter. "Finding Elizabeth and Trent could do more harm than good. It would reopen the case and put Logan's name back in the news. It was a horrible time. His friends abandoned him. Even his own father acted like he didn't know Logan. Not once did that jackass come to court to support his own son."

"Or finding them and bringing them back could clear him."

He stated it so matter-of-factly. "You said he'd never regain public trust."

"Even with a full confession, there would always be a cloud of suspicion. In my opinion, Logan needs this more for personal satisfaction than public forgiveness. He's happy with his job here. I don't think he'll leave it—even if he hasn't admitted that to himself yet."

"You think he's happy here? And that he won't go back to Charleston?"

"Yes, I do. He enjoys being on the water. He has my boat out today, in fact. You can take the boy out of the Keys, but you can't take the Keys out of the boy."

If Ignatius was right, then the letter from Logan's ex-wife might help. *Or* it could cause him tremendous harm. Why hadn't she destroyed it? If she had, she wouldn't be so torn about giving it to Ignatius.

She'd accused Logan of meddling in her life and smothering her. Was she any less guilty of trying to manipulate his life? No. She pushed away from the table.

"Aren't you going to finish your dinner?"

"In a minute. Maybe." She wheeled into her bedroom, reached under her mattress and dragged out the letters. When she turned around, Ignatius stood in her doorway.

"You okay, Miri? You got mighty pale."

His concern was touching. And she didn't deserve it. "I've been impeding the investigation."

She held out an envelope. He came forward and took it from her and scanned the front. "This is addressed to you."

"There are two letters. The first is to me from Elizabeth. She sent it six months ago and asked me to forward the enclosed second letter to Logan. He'd sold their old house and she didn't know how else to reach him.

"I opened his letter and read it, then decided not to give it to him because I didn't want that selfish bitch to hurt him again. I want him to quit living in the past and forget Elizabeth and the heartache she caused. But maybe I'm the one who's being selfish."

"May I?" he asked. She nodded and he opened the envelope, unfolded then scanned the first set of pages. When he was done, he opened and read the second. Then he whistled, refolded both exactly as he'd found them.

"An apology and a full confession. She wants to come home and wants him back. No wonder you kept it. You're sure this is her handwriting?"

"Yes. She used to address all their Christmas cards. I saved them because they were all we ever got of Logan after he hooked up with her. Will I be in trouble for interfering with mail delivery and concealing evidence? Will I get arrested?"

"Don't worry about that. What do you want to do with these?"

"You mean you're not going to rush to give them to Logan?"

"Your letters. Your decision. I can pretend I never saw them."

"You'd do that?"

"For you, yes. Do I think it's the right thing to do? No."

What *did* she want to do? If there was any chance of Logan finding the happiness she'd found with Jack, she wanted that for him. A girl like Jessie was exactly what he needed.

"I'll pay you to find her. I want this over with

once and for all. You're right. Logan will never completely be free of the past until he confronts it."

"Good choice. But you don't have to pay me. This one's on me. I'm good at what I do, and it's bugged me that I couldn't crack this one. But if you don't mind, let's keep this between us until I have answers. Postmark is six months old. She's likely moved on. No need to get Logan's hopes up."

She searched his face and realized he was on her side. They both wanted what was best for Logan. And that mattered. A lot.

EARLIER, LOGAN HAD been certain how this day would end. Now he wasn't. His arousal and anticipation had turned to confusion.

At Jessie's request he'd taught her how to fillet their catch. Then she'd invited him into the house to shower. He'd been disappointed when she showed him to the guest room and left him, but he'd handled it without complaint. He accepted that women had rituals of preparation he'd never understand. After cleaning up, he'd put on the spare clothes he'd packed in a duffel bag and stowed on I's boat and rejoined her in the kitchen.

Her agitation had been palpable. He'd parked her on a bar stool to watch while he prepared the lobster, hush puppies and lemony asparagus. The meal had lacked this afternoon's easy camaraderie, then after dinner she got to her feet and hadn't quit flitting around the kitchen since.

While he'd been relishing the prospect of learning every inch of her front the way he had her back while applying sunscreen this afternoon, she'd loaded the dishwasher, wiped counters so hard she'd nearly rubbed a hole in the marble and checked and rechecked the clock. It currently read 9:00 p.m.

Even with running lights and spotlights, he'd prefer not to try to maneuver the boat down I's tricky canal at this time of night. It was doable, but with so little moon, risky.

He stepped into Jessie's path, blocking her forward momentum. But he resisted the temptation to touch her soft, fragrant skin. It wasn't easy.

She wet her lips and met his gaze. The pulse at the base of her neck fluttered wildly. "Should I drive you home or...?"

Back in Charleston, he'd excelled at reading clients, anticipating their needs before they voiced them. He wasn't having that kind of success interpreting Jessie's mixed signals. "That's your call."

She blinked. "I—I—"

Did she want him to stay? Or go? He'd have to lay his cards on the table. "Jessie, there's nothing I want more than to pick up where we left off this afternoon and not stop till we are both satisfied and too weak to move."

Her breath hitched, and her pupils expanded.

Damn, her eyes were beautiful. He couldn't imagine why she'd want to change the pale silvery blue to brown.

And then because he couldn't help himself, he lifted a hand and brushed back her still-damp hair. She shivered. Encouraged, he dragged a fingertip down her cheek, her neck, her arm, then he laced his fingers through hers and squeezed.

"I want more days like today, and if rushing you is going to mess that up, then I'll wait till you're ready. But make no mistake about it. We will make love, Jessie. The only question is when."

Her hand trembled in his. Emotions chased across her face too fast for him to interpret. She inhaled then exhaled, taking so long to respond that his hunger turned to frustrated, reluctant acceptance. "I'll sleep in the guest room and be out of your hair at first light."

"No!" Her eyes rounded and her fingers tightened on his. She looked as surprised by her protest as he was. "Logan... I w-want you to s-stay... with me."

Elation flooded him despite the uncertainty in her voice. If she was nervous, he'd put her at ease. He gently cupped her waist and tugged her closer. Her breasts brushed his chest like live wires. He whistled through clenched teeth then dotted a kiss on her forehead. He added a second one to the tip of her nose. "Are you sure?"

She quivered then gulped and nodded.

But still, he sensed reservations. His next kiss flirted with the left corner of her mouth. He relished the faster tempo of her breathing and the way she leaned into him. "Be very sure, Jessie."

He slanted his head to sip from the opposite side of her exquisite mouth, but before he could make contact, she shot to her toes and awkwardly bumped her lips and nose against his. Hallelujah. That response he understood.

"Oh, I'm sorry. I—"

He wrapped his arms around her, capturing her apology with his mouth and crushing her breasts to his chest. She felt good in his arms, and he'd been aching for this all day. Her words turned into an *mmm* that he silenced by parting her lips to tangle with her tongue.

Her hands gripped his hips and then her short nails skimmed up his spine to loop around his neck, eliciting a groan from him. Because he ached to go fast, he forced himself to go slow, to concentrate on her pleasure more than his.

He slid his palms upward, stopping just below her breasts to buff his thumbs back and forth beneath the soft swells. He hadn't thought the thin straps of her sundress allowed for a bra—he'd been right. Just a single thin layer of flowered fabric between him and her. She shuddered and leaned back, inviting his touch.

He skimmed the pads of his thumbs over the

curves, locating and caressing the tips. She broke the seal of their lips to gasp.

"Feel good?" he asked even though her stiff nipples, flushed cheeks and panted breaths gave him his answer.

"Yes."

"I want to taste them."

Her lids fluttered upward, and the passion in her eyes and the sight of her wet, swollen, parted lips nearly snapped his control. If he blew this in an adolescent rush, there'd be no follow-up. And he wanted follow-ups. A lot of them.

"Let me, Jessie."

Her chin dipped in agreement.

He caught her hand and led her to the guest room where he'd showered—and where he'd left his bag and the protection he'd had the good sense to pack. She paused in the doorway, looking around as if she'd never come in here. Then she let him tow her to the bedside.

He yanked back the covers, turned and spotted white teeth pinching her tender flesh. He rescued her bottom lip with his finger, then soothed it with his tongue before her second thoughts could derail them. It took three seconds for her to relax into him. He savored her mouth, her tongue, then her jaw, her earlobe and the soft skin behind it. Her quiet whimper set him ablaze. She threaded her fingers through his hair, holding him close and tilting her head to give him better access.

He bunched her sundress in his fists and swept it over her head in a quick motion. She stood frozen in front of him, wearing only tiny pink panties. Her hands hovered self-consciously at her waist as if she didn't know what to do with them. Her breasts were round, the perfect size to fill his palms, and crowned with puckered dusky peach tips. His mouth watered. He captured her wrists and pulled her hands out of the away.

"You're beautiful, Jessie."

Something flickered across her face, but he was too far gone to decipher it. He bent to outline one perfect circle with his tongue. Her head fell back, arching her spine and lifting her breasts to his mouth. He took her inside, licking and suckling until she whimpered again. Then he lifted her and laid her in the center of the white sheets and followed her down. He kissed her mouth again then sampled the neglected nipple, sipping then grazing it gently with his teeth.

Her heels dug into the bed and her back arched. He smiled against her. She'd liked that. He repeated the process, dividing his attention between the perfect pair. All the while he traced the length of one leg then the other, drawing closer to her panties with each agonizingly slow pass. He wanted her as near to the edge as he was.

He traced the elastic leg opening, first the right, then the left. She squirmed, lifting to his hand, asking without words for him to touch her center. Instead, he traced the band around the top, dipping slightly behind it and finding curls. He swirled his finger in them and her muscles clenched. He had to know her natural hair color.

He hooked a finger over the edge and tugged them down to expose golden-blond whorls. Why color her hair and wear contacts, his subconscious nagged. But he was too aroused to pursue the thought. He pitched her panties onto the floor and leaned closer to inhale her scent.

She stilled. He stroked her. Finding her folds slick and ready made him impatient to be inside her. But he forced himself to wait and allow her time to get used to the intimate caress of his fingers before he took what he wanted. When she relaxed her legs, letting them fall open, he tasted her. Her body jerked and a gasp rent the silence of the bedroom. He didn't give her the chance to roll away, but gently held her while he licked until she trembled. Her fingers tangled in his hair. Moments later an orgasm shuddered through her. At her cry, pressure built in his groin until he thought he'd lose it solo. He slowed his strokes, giving her a moment to regroup before increasing his tempo and sending her over the edge again.

He worked his way up her body, leaving a trail of damp kisses across her belly, her breasts and her neck before brushing his mouth over hers. He looked into her passion-glazed eyes. "Don't go anywhere."

Then he swung around, shed his clothes and retrieved a condom. Seconds later, he returned to her. She lifted her arms and welcomed him. He sank into her damp curls, into the hot, slick sleeve of her body, and pleasure so intense he thought the top of his head would explode overcame him. He withdrew, plunged again and again. Her nails lightly scored his back as she pulled him closer—to her body and to climax.

He groaned and shook, fighting to make it last. But when she nipped his earlobe, he lost it and went off like a Roman candle. Too soon. Too intense. His release seemed to last forever. And then he was done. Empty. Drained.

He eased down beside Jessie and tried to fill his burning lungs. When he regained control of his spent muscles, he rolled to face her. She lay beside him, eyes closed and a blissful smile on her face. He wanted to believe his over-the-top response to her was due solely to his long abstinence. But he knew better. The craving for her company, the urgent need for her smiles was more than horniness, otherwise any of the happy hour women would have sufficed.

He'd fallen for Jessie. The realization slammed his heart against his chest. Given his history, how could he have let himself fall for a woman he knew next to nothing about? He didn't even know her last name.

A relationship with her would be one based on

trust, not facts. And trusting was hard for him. Could he accept that her past might be too painful for her to ever feel comfortable discussing? But even if she didn't share hers, he'd have to tell her about his, about Trent and Elizabeth, their embezzlement, the dismissed charges against him and that he'd almost gone to prison. He'd have to risk rejection. The idea filled his gut with dread.

He wouldn't tell her yet. First, he would show Jessie how good they were together. Then maybe she wouldn't turn away.

CHAPTER SIXTEEN

JESSIE FEIGNED SLEEP until she heard Logan's breathing deepen. Only then did she turn her head and study the man beside her.

His hair was a spiky mess. Her fault. Her face warmed. She'd never grabbed Aaron by the head like that, nor had she ever experienced so much pleasure with him that she'd lost control and been noisy while making love. Sex with her former fiancé had been pleasant, but silent.

The intimate act with Logan was the intense event about which novels were written. The sounds that had gurgled from her throat and the cries that escaped from her lips had been uncontrollable.

Could this be love? They'd known each other less than a month, and the better portion of that had been filled with animosity. Yet she already knew that a few more weeks with him would not be enough. She and Aaron had dated almost a year before she'd deemed her slow-growing fondness love. She now wondered if it had just become habit.

What she felt for Logan was explosive and exciting and yet fun and comfortable, too. Today had been one of the best days of her life—if not *the* best. She admired his protectiveness of Miri, his loyalty to his clients and his patience with her. She genuinely liked Logan, as well as desired him.

Would her family like him, too?

Tension erased satisfaction. How could she tell her family about Logan when that meant revealing the double life she'd been living? She'd been lying to everyone—Logan included. And all of them had the right to be angry with her.

Would Logan forgive her for lying? Would he understand her reasons? Having money was a good thing. It wasn't like she'd lied about a criminal past.

As her granny used to say, she'd dug herself a hole that was going to be difficult to climb out of.

The only way for her to even have a chance at a happy ending with Logan was to come clean. Tomorrow, she'd tell her family everything. Then she'd tell Logan. Once everyone was on the same truthful page, she'd take him home to meet her parents, and she'd pray they loved him as much as she did.

JESSIE FLOATED BACK up the dock after seeing Logan off Thursday morning. Waking up beside him, then making love with him and showering together had put a spring in her step. Then his hot kiss and his promise to come back tonight after work had put a smile on her face that felt brighter than the sun rising behind the house.

Determined to get the call to her mother out of the way, she went in search of her beach bag. She'd set it down somewhere last night, but she'd been so nervous after cleaning the fish that she couldn't remember where she'd dumped it. She'd wanted Logan to stay last night, but she'd been raised with old southern manners. Girls didn't call boys on the phone, let alone ask them to spend the night. It seemed so...forward.

She'd hoped Logan would take the decision out of her hands, but he hadn't. He'd made her say it. And it hadn't killed her. In fact, speaking her mind made her feel a little braver, more confident she could handle the call home she had to make.

She found her oversize tote in the laundry room. She hadn't put it here. Logan must have. She pulled out the dirty beach towels and pitched them in the washer. Next came her hat and sunscreen. She shivered at the memory of Logan slicking lotion across her back. Then finally, at the bottom of the bag, she located the waterproof box Logan had loaned her to put her phone in.

She fumbled the tightly sealed case open and retrieved her phone. Four missed calls. Two voice mails. She'd never heard it ring. Her stomach plunged to her toes. Had something happened to her father or mother?

All the calls and messages were from Brandon. She played the first one. "Jessie, where are you? Pick up… Call me." The second: "Damn it, Jessie, I told you not to pull this crap. Answer your phone. Call me before I get on a plane."

She gulped and hit Call Back.

"Where in the hell have you been?" he shouted without a greeting.

She took a deep breath. "I was out on a boat all day with a friend yesterday. I had my phone in a waterproof—and apparently soundproof—case. I'm sorry I didn't hear it ring."

"I called four times. You should have checked your messages when you got home."

When she'd gotten home she'd been otherwise occupied. "Yes. I know."

"Is she okay?" she heard her mother ask in the background. Brandon must be at her parents' house.

"She is until I get my hands on her," Brandon groused. "What kind of friend? You're supposed to be lying low."

"I was. But I got tired of solitary confinement and I…" This wasn't going to be easy or good. "And I was running low on cash. So I…took a job."

Anticipating his reaction, she held the phone away from her ear, but his, "You what?" blasted through loud and clear.

"I dyed my hair and bought colored contacts.

I told you that even you wouldn't recognize me. And I took a job waiting tables. I work for tips only. No paper trail."

"Of all the stupid—"

"Don't call your sister stupid," her mother chimed in.

He took an audible breath. "Jessamine, that was foolish and risky. Who is this friend?"

"You told me not to use a cash machine and you hustled me out of town so fast that I didn't give you power of attorney so you could access my accounts. I needed money, Brandon, for food. For gas. For toilet paper. Everything is more expensive down here."

"You should have said something."

"What if I had? Can you afford to send me money?" She didn't give him time to argue. She had to take control of her life. And this was the moment to do it. "My friend's name is Logan Nash. He does taxes in Key West. I work for his aunt, Miri Evans, at the Fisherman's Widow. They're good people, Brandon. I wouldn't have taken the job if they weren't."

"What do you know about him?"

Typical Brandon. He'd gone into investigator mode. "I know he was raised here and had a business in Charleston for a while. And I know..." She took a deep breath. This was a biggie. "I know that I'm in love with him."

The words felt right in her mouth and in her heart, and she felt empowered just by saying them.

Her brother cursed, fluently. And her mother scolded him for his language.

"Jessamine, you're lonely and too damned trusting. You have a lot at stake right now. Have you told him about the money?"

She winced. "No. Not yet."

"For your own safety, don't, and don't do anything stupid like marry the man until I've had a chance to check him out."

"Oh, for pity's sake, Brandon, that's not necessary. Please stop playing cop for one minute and trust me."

"Like we were supposed to trust your judgment about Aaron?"

She shrank in shame. "I know you're all used to making decisions for me, but you can't baby me forever. I'm twenty-six years old. It's time I started making decisions for myself. I love you all. But I have to go."

Then, for the second time, she hung up on a family member.

It was liberating. But also terrifying.

She'd told her family. That left the most important person. Logan.

"You said to dress nicely," Jessie said Thursday afternoon as Logan helped her into his car. "I guess that means we're not going fishing?"

He flashed a knee-weakening smile. "No. And I like the sundress. You have great legs."

The compliment warmed her. "Thank you. Are we going to one of your locals' hangouts?"

"No. I'm taking you to meet one of my clients."

"Why?" she asked when he slid into the driver's seat.

"He'll explain when we get there."

He turned north on the Overseas Highway. They rode in silence, but not the usual comfortable one they shared on the boat. Guilt and worry gnawed at her. She needed to tell Logan the truth. And she'd planned to do so as soon as she saw him tonight. But doubts had encroached after her call home.

What if she saw that greedy light enter in his eyes when he heard she had a substantial income guaranteed for the next fify years? She'd seen it in Aaron's, and then in her friends' right before they'd started listing all the ways she could spend her windfall—on them.

She wanted to believe Logan wasn't like that. But what if she was wrong? Maybe if they'd known each other longer, she wouldn't have these doubts. Maybe time was all they needed before she could be sure. She chewed her bottom lip.

He reached out and touched her tender flesh. "Don't do that. You'll like these people."

She hoped he was right. At mile marker twenty-five he exited onto Summerland Key and drove toward the ocean. He passed rows of expensive houses before turning into the driveway of a mansion. He pushed the button at the gate box. Then the iron gates swung silently open.

The house, shaped like a big comma, was large enough to be a small hotel. Beyond it the ocean looked like a swath of undulating teal silk.

"Your client lives here? It's huge! It must have cost millions."

He nodded. "Twenty-six million."

Her mouth dried. Words vanished. She'd never met anyone with that kind of money. Although she could have been someone with that kind of money if she'd taken the lump sum instead of the annuity.

A man she guessed to be in his late fifties with silver hair and wearing expensive clothing greeted them. "So glad you could make it, Jessie. I've heard great things about you. I'm Reed. The wife and I are sitting out by the pool enjoying a cocktail. Join us."

Numbly she followed her host down a flagstone walkway as wide as the halls of her school and the length of a football field. The pool, when it came into view, was larger than any public pool she'd ever seen. It had a waterfall at one end and a spa at the other. In the center a huge leaping copper fish spouted an arch of water. There was so much to see she couldn't take it all in.

Logan kept company with millionaires? She

never would have guessed. His clothes, though from an expensive label that she couldn't have afforded on a teacher's salary, were not new. And his car, while clean and well maintained, was not new, either, or a pricy model.

The woman, also fiftyish, was so beautiful she could have been a model, and her clothing looked like something right off the fashion runway. Her swept-back dark hair revealed not one wrinkle on her face. Even her teeth were perfect. She swept out a graceful, jeweled hand. "I'm Ana. Please, sit. Let me pour you a glass of wine."

Feeling very out of her element, Jessie accepted the wine and perched on the thickly cushioned settee indicated. Was the furniture teak? It looked like something off the yachts she used to watch at the marina. Logan sat beside her, his thigh nudging hers.

"Reed and I are frequent visitors to the Fisherman's Widow. We've seen and admired your work."

These people who could afford anything liked her work? "Thank you."

"Have you ever done a mural?" Reed asked.

"Yes. I painted halls at m—" She glanced at Logan and found his gaze pinned on her. Cowardly, she turned her attention back to her hosts. "I've painted several murals at the elementary school near where I used to live."

"You're very talented," Ana said. "Would you consider doing one for us?"

"A mural? W-where?"

"Our daughter and our grandchildren are moving in with us. The girls are three and five. We'd love to fill their suite with the birds and animals of the Keys. I particularly loved your Key deer, but it sold before I could purchase it."

They wanted her to paint a mural in a twenty-six-million-dollar mansion? At a loss for words, Jessie sipped her wine and tried to make sense of the request. Murals took weeks, sometimes months, depending on their complexity. Agreeing would mean not returning home in January. It would mean more time in Key West. More time with Logan.

"Could I see the room?"

Ana rose with the grace of a ballerina. "Certainly. This way. We will leave the men to talk about fishing or sports or whatever."

The house was unbelievable—like something you'd see in a documentary about Hollywood movie stars. She knew she was acting like a tourist with her head swiveling in every direction as she took it all in, but she couldn't help it.

They climbed a marble staircase and traversed a long hall. Finally, Ana threw back double doors. She flipped a graceful hand to the right. "The girls will sleep in this room. And this will be their playroom. I'd like you to start here. If time permits, I'd like for you to decorate their bedroom, as well."

Two rooms. In a mansion. She couldn't get over it. She'd begun to believe she had some talent when her pieces sold at the restaurant. Yet she'd considered that mostly tourist trade. But this…

Her hostess looked at her expectantly. Jessie nodded. "If you'll give me an idea what you'd like, I can sketch something for your approval."

"Excellent. I look forward to working with you, Jessie. Let's go tell the men." They rejoined the others as if nothing out of the ordinary had just occurred.

But so many things had. The incredible job opportunity made her feel like a real artist—not just one who produced tourist fodder. And it also meant she had to quit stalling and tell Logan her whole story. Because if she'd guessed wrong about his lack of interest in her annuity, then there was no way she could stay in the Keys to take this job of a lifetime.

LOGAN PARKED BENEATH Jessie's house and helped her from the car. He had it all planned. Tonight was about showing her how much he loved her, then tomorrow he'd tell her about Charleston, Elizabeth and Trent. If she accepted his past, they'd move forward. If she couldn't— His chest tightened. Not an option he wanted to consider.

"We need to celebrate."

The excitement in her smile encouraged him. "How…how did that just happen, Logan?"

He opened the trunk and withdrew the cooler containing the fruits of his careful planning.

"Reed is the client I had to meet this morning. I was talking about your work, and when he realized you were the same artist he and Ana had been admiring at the Widow, he asked me if you'd be willing to do a mural for them. We arranged the meeting. The rest you know."

"You told a client about me?"

He felt the burn crawling from his chest to his hairline. Talked about her? No. He'd yammered like a love-struck fool. He had it bad. "Jessie, I'm proud of your work—even if I can't take any credit for it."

She wound her arms around his waist, rose on tiptoe and kissed him. The soft press of her mouth combined with the brush of her breasts as she slowly sank back to her heels sent need pulsing through him and almost derailed his plan.

"But you can take credit, Logan. Without your encouragement I'd never have displayed or sold any of my paintings, let alone agreed to consider a mural."

"Yes, you would've. You're that good." He grabbed her hand. "Let's enjoy the sunset."

He led her to the double-size lounger between the pool and the cabana. Ever since he'd seen this place he'd wanted to have his way with Jessie out here where the evening breeze could dry the sweat from their skin. He angled the lounge toward the west and the sun sinking behind the trees of No Name Key, then double-checked to make sure they were screened from the road by the tiki hut. "Have a seat."

He lit each of the citronella torches, and the pungent aroma filled the air. Then he returned to the cabana, hit a switch and soft music from the outdoor speakers filled the air. Next, he turned on the pool lights and then the spa. The water bubbled to life with a low rumble.

He opened the cooler and extracted his goodies. First, the bottle of champagne, then the flutes. They clinked when he set them on the small table. A slow, sexy smile curved her lips. She bent one knee and the skirt of her dress fell to the top of her thighs, revealing a sliver of red panties. He popped the cork—literally and almost figuratively—before collecting himself and filling both glasses.

He had never wanted a woman the way he wanted Jessie. Thoughts of her intruded into his work. That was a first. Not even Elizabeth had come between him and crunching numbers.

He blocked off the past. He'd deal with that in the morning. He wasn't going to let his ex spoil tonight. Then he pressed a glass into Jessie's hand.

"To your success. May it be the first of many." He clinked his rim against hers. She sipped, her eyes overflowing with emotion that he hoped matched how he felt.

After drinking, he stared into the liquid, trying to find the words to say what he needed to say, and hoping she understood what a big step this was for him. Then he lifted his gaze to hers. "If you do the mural, you'll need to be in Florida beyond your lease on this place. I want you to move in with me, Jessie."

Her lips parted. Her chest rose on a deep breath.

Before she could respond, he rushed to present his case. "My house isn't much. It's certainly nothing like this. But it is on the water with a great view of the sunset. I have a screened porch that I can enclose and turn into a studio for you. I'll leave you alone to paint during the day. Then we can be together every night."

His pulse kicked in anticipation of those nights, but his gut clenched with worry that she'd reject him—especially after she heard about Charleston.

She set her glass on the concrete beside her chair, then rose to her knees and took his face in her hands. She kissed him again, but this time was different. Her lips clung, and when she lifted her head, love shone in her eyes like a lighthouse beacon.

"I love you, Logan. And I would love to move in with you."

His heart pounded. Love. She'd said the word.

He wanted to say it back. But he didn't. His pride had been ground in the dust once before—he wouldn't lay it out there for another tromping. If Jessie changed her mind about her feelings in the morning, then at least he'd have the satisfaction of knowing he hadn't bared his soul.

SHE'D SAID IT and it felt good. Dredging up the courage to take the initiative, Jessie took Logan's glass and put it on the table.

Then she leaned in and kissed him again. She savored his mouth, the taste and texture of his jaw, now studded with five o'clock shadow. The silkiness of his hair tickled between her fingers.

His hands clasped the backs of her thighs and stroked upward, stopping just below her panties, then he delved beneath the elastic and cupped her bottom. The heat of his hands spread through her. He held her close while he tickled her neck with his tongue then kissed his way down the strap of her sundress.

"Take it off," he murmured against her sternum.

She reached up and untied the halter straps. They fell, snagging on her erect nipples. He nudged the fabric aside with his nose and night air caressed her flesh a moment before his breath warmed her, then his tongue circled her. He suckled and swirled and grazed. She shuddered as he pulled a response from deep inside her.

His caresses made her hungry and bold. She dragged her fingers from his hair and unbuttoned his shirt, then pushed it aside and bent to torture him the way he had her. He groaned, and the sound rumbled through her.

She worked her way down his chest to his belly then flicked open the button of his pants to reveal his navel. Remembering how it had felt when he'd done it to her this morning, she swirled her tongue around his navel. His stomach muscles contracted and his erection pressed against his zipper. She eased down the teeth and pulled his boxers aside, then she tasted him.

His breath hissed. His back bowed. She circled and teased him until he growled her name. Then he flipped her onto her back, lifted her skirt and tossed aside her panties. Seconds later he was sheathed and inside her, riding her to a release more powerful than any she'd ever experienced. His own quickly followed.

She stroked his back and stared at the stars, trying to catch her breath. She loved this man. And she prayed he loved her. He hadn't said it, but he'd shown her in so many ways. If he loved her, they could get through anything—even the lottery headaches.

He chuckled, his chest rumbling against hers. "I wanted to have my way with you, but I thought we'd at least get undressed first."

She smiled and nipped his earlobe.

The sound of car doors slamming cut through the music. He stiffened above. "That sounded close."

Too close. She scrambled out from under him, grabbing the straps and retying her dress then batting down her skirt. He zipped his pants.

She heard the crunch of approaching footsteps. Her heart rose in her throat. Who knew the gate code? Who could have gotten into her compound? Her brother's warning raced through her head. Before she could figure out if they needed to run for the house, Brandon, followed by her father and mother, came around the corner of the tiki hut.

Shock rocked her. Why were they here? Then embarrassment filled her. She was sure what she'd just been partaking in was written all over her face. "What are you doing here?"

"Is this him?" Brandon barked. "Is this the embezzler?"

Confused and embarrassed, she glanced at Logan then back to her brother. "I— No—this is Logan. What are you talking about?"

"He hasn't told you he was a hot-shot financial adviser whose Charleston firm stole funds from clients and wiped out dozens of peoples' retirement accounts?"

A chill raced through her. No. *No!* She turned to Logan. He looked pale under the tiki lights. "Logan, tell Brandon he has the wrong man."

Logan's jaw locked. A muscle in his upper lip twitched. His fists clenched at his sides.

"You are Logan Chancellor Nash. I recognize your picture," Brandon continued in his most intimidating tone.

That was Logan's full name. She'd heard Miri use it. Dread coiled like a copperhead in her belly. "Tell him, Logan. Tell him he's wrong."

"He's not."

She couldn't breathe. Her head spun. "But… but you're an accountant."

"He is now," Brandon said. "Because no one will trust him with their investments."

"The charges were dismissed," Logan stated flatly.

"For lack of evidence. Not lack of guilt. Has he told you about his fugitive wife and business partner? How about the missing millions? Did they cut you out of the deal, bud? Screw you while they were screwing each other? That's what the newspapers claim. Is that how it happened?"

Logan had told her about his ex-wife and ex–business partner's affair and how they'd run away together. Jessie felt sick to her stomach. Had he been using her sympathy to connive her? She didn't want to believe that.

"And now you're trying to swindle my sister out of her winnings. Did you recognize her from the lottery announcements despite this—" he gestured to her hair "—thin disguise? Was an elementary-school teacher easy picking to a professional thief like you?"

"That's not how it was." She denied to herself as much as to her family then covered her mouth to hold back a sob. Had she done it again? Fallen for and been completely fooled by someone?

Brandon turned his sneer on her. "Are you trying to tell me there's no way he found out that you're East Coast's biggest lottery winner? That none of the press that's been hounding you and drove you into hiding could have found you or tipped him off? He just happened to single out a waitress with a bad dye job and sweep her off her feet?"

His private investigator knew who she was and why she was here. Had Ignatius told Logan?

Tears of heartbreak and humiliation burned her cheeks. She didn't want to believe Brandon. But he was family. He'd always been there for her and protected her the way big brothers did.

She faced Logan. "Tell me it's not true, Logan. Please, tell me it's not true."

The deadness in his eyes as he met her gaze crushed her. "You've already made up your mind."

Then he strode past her family. She heard his car door slam, then the engine fire and pull away.

Her knees buckled. She landed on the lounger—the same lounger where she'd made love to a man who'd lied to her as much as she'd lied to him.

Only he'd been hiding a criminal past and his intentions to hurt her.

Or had he?

CHAPTER SEVENTEEN

THE DOUBTS IN Jessie's eyes ate at Logan all the way home. And they brought the past flooding back. Friends and even his own father had refused to vouch for him or come to court to support him. Only Miri and Jack had been there for him through the long, humiliating trial. It had cost them time and money—he could never repay them.

Then he processed the rest of her brother's story. The East Coast's biggest lottery winner? Jessie must have millions. She'd told him she needed the money from her tips and painting sales. She'd even held on to the measly five hundred in case the buyers wanted it back. What a load of crap. And he'd fallen for her fake vulnerability.

Ha. No wonder I had told Logan not to worry about Jessie taking from the till.

He felt like a gullible fool. He'd believed she was hiding from a bad relationship and had worried about the asshole coming after her. Instead she was hiding from the press, and if the media found her, they'd find him. Worse, if they found him involved with a lottery winner, he'd be crucified. Again. It wouldn't matter that he hadn't known about her money. Just like her brother, the rest of the world would think him a crook. He couldn't face the press until he could clear his name.

He loved her. Or thought he did. But he couldn't be with someone who didn't trust him and who would always wonder about his motives for being with her.

He'd learn to live without her. The same way he'd learned to live without Elizabeth.

"WHERE IN THE hell are you going?" Brandon asked Friday morning when she entered the den wearing her uniform.

Jessie was tired and cranky. She hadn't slept all night. She kept replaying Brandon's ugly accusations and weighing them against her days with Logan. They didn't add up. Why would he help her land a dream job with his friends if all he wanted to do was rip her off? And what about Miri? She was such a giver. Jessie couldn't believe she'd love and forgive someone who stole from others. And why would Logan have a private investigator working for him if *he* was the guilty one? Ignatius had been on the scene long before Jessie came around.

Then she kept recalling the look on Logan's face when her brother mentioned her lottery win.

She'd seen shock. Not greed. Not excitement. Not even a twinkle of anticipation over spending a chunk of cash.

But he'd admitted he had been on trial for embezzlement. Should she trust her own instincts or her brother's? He was, after all, a professional interrogator. And she had a lousy track record. But he didn't know Logan.

Did she? Did she really know him or only what he'd wanted her to see?

"Jessamine," Brandon snapped.

The name rankled. "It's Jessie. And I'm going to work."

"You don't need a job."

She opened her mouth to object then shook her head. Why waste her breath? Brandon wouldn't listen. "Miri needs me."

"Jessamine," her mother crooned. "I know you're hurting. Come home with us. We want you to be safe."

"I was never in any danger, Mom, and I'm still not. You're the one who taught me to always honor my word. I made a promise to help a friend, and I'm going to keep it." She held up a hand when she saw the protests forming from all three of her guests. "I know I usually do everything you tell me to do, but I'm not going to give on this. So don't waste your breath. Y'all can go home or stay and enjoy a few days here. That's up to you."

Walking out on her family was one of the hardest things she'd ever done. She worried all the way to the Widow that she was making a mistake. She wasn't ready to face Logan until she figured out the truth, but he shouldn't come in until closing. By then she'd have helped the rest of the staff through the rush, and she could duck out before he arrived. To her broken heart, that sounded like her best bet.

"I WANT TO go to the Widow," Miri announced Friday morning as soon as her nurse left.

"Forget about it," Ignatius replied instantly without looking up from his laptop computer.

"I won't do anything. I just need to be there."

He turned his pugnacious face on her. She smiled and gave him her most pitiful, begging eyes—the ones his granddaughters had used successfully. His grouch face melted. "Fine. If Jessie and Sue promise to make you behave. I could use an hour or two to do a little business. But let me warn you, goldie, if you misbehave, I'll make sure you don't leave this yard except for doctor's appointments for the rest of your six weeks."

"Goldie?"

"Your hair turns to gold in the sunshine. It's pretty."

The compliment took the wind out of her sails. "Thank you?"

"You're a beautiful woman. You need me to tell you that?"

Flabbergasted, she stared at him. "It's not something I hear every day."

"You should." He called the restaurant and must have received affirmation, because he rolled her chair down the ramp and to his car. When he turned to open the door, she scooted forward in the seat.

"Freeze," he barked commandingly, and she froze in shock.

"Is that your cop voice?"

"Yeah."

"It must have been effect—" Before she could guess what he was doing he swept her up as if she weighed no more than a child and put her in the passenger seat, then he leaned across her and buckled her belt. It was over before she could process her response to all the brushing and touching. Her nipples were embarrassingly tight from the scrape of his arm.

"Have you found anything on Elizabeth?" she asked to hide her reaction. She hoped he missed the throatiness of her voice.

"Nothing firm."

"Did the letter help?"

"Yeah."

He was preoccupied and had been since she'd given him the letters two nights ago. She hadn't realized how much she enjoyed his company until she didn't have it. Not that he'd physically left, but mentally, he'd been miles away, staring into his computer screen. She missed him, she realized. Missed his nagging. Missed his overprotectiveness. Missed him watching her every move. Missed the crazy way he pampered her.

Who'd have thunk it? She actually liked having the buttinsky in her house.

They reached the Widow. The parking lot was already filling with the early lunch crowd. She couldn't wait to get inside and feel useful. He opened her door, planted his big paws on either side of her and leaned into her face, stopping scant inches away. His aftershave filled her lungs with its pleasant, manly scent, and her tummy fluttered.

"Stay out of the kitchen. There's no room in there for folks to move around without bumping your leg. And don't do anything to hurt yourself. Because, so help me, if you do, Miriam Louise, I'm not letting you outta my sight again. Got that?"

His nearness scattered her thoughts. She scrambled to find them. "I hear you."

He scooped her up as if she were delicate china and set her into her wheelchair, then he bent over her from behind. His minty breath tickled her ear. "I have plans for you and me when that cast is off. And I want it off soon. So don't screw up your healing."

Then he straightened and wheeled her inside. Excitement skittered through her. She'd sworn when she lost Jack that she'd never look at another man, but this one, this supposedly jaded former detective who cowered in the face of his granddaughters, rescued kittens and played both chef and nursemaid, definitely had her attention.

He wheeled her into the Widow. The entire staff was waiting for her and cheered. She teared up, pressing her hands to her chest. Lordy, she'd missed her family. Ignatius parked her by the hostess stand and locked her tires.

"Don't let her move from this spot," she heard him order over all the greetings and hugs. Home. She soaked it in: the smells, the wooden walls, the chatter of people and clink of utensils.

"Thank you all," she told them. "Now get back to work."

Grinning, she looked over her shoulder to thank Ignatius for bringing her in. But he was already gone. A little of the air from her happiness balloon leaked out. Then a customer came up. She squashed her disappointment and greeted them.

Even if she couldn't work and couldn't be part of the kitchen chaos, she was happy to be here. An hour later her energy was flagging, though. She was debating retreating to the empty private party room when someone called her name.

Ignatius's daughter walked up. "Miri, I want to

thank you for keeping the girls the other day. They have talked nonstop about their visit ever since."

"It was a joy to have them." Then Miri realized there was a way to repay Ignatius for what he was doing—for her and for Logan. "Bethany, do you have a moment?"

"Um…sure."

At the risk of inviting Ignatius's wrath, Miri released the brakes and wheeled her chair into the private room. She spun to face Bethany. "Your father loves you very much. And he adores those girls."

Bethany shifted and her gaze bounced away. "I know."

She didn't sound convinced.

"He's told me how much he regrets never being there while you were growing up, but it wasn't because he didn't care for you or your mother. It was because he wanted you to have nice things. Sometimes, we get so caught up in proving our love by giving material things that we forget our time is the most precious gift we can share with the ones we love."

Bethany mashed her lips together, blinked and nodded.

"I hope you'll give Ignatius a chance to give you and the girls the gift of his time now. I'm not going to lie. He's absolutely terrified of Sydney and Chloe, but it's because they mean so much to him and because in seeing them, he's realizing what he missed with you."

Tears streaked down Bethany's cheeks. "Thank you. Thank you so much for telling me that. I grew up only hearing Mom's side of the story, so...I didn't know. And he has been trying... really hard." She bent down and hugged Miri. "Whatever you are to my dad, I hope you're part of his future."

A knot formed in Miri's throat. "You and the girls are welcome at my house any time—with or without Ignatius."

A throat clearing drew Miri's attention to the doorway. Ignatius stood there. She hoped she hadn't overstepped her bounds. But she couldn't tell. His face was a blank mask.

Bethany launched herself at him, throwing her arms around his neck and squeezing him until his face turned red. His eyes filled as he hugged her back. The gratitude Miri saw when he met her gaze filled her with as much satisfaction as returning to the Widow today had. She wanted a ringside seat as he rebuilt his relationship with his daughter. And she wanted to be a part of Ignatius's future, too.

An immediate sense of disloyalty to Jack rushed over her. Jack had been the love of her life. Without him she would never have built this place that filled her days and her heart. And she could never forget that. Or him.

But if she clung to her memories, was she doing any different than what she chastised Logan for? She couldn't move forward if she continued looking back. And what she had with Ignatius was so…different than what she'd shared with Jack.

Bethany said her goodbyes and Ignatius aimed those green eyes at Miri. "You moved. There will be a penalty for that."

She scowled. "You can't ground me. I'm not a child."

"No. You're not." He wheeled her out the front door and to his car then lifted her and set her in the passenger seat. He leaned over her to fasten her seat belt but didn't pull back. As he'd done this morning, he paused with his face only inches away.

"You're the woman my daughter wants to be a part of my future. I want that, too."

Miri gasped. "You have a fine way of showing it. You didn't even kiss me goodbye after you took me to lunch."

"I don't make a habit of kissing women I'm not dating. But as of now, you and I are dating." Then he planted his mouth on hers.

Shock held her immobile. Then a tidal wave of sensation crashed over her, rolling her as if she'd been caught in the surf. His lips were gentle and soft. She wouldn't have expected that from the big goon. He cupped her face even more gently, then feathered his fingers through her hair. Her pulse roared in her ears and a whirlpool of desire formed in her stomach.

Then he lifted his head. His bemused expression turned to one of satisfaction. Hunger glinted in his eyes. "Get used to it. There's more where that came from."

She gathered her shattered composure. "Says you."

His smile turned smug. "Yeah, says me. You're a fireball, Miri, with a big heart. You never met a stranger and you're too generous for your own good. I figure you're exactly what a jaded ol' detective like me needs. I'm mighty fond of you, Miriam Louise, and I plan to court you. I had planned to wait until you got rid of the cast, but you jumped the gun on that one. But I'm telling you, no matter how much you beg, I'm keeping my virginity until after you get that hunk of plaster off."

She snorted. "You haven't been a virgin in a lot of years."

He blushed. "You make me feel like one. Like I'm falling in love for the first time. I don't know what to say or what to do and I—"

Her heart turned into a big puddle of mush. She put her finger to his lips. "You're doing just fine, and ready or not, I think I'm falling for you, too, Ignatius Smith."

Jessie had parked across the street from the Widow. She waited in her car until she saw Logan turn into the lot, then she headed for Miri's. When she got there she climbed the ramp and knocked on the door. Ignatius opened it.

"Come in," he said with no trace of malice.

"Has Logan been by?"

Miri waved her in. "Haven't seen him today."

"Then I guess he didn't tell you about...meeting my family last night."

Miri and Ignatius shook their heads. Oh, boy. "My brother found out about Logan's past and... it wasn't pretty."

"He's an agent with the South Carolina Law Enforcement Division," Ignatius explained to Miri, reminding Jessie he'd done his own investigating of her. "Thinks Logan's after your money, doesn't he?"

"Yes."

"What money?" Miri asked.

"Jessie's got a little lottery money coming her way. What do *you* think, Jessie?"

A little. She liked the way he'd understated that. "That's why I needed to talk to you and find out if Logan knew about my...income."

Ignatius shook his head. "I'm not giving you anything. You either trust him or you don't."

She looked from Miri to Ignatius and realized she'd wanted them to tell her whether or not she could trust Logan. Because then if they were wrong it wouldn't be her fault.

Her muscles went rigid. She'd always told her

students not to fear failure. But she'd spent her life doing exactly that. A sickening feeling turned her skin clammy. Because of her fear she'd relegated herself to being the backseat driver of her own life. And unless she wanted to continue meekly following others' directions, she had to take a risk and take the wheel. This was her life. It was time she started living it on her terms.

Even if she failed, it couldn't be as bitter as looking back on her life and knowing she hadn't tried.

"Do you think there's a way to prove Logan's innocence?"

"For yourself or him?"

"For him. I want to help him do that."

"Why?" Miri asked.

"Because I love him and I believe in him."

Ignatius glanced at Miri, then faced Jessie. "There might be."

"Then I need his address. Please."

Miri and Ignatius shared another look then Miri took a pad of paper and wrote. "Don't hurt him, Jessie. He's been hurt enough for a lifetime."

Jessie took the paper, nodded her thanks and left.

Tomorrow the Widow was closed for the holiday, and she was going to visit Logan and get his side of the story.

LOGAN SAT ON his back porch, staring at the water and watching the sunrise. It didn't feel like

Christmas Eve morning. It felt like Christmas Day morning and he'd woken up to find Santa had left him a stocking full of coal. Everything he'd hoped for with Jessie was an impossibility.

He'd spent the night scouring the internet for articles about her—about *Jessamine*—and her lottery win. Seeing pictures of her with blond hair had been a shock. She hadn't looked like his Jessie.

Because she wasn't his, he reminded himself bitterly.

He'd read the stories about multiple break-ins of her car, home and school, and her subsequently getting let go from her job. The strain on her face in the photos had increased as the weeks and incidents passed until she'd resembled the woman he'd first met. The one without the easy smile or the childlike joy in the simple things he took for granted. The one she'd become in the past few weeks.

Apparently, the press enjoyed seeing winners suffer. They'd gone into great detail about how bad the "poor little rich teacher's" life had become before she'd vanished. Then they'd speculated about whether she'd committed suicide or fallen victim to foul play. They'd listed numerous lottery winners who'd done exactly that. The statistics were not good.

His protective instincts kicked in. He didn't want that for Jessie—Jessamine. Then he reminded himself again that she was not his anything. But at least now he understood why she'd dyed her hair, worn colored contacts and omitted mentioning she had money. That didn't change the facts. She thought he was after her winnings. And he couldn't prove otherwise. That meant they were done.

Someone knocked on his front door. It was too damned early for visitors and he was in no mood for company. He ignored it. The persistent pest knocked again and didn't stop. He'd get no peace if he didn't send them on their way. He stomped inside, crossed the small living area and yanked open the door.

Jessie—Jessamine—stood on the other side. Her hair was the same pale golden shade he'd seen online, and her eyes were the same blue. She was so beautiful she took his breath away. Even prettier than she'd been as a brunette. But still off-limits.

"May I come in?" she asked.

"Why?"

"Because I want to hear your side of the story."

"I spent three years defending my innocence. I'm done."

"I know you didn't do it, Logan. I want to hear what happened—from your side."

A balloon of hope inflated in his chest. He popped it. "I got screwed by people I trusted. Nothing more to say."

"I understand betrayal. I was betrayed by people I thought I could trust, too, although my so-called friends just wanted me to buy them things. They didn't try to frame me for a crime I didn't commit. Tell me about it. Please."

She believed him. It didn't change anything. "Your brother pretty much summed it up. My exes took off with our clients' money and left me to take the fall. They haven't been seen since. Neither has the money."

"And you hired Ignatius to find them. To clear your name?"

"He tell you that?"

She laughed. "No. He wouldn't tell me anything. I had to figure it out by myself. Now, may I come in or am I going to be a blood offering to your mosquitoes?"

He opened the door. She walked past him, trailing a hint of strawberries. He would never be able to see a stupid strawberry again without thinking of her.

She turned a circle in his den then walked to the wall of windows looking over the water. "I like this."

"It's not much. It was Jack's old fishing shack before he married Miri. He held on to it for sentimental reasons, and I bought it from him back before the shit—before everything went wrong. It's the only thing I was able to hold on to."

"Pretty nice for a fishing cabin."

"I did some renovations when I moved in three years ago." Why was he telling her this? "What do you want, Jessamine?"

"I prefer Jessie." She faced him, looking as defiant as she had the first time she'd confronted him about smothering Miri. "I love you, Logan, and I believe in you, and I want to help you clear your name."

He refused to play this game. "No."

"Do you love me?"

He said nothing.

"I think you do. You showed me your world, and you forced me out of my comfort zone. Because of that, I grew in ways I didn't even know I needed to grow. Until you made me see it, I had no idea I'd let my family make every important decision for me—from what to study in school to which house to buy and which car to drive. Me being a doormat wasn't their fault. I was a coward and afraid to fail.

"You are the first person who's ever encouraged me to follow my heart and do what makes me happy. That happened to be my painting. You validated my dreams by helping me sell my work. Then you introduced me to your friends, who offered me the job of a lifetime. And what did you get out of it? Nothing. So let me give you something in return. Let me hire the best investigators we can find to clear you."

He jumped back as if scalded. "I'm not touching your money."

"But I could help."

"No."

Her eyes filled with hurt. "Then at least admit you love me. I need to hear it."

He'd shown her in every way he knew how. "Jessie, the press still haunt me. If they find you, they'll find me. Your name will be dragged through the mud and you'll be made a laughingstock for falling for a swindler. I won't let that happen."

"If I believe you, then what does it matter what anyone else thinks?"

She was killing him. He wanted nothing more than to greedily soak up the love she offered. "You deserve a man who won't always be viewed with suspicion. One your family can…accept."

Her color drained. The pain on her face eviscerated him.

"Jessie, it's because I…care about you that I have to let you go."

Her breath came in hiccups and she blinked furiously. Then her shoulders drooped. "Then help me find a way for us to be together."

She turned and walked out his front door. He felt as if she'd gaffed him through the chest. He followed her, wishing he had the answer.

And then he did. "Jessie."

She stopped, turned and waited.

"I can only think of one way for us to be together. I'll sign a prenuptial agreement stating I have no claim on your money or anything bought with your money."

"That's not necessary."

"It is for me." He had to say it. She needed to hear it. "I love you. And I want to marry you and spend the rest of my life showing you how much. But I don't want anyone—especially your family—to doubt that it's you I love and not your annuity."

Her lips quivered and her eyes filled with tears. Then she laughed and pressed her fingers over her mouth.

"What?" he asked.

"My family insisted Aaron, my former fiancé, sign a prenup. He refused and threw a tantrum. He said if I really loved him I wouldn't ask that of him. He tried to make me choose between my family and him. You're doing the opposite. My family is going to love you, Logan. Almost as much as I do."

He brushed her golden hair back. "Then marry me as soon as your lawyer can draw up the papers. Let me spend the rest of my life showing you how much I love you."

She threw her arms around him. He banded her close and drank in her scent. This was real love, and he'd found it in the arms of a woman too stubborn to give up on him and on them.

He eased her back. "You were voted teacher of the year twice back in South Carolina. You must love teaching. I've started over before. If you want to go back home, I can start over again."

She smiled. "You've been doing your homework. I do miss my students. And I did love my job. But teaching doesn't allow me time for my art. I wish I could do both…but I can't see a way to make that happen. And this is your home. Your clients are your extended family. I won't take you away from them."

He kissed her temple. "I'm very good at seeing the big picture. Let me work on it and see if we can find a way. Because helping you make your dreams come true is my job now."

EPILOGUE

JESSIE COULDN'T STOP smiling as she and Logan climbed Miri's ramp hand in hand Christmas morning. Logan had indeed found a way to make her dreams come true.

Ignatius opened the door. "Damn, you're early. But that's good. Saves me a call. Come in."

Miri, still in her nightgown, looked from Logan to Jessie and back. "You look like Santa's been good to you."

Logan squeezed her hand. "He has. He brought me a woman to love, and one who loves me. Jessie's agreed to marry me."

Miri clapped her hands. "Then Ignatius and I would like to give you your first wedding present. Dear?"

"I'll get it." The PI left the room.

Jessie and Logan exchanged surprised glances at the endearment, then Logan said, "So you two…?"

Miri beamed. "I've been harping on you to put the past behind you. I decided to take my own advice. So, yes, Ignatius and I are keeping company."

Ignatius returned and handed Logan a sheaf

of papers. "A buddy at the FBI faxed these reports this morning. Elizabeth is in federal custody. She's confessed everything and is willing to turn over Trent's location and their bank account information in exchange for a lenient sentence. No honor among thieves, I've always said. And by the way, she completely exonerated you."

Logan went still beside her. "You found her?"

"With Miri's help. Her clearing you means you can go back to your old life if you want it."

Logan shook his head. "I'm right where I need to be. Together Jessie and I are going to build an art camp for disadvantaged kids. She can teach all summer and paint the rest of the year."

Miri beamed. "You're a teacher? I knew there was a reason you were so good with our little customers."

"Logan, if you want to see Elizabeth, I can make it happen," Ignatius added.

"No. Elizabeth and I are done. That chapter of my life is closed. I see nothing but a bright future ahead. There's no need to look back."

Jessie squeezed his arm. "If you've been exonerated, we don't need to wait for the prenup."

He kissed her forehead. "Yes, we do. I'm leaving the world no doubt about my love for you. I's right. The cloud of suspicion will always be there. I want everybody to know—especially your family— that I'm the luckiest man in the world, not because I found a woman with a nice bank balance, but because I found one who stole my heart and promised not to give it back."

Jessie didn't need guarantees. But she didn't protest, either. She loved Logan enough to let him have his way in this. "Speaking of my parents, I can't wait to tell them, but no matter what they think, I say this is the best Christmas ever!"

* * * * *

LARGER-PRINT BOOKS!

GET 2 FREE LARGER-PRINT NOVELS PLUS
2 FREE GIFTS!

HARLEQUIN®

Romance

From the Heart, For the Heart

LARGER-PRINT BOOKS!

HARLEQUIN

Presents®

GET 2 FREE LARGER-PRINT NOVELS PLUS 2 FREE GIFTS!

PASSION
GUARANTEED
SEDUCTION

YES! Please send me 2 FREE LARGER-PRINT Harlequin Presents® novels and my 2 FREE gifts (gifts are worth about $10). After receiving them, if I don't wish to receive any more books, I can return the shipping statement marked "cancel." If I don't cancel, I will receive 6 brand-new novels every month and be billed just $5.30 per book in the U.S. or $5.74 per book in Canada. That's a saving of at least 12% off the cover price! It's quite a bargain! Shipping and handling is just 50¢ per book in the U.S. and 75¢ per book in Canada.* I understand that accepting the 2 free books and gifts places me under no obligation to buy anything. I can always return a shipment and cancel at any time. Even if I never buy another book, the two free books and gifts are mine to keep forever.

176/376 HDN GHVY

Name _____
(PLEASE PRINT)

Address _____ Apt. #

City _____ State/Prov. _____ Zip/Postal Code

Signature (if under 18, a parent or guardian must sign)

Mail to the Reader Service:
IN U.S.A.: P.O. Box 1867, Buffalo, NY 14240-1867
IN CANADA: P.O. Box 609, Fort Erie, Ontario L2A 5X3

**Are you a subscriber to Harlequin Presents® books
and want to receive the larger-print edition?
Call 1-800-873-8635 today or visit us at www.ReaderService.com.**

* Terms and prices subject to change without notice. Prices do not include applicable taxes. Sales tax applicable in N.Y. Canadian residents will be charged applicable taxes. Offer not valid in Quebec. This offer is limited to one order per household. Not valid for current subscribers to Harlequin Presents Larger-Print books. All orders subject to credit approval. Credit or debit balances in a customer's account(s) may be offset by any other outstanding balance owed by or to the customer. Please allow 4 to 6 weeks for delivery. Offer available while quantities last.

Your Privacy—The Reader Service is committed to protecting your privacy. Our Privacy Policy is available online at www.ReaderService.com or upon request from the Reader Service.

We make a portion of our mailing list available to reputable third parties that offer products we believe may interest you. If you prefer that we not exchange your name with third parties, or if you wish to clarify or modify your communication preferences, please visit us at www.ReaderService.com/consumerchoice or write to us at Reader Service Preference Service, P.O. Box 9062, Buffalo, NY 14240-9062. Include your complete name and address.

HPLP15

REQUEST YOUR FREE BOOKS!
2 FREE WHOLESOME ROMANCE NOVELS
IN LARGER PRINT
PLUS 2
FREE
MYSTERY GIFTS

⚜⚜⚜⚜⚜⚜⚜⚜⚜⚜⚜⚜⚜⚜⚜⚜⚜⚜⚜

HEARTWARMING™

⚜⚜⚜⚜⚜⚜⚜⚜⚜⚜⚜⚜⚜⚜⚜⚜⚜⚜⚜

Wholesome, tender romances

YES! Please send me 2 FREE Harlequin® Heartwarming Larger-Print novels and my 2 FREE mystery gifts (gifts worth about $10). After receiving them, if I don't wish to receive any more books, I can return the shipping statement marked "cancel." If I don't cancel, I will receive 4 brand-new larger-print novels every month and be billed just $5.24 per book in the U.S. or $5.99 per book in Canada. That's a savings of at least 19% off the cover price. It's quite a bargain! Shipping and handling is just 50¢ per book in the U.S. and 75¢ per book in Canada.* I understand that accepting the 2 free books and gifts places me under no obligation to buy anything. I can always return a shipment and cancel at any time. Even if I never buy another book, the two free books and gifts are mine to keep forever.

161/361 IDN GHX2

Name _____ (PLEASE PRINT)

Address _____ Apt. #

City _____ State/Prov. _____ Zip/Postal Code

Signature (if under 18, a parent or guardian must sign)

Mail to the **Reader Service:**
IN U.S.A.: P.O. Box 1867, Buffalo, NY 14240-1867
IN CANADA: P.O. Box 609, Fort Erie, Ontario L2A 5X3

* Terms and prices subject to change without notice. Prices do not include applicable taxes. Sales tax applicable in N.Y. Canadian residents will be charged applicable taxes. Offer not valid in Quebec. This offer is limited to one order per household. Not valid for current subscribers to Harlequin Heartwarming larger-print books. All orders subject to credit approval. Credit or debit balances in a customer's account(s) may be offset by any other outstanding balance owed by or to the customer. Please allow 4 to 6 weeks for delivery. Offer available while quantities last.

Your Privacy—The Reader Service is committed to protecting your privacy. Our Privacy Policy is available online at www.ReaderService.com or upon request from the Reader Service.

We make a portion of our mailing list available to reputable third parties that offer products we believe may interest you. If you prefer that we not exchange your name with third parties, or if you wish to clarify or modify your communication preferences, please visit us at www.ReaderService.com/consumerchoice or write to us at Reader Service Preference Service, P.O. Box 9062, Buffalo, NY 14240-9062. Include your complete name and address.

HW15

LARGER-PRINT BOOKS!

GET 2 FREE LARGER-PRINT NOVELS PLUS
2 FREE GIFTS!

◆ HARLEQUIN®

INTRIGUE

BREATHTAKING ROMANTIC SUSPENSE